PRAISE FOR **THE DEVIL'S SMOKEHOUSE**

"A work of fiction inspired by the author's childhood, *The Devil's Smokehouse* is the inspiring, painful, exhilarating, disturbing, and at times hilarious journey of a child survivor. One who must cross a line in order to keep surviving. Jones weaves plot twists that are fantastical but believable, as only a survivor could."

— **FURY YOUNG**, *founder of Die Jim Crow Records*

"It's a struggle to survive childhood, and that's the conundrum faced by Jenkins, the narrator of Justin Jones's coming-of-age mystery novel, *The Devil's Smokehouse*. Jenkins underrates the prevalence of evil in his hometown, an impoverished rural community in the middle of the country. Everyone knows everyone in this hamlet where even the local pervert's identity is an open secret. As he matures, Jenkins uncovers more dark secrets, learning that the twisting threads of big-city drug culture have a stranglehold on some local powerbrokers. Even his own road to nowhere takes an unexpected turn. *The Devil's Smokehouse* is a page-turner that is hard to put down."

— **SUE HINTON**, *retired English professor, Oklahoma City Community College (OCCC)*

"Justin Jones captures the raw essence of humanity in all its beauty and grit. Characters leap from the page with intensity, as they grapple with love, violence, loss, and redemption. Instantly compelling, Jones's writing is full of wisdom and depth as it goes to people's darkest struggles, and also their most glorious moments of triumph."

— **ROYAL YOUNG**, *author of* Fame Shark

Published by River Grove Books
Austin, TX
www.rivergrovebooks.com

Distributed by River Grove Books

Design and composition by Greenleaf Book Group and Brian Phillips
Cover design by Greenleaf Book Group and Brian Phillips
Cover images copyright NKmotion. Used under license from Shutterstock.com, ©iStock.com/cruphoto, and ©iStock.com/Mountain Creek Imagery, 2023.

Publisher's Cataloging-in-Publication data is available.

Print ISBN: 978-1-63299-720-3

eBook ISBN: 978-1-63299-721-0

First Edition

THE DEVIL'S SMOKE HOUSE

A NOVEL

JUSTIN JONES

RIVER GROVE
BOOKS

Hell is empty and all the devils are here.

—*William Shakespeare,* The Tempest

CONTENTS

1 First Memories *1*

2 The Happening *15*

3 The Experiment *23*

4 Another Option *31*

5 The Plan Started *39*

6 The Waiting *45*

7 Doubt *53*

8 Inquiry *57*

9 Rinse and Repeat *67*

10 A New Level *73*

11 The Art of Lying *85*

12 1969 *95*

13 Crazier *103*

14 A Good Deed *111*

15 It's Complicated *123*

16 Lord on My Side *137*

17 It Thickens *149*

18 Grim Reaper *159*

19 Chit-Chat *167*

20 Buried Treasure *177*

21 Answers *187*

22 Renaissance *195*

23 Reckoning *205*

24 Time for Change *217*

25 Horizons *223*

26 The Adult Education *231*

27 Step Back *245*

28 The End Game *255*

About the Author *263*

CHAPTER ONE

FIRST MEMORIES

A STOIC CORRECTIONAL OFFICER DREW THE CORD, AND THE pale-blue blinds slowly opened, exposing the execution chamber. There was no dust on the aging metal blinds. You will never see dust on the blinds or, as a matter of fact, anywhere else in a well-operated prison. The soon-to-be deceased was strapped to a medical gurney. There were no distinct colors or transition of blanket textures distinguishing the apparatus from any other. The expressed purpose for this chariot of demise was to provide an appropriate position to deliver death. When the blinds were drawn, most witnesses in the viewing seats fixated on the gurney without fully comprehending it. Aside from the prison staff and the usual viewers, such as the arresting law enforcement agency and the prosecutor, few knew what to expect when they first gazed into the death chamber.

The strapped man turned his head to the left to see who would look back at him. He smiled as if to say hello, or perhaps show his pleasure that some family had come to witness his death. Maybe he was just pleased to have anyone present. His body was strapped tightly to the gurney, so he strained his neck to the side and then moved his head up and down to canvass the entire viewing area. Once he saw the government officials straight across from where his head was positioned, he never looked in that direction again.

"You have two minutes for any last words, *and* I will advise you when the two minutes are up." The tall, heavyset warden with a pencil-thin mustache announced the official time limit. "At that point, if you continue speaking, I will give the order to let the execution commence anyway."

The man now stared at the ceiling as he appeared to flex his muscled-up chest and attempted to stretch his short, stocky body as much as the restraints would allow. "I know I must die," he said. "I'll die here today as not the same man who committed a senseless, horrible crime, but one who has become a better person than that 19-year-old drug addict that I was. I can't even fathom that other person, the one I was then. No excuses. I hope my death brings some liberation from the grief I have inflicted on the victim's family, but I doubt it will."

He was calm, his voice soft, and his eyes repenting. He thanked the correctional staff for the respect they had bestowed upon him while on death row. Little did he know that he would become a vehicle, an inspiration for my story.

So, let us start from the beginning.

———

My heart was beating furiously, and I was afraid it would explode through my chest. There were always two options: the closet or under the bed. The bed gave more escape options. If he came after me from one side, I could crawl out the other to make my escape. Like all of our furniture, the worn-out bed had been passed down through generations of family. It was huge, or at least seemed so to me when I was a child. I was thankful for the hiding place and safety the bed provided.

Sometimes the flight from fear would continue through a window. Our windows had screens to keep flies out in the summer. An old-fashioned hook latch was supposed to keep the window screen secure. There were ragged holes around the latch where my sister Jill and I would have to tear the screens to unlatch them from the outside. This was necessary to get back into the house on the many nights we would escape through the front door but have to return crawling silently through the windows.

The house had no air-conditioning, so we needed the open windows to fight the stifling summer heat. Any cool breeze was a blessing. I would lay face down on the hardwood floors under the bed, waiting for the monster's approach. My breath would cause the dust balls that lived between the cracks in the floor planks to roll as if they had a thousand tiny feet propelling them. I loved the coolness of the worn natural wood floors. Not like you have nowadays, where such floors are expensive and in vogue. Rich people had carpets. These floors were an intricate part of the frame, making it a structurally sound house. I would use my pocket knife to dig the goody from between the wood floor planks. Goody was what I called the mixture of dirt, floor wax, and fuzz balls that lived in the cracks and spacing between planks. If I dug too deep, I would create a passage for light to illuminate the dirt foundation below. The dirt road just a few yards from our house contributed to the ample dust supply. It was like a high-speed freeway for oil tanker trucks. Occasionally my mother would flag one down to see if the driver could drop some oil slush from their tank onto the road. At least for a few days, this would reduce the red dust flying through the house. My sister and I drew pictures in the red dirt that settled and collected on the floors.

The army-green 1962 Chevy pickup had a distinct sound as it pulled onto our dirt and gravel driveway. The sound was our warning, our siren of sorts. A signal that the monster had arrived. The muffler had been torn off and replaced several times. Once, the monster decided to rid our pasture of its thicket of wild plum and persimmon trees. He chose to use the 1962 Chevy as his choice for this mass destruction. With the pickup, he mowed down the weak and smaller trees, but the larger ones eventually stopped his progress. A tractor was required to remove the Chevy from the high center atop a group of trees that bent but would not break. Neighbors would always assist, as they either felt sorry for my sister and me or were too afraid of the monster to refuse.

The Chevy was also used many times as a battering ram. The pickup didn't care for our mother's new stripped-down white Chevy Malibu. The monster commanded the pickup to attack the Malibu. Over and over again, he would ram it, back up, and ram it again. With satisfaction in his growl, the monster would exit the pickup, stare at the Malibu, call it a lying motherfucker, and proceed to his bedroom, his chamber of horrors.

I liked that old pickup, the toughness. It was what I learned to drive on. Then it became a killing machine, when the monster intentionally ran over my dog while it was asleep in the front yard. He hated that dog as I had taught it to hate him. It was very protective of me and would growl and bark whenever the monster prepared to bring his wrath down on me. I looked for days for my dog. Jill and I found out later that my mother had witnessed the murder but didn't want to tell me for fear of what I might do. I was maybe eight years old at the time. What could I do? I eventually found the bloodstained ground barely hidden by the drying grass of autumn. I wanted revenge—my favorite dog of all time. Maybe this was what my grandpa and Mom were talking about when I eavesdropped and heard them discussing how I would grow out of my anger issues. The monster was responsible for my rage, so why couldn't they see that?

One day I exchanged bedrooms with Jill. Now my room was the only direct path the monster could take to his bedroom or the only toilet we had. I started calling the monster's bedroom a den. The thunderous snoring and earsplitting farting echoed into my bedroom. My sister had occupied the middle bedroom for years but never told me how loud those sounds could be. Only an animal could make those sounds. After the move to the middle bedroom that served as a corridor to the monster's den, I now believed it was my turn to suffer more, and suffer I did. Jill had suffered enough.

Our house was a prefab, even though we did not call such homes by that name in the 1960s. It sat on cement blocks with exposed plumbing underneath. Some blocks were removed to allow the dogs to shelter under the house. Our female dog would have puppies somewhere under the house; it was always like a treasure hunt mixed with Christmas for Jill and me to crawl under that place under the house to find them. We never knew how they were going to look. All dogs roamed free in the rural county we lived in, so there were many colors, sizes, and shape options from various suspecting dads. Spaying a female dog was expensive and frowned upon. If an owner couldn't give pups away or didn't wish to raise them, they were stuffed in a tow sack and thrown in the creek or pond.

Our elongated house was like a trailer made of wood. The three bedrooms were in a row with a tiny bathroom as you entered the hallway. The monster could go through the kitchen and the add-on back utility room, but rarely exercised this option. If he was in a melodic mood, he would come through the middle bedroom. There he would batter and beat on the old upright piano that Jill played. The central bedroom was the only place where this monstrosity of a musical instrument would fit. It was another reason why I should have never traded rooms with my sister.

The house leaked like a sieve when it rained. Buckets, pots, and pans were placed throughout to catch the water. Sometimes the beds had to be shifted to avoid new leaks. The monster would march through, kicking over the captured water in a defiant attempt to remain upright despite his wobbly spaghetti legs. Sometimes he caused more leaks. Sometimes a single-shot .22-caliber Montgomery Ward rifle gunshot would ping through the house. The fool monster would sit quietly in the dark and shoot at mice as they scampered across the floors. We had mouse holes in our baseboards that reminded me of those in the Tom and Jerry cartoons. Not sure if he ever hit one. The small-caliber shells would ricochet many times before coming to rest in the ceiling. This made more rain holes, and we'd have to move the beds again. There was no insulation to slow the bullets or divert the rain.

All walls and doors had multiple holes created by the power of the monster's fist. After a night of drunken wall and door beating, my mother would mix plaster with newspaper and sometimes chicken wire and patch the holes. There was no patching of the doors. The doors were cheap, as were customary for prefabricated homes; they were hollow and not patchable. The lack of insulation caused our little house to swelter in the summer and freeze in the winter. One small gas stove in the front room was all our heat for the entire house, and the water pipes would stay frozen most of the winter.

Jill and I would ask our mom if friends could come over, but she would almost always say no. We didn't understand then, but she knew our friends' parents would not let their child come to our house. At that time we were unaware of the monster's evil notoriety. Still, our unabated imaginations created unusual explanations for all the puffy wall plaster and holes for the rare occasions when we did have a guest. Jill once explained to a friend that our house was damaged by shrapnel when a tornado came tearing across the yard. I countered her tornado story by explaining that moonshiners had knocked holes in the walls looking for a magic potion they had mistakenly sold to the monster.

My stories always had some link to a memory. I must have been around four or five, but I could vaguely remember riding in the back of a pickup. We would raise our small faces and peer over the pickup bed edge when the bell rang. The bell hung in a tree tied to a string that ran to someone's house. The monster would pull the line and the bell would ring, and eventually a burly, slow-walking bowlegged man would drop two one-gallon jugs in the back of the truck. We somehow understood what was occurring was clandestine and wrong, but we didn't know why. Our mother sat in the pickup's front seat, stoic and staring straight ahead while sucking hard on her Salem cigarette. As the man slowly shuffled back into the shadows, Jill and I would whisper to the wind *troll, troll* as he turned to leave. Trolls were another explanation for all the patched walls. Jill and I could explain anything away.

The monster entered the house. I whispered down the hallway to see if Jill had heard him. She had. Being in the monster's least direct path, she rarely retreated to the closet or under the bed. Her mode of security was to hide under the blankets. Even on a hot August night, she would rather sweat to her death than face the monster. That night, like many others, I trembled and allowed my heart to race, scared to death of the monster. I held my breath and waited. Seconds later, the wrath of hell rained down.

He started in the kitchen, breaking all the dishes and slinging the food out of the icebox. His fist blasted through the cheap sheetrock wall from the kitchen into my bedroom. His knuckles must have partially hit a wood stud in the wall because he cried out in pain. The pain only made him angrier. He stomped down the hallway with fists, punching holes in both sides of the hall. It was astonishing that any sheetrock was left from all the previous rampages. He was like the Hulk, easy to anger and strong enough to do real damage. But unlike the Hulk, there was no good side, no alter ego. I retreated to my false safe place, under the bed.

I saw his steel-toed work boots stop beside my bed. The torn leather exposed the shiny steel embedded in the shoes to protect them from falling objects. When he did work, it was as an oil field machinist. I could smell the oil on the leather boots and see the sheet metal shavings stuck in the soles. Pure silence waved through. I crawled backward until the wall impeded my withdrawal. He reached under the bed and pulled me out by the hair of my head.

"You goddamn little motherfucker!" he yelled. Then his belt came off, and he beat me as I attempted to crawl back under the bed. Again he grabbed me, this time by my feet. "Don't run from me, Jenkins, you sorry son-of-a-bitch!"

He let go, and I ran into the closet—more silence. Then I heard the mattress and springs of his bed. Compressed by his flopped, plump body, the urine-stained sheets and 20-year-old mattress emitted an ungodly odor. The flicking sound of a cigarette lighter flinging open then shut indicated he was having a smoke from his filterless Camels. The cigarette would soon fall from the monster's hand when he fell asleep, burning the hardwood floor, and joining a thousand others in a burned offering of abstraction. The yelling, cursing, and screaming at imaginary people continued.

It was a pattern Jill and I knew so well. The monster would fall asleep, then awaken, and stumble through my room in his dirty yellow pee-stained Fruit of the Loom underwear on his way to the toilet. He would end up pissing all over the walls and floor. The bathroom wallpaper was brittle from it. Then the cussing, wall-thrashing, and window-breaking fits would commence. This would repeat itself over and over again until the sun came up. On many of these nights I would not come out of the closet until morning. By dawn the rampage would subside, and eventually the monster would become comatose. Mom would come home from her night-shift job. We would clean the devastation and prepare for the next rampages. Then we went off to school with no sleep. As always, we never discussed the night with anyone.

Our morning alarm clock was sometimes the clinking sound of him flicking open his stainless steel cigarette lighter and then slapping it closed. The monster could do this all with one hand. Our version of a backup alarm was his subsequent coughing, hacking up phlegm, and spitting it on the floor. Then we would hear the metal shavings in his shoes scrape across the floor, causing small paisley-like indentions. Like the fuzz balls, these indentions on the floor became just another plaything for me. I would pretend they were stars, comets racing across the sky, or missiles and bullets. My little plastic green army men figurines had to dodge all the projectiles or die.

There were never any photographs or pictures on our walls. I didn't even know that other families put photos on walls until I got much older. I did put up a Buffalo Springfield concert poster once. I had ordered it from the back of a magazine and was careful where I tacked it to the wall. I selected a location not easily noticed by the monster. It covered two huge holes in the wall. The poster survived a week before the monster snatched it off the wall and cursed the long hair and the Communism it represented. There were now too many holes punched through the walls to hang anything else.

He never injured himself while punching through walls or hitting a stud. Another confirmation he was an indestructible monster. To a child's mindset, he was not human. I do recall the few times we had visitors to the house. There was a vain attempt to conceal the holes with whatever was available. We probably had more calendars on the walls than anyone else. The calendars just made all the walls appear to have pimples. The plaster always protruded outward and the calendars couldn't hang flush.

The cramped kitchen, with its small dining table, also served as the torture room. Here we were forced to eat and face the monster. Curtains covered the cabinets, because the doors had been torn off during his rampages. We were forced to eat everything we put on our plates or receive a beating. My favorite food was red beans and cornbread with a side of raw onions. I could never get the portions correct, so countless beatings occurred. I learned that tears could be caused by anger. Tears would drip into my plate as the monster stood over me yelling, "Eat everything on your goddamn motherfucking plate. You try to get up before that fucking plate is clean, and I'll beat your ass off!"

The kitchen table also was where Mom would tell on Jill and me. A tribunal. She would only do this if the monster had been sober for a few days. He would acknowledge that Mom had spanked us for whatever offenses we had committed, then continue eating as if it was no big deal. Hell would arrive days later when the monster came home drunk and determined we required additional punishment. For some reason, the monster only seemed to remember our need for a beating while eating in the kitchen. In his alcohol-induced stupor, he would beat us with his much-beloved weapon, a 100 percent raw cowhide belt. Being punished twice for the same offense was our form of double jeopardy.

Sometimes the monster had visitors. Most were from the demon world. Alcohol brings out the demons in those who are possessed. For the rest of us, the unpossessed, alcohol dulls the senses and reduces oxygen to the brain. For others, it makes them invisible. They are invisible in that they don't seem to think anyone can see what they are doing. I learned that demons hang out with demons, and our monster was the ring leader.

They all had smaller and darker eyes than most people. You could look into their eyes and see nobody was home in there. Their nostrils flared when angry. The monster learned who had demons in them and cultivated them.

Mr. U was one of the possessed who would occasionally visit our house. Remarkable, at my age now, how vivid imagery ingrains in the memory. The demons would go fishing but rarely brought any fish back. They had thrown some snapping turtles in the back of the old '62 Chevy on a sunny spring day. Only the larger turtles could not escape through the cracked and hole-infested wooded pickup bed. Growling with a cigarette dangling from the corner of his mouth, loosely stuck to his lower lip, Mr. U declared, "You see those fucking eyes? The motherfucker needs to die." The other demons from the fishing trip gathered around.

Mr. U continued staring at the turtle while the others passed around a bottle of cheap whiskey. Finally, the turtle hissed and snapped as if to say, "Fuck you, bring it on." Mr. U, in a calm demon voice, spoke to the turtle and said, "Okay, you son-of-a-bitch." Then he bit its head off. He spat it out and delivered a tremendous laugh, with blood running down the corners of his mouth. This confirmed to me, at the age of seven, that there were demons all around me. Even Ozzy Osbourne wouldn't bite a snapping turtle's head off. After they left, I buried the turtle with its severed head. I said to God, "If there is a turtle heaven, this one deserves it." I carved the name I gave him in a small sandstone, "Danny," and made him a headstone. Turtles became my favorite creature, maybe because of guilt, for I didn't do anything to save this one.

The demons loved to create sports for their amusement and demented entertainment. Again, Mr. U was the demon of creation, the patron saint of sport for demons and monsters. Sarsaparilla was my pet raccoon. Jill and I found her when she was only about a month old.

Hunters had killed her mother. Once she was full-grown she was no longer allowed in the house. Being kids, we always sneaked her inside to sleep in one of the closets during the day. We didn't know the word *nocturnal*, but it didn't take long to understand that a raccoon was ready to play when the sun went down.

"Jenkins, you little fucker. I hear you keep a coon sow in the house. Why don't you bring her out here," Mr. U chuckled one day as he stood in our front yard. I was constantly being called a little motherfucker by the monster's friends. I was small, skinny, and probably looked like a poster child for malnutrition. Everybody looked large to me, and Mr. U was one of the largest.

He had killed the turtle only a month before, and I wanted no part of him. He had arrived with the monster and four other demons. I fixated on the ground, not wanting to make even the slightest eye contact. Eventually, I shuffled away toward the hog pens. Jill was playing with dolls out by the cellar. The next thing I heard was a dog barking. Mr. U and the monster had taken one of Mr. U's hunting dogs out of his truck. The barking was insidious.

"Tell you what we are going to do. First, we can bring old Sarsaparilla out and see if she can get away from Bomber here." The monster took control and started giving instructions to his demon followers.

"No, just throw the dog in the closet with the sow, and winner takes all," Mr. U countered. The other demons agreed with Mr. U. They started capriciously throwing their money on the porch, with most betting on the dog.

I ran as fast as I could toward the house. As I entered the yard, the monster's colossal hand stopped all my forward motion. I fell forward and gasped a mouth full of chicken-manure-infested dirt. The monster held me in a breath-defying grasp. "Don't be a pussy, be a man," the monster screamed at me. I heard barking, growling, whining—and then silence.

Mr. U stumbled out of the house holding his beloved dead Bomber. The dog's eyes were gone, and his nose was hanging on with a few hairs. Blood dripped from his mouth like slow ketchup leaving a bottle. His mouth froze in a snarl. They'd found Sarsaparilla in a closet, where they threw Bomber in and closed the door. Unbeknown to me, raccoons fight a dog by wrapping themselves around its face. The dog never had a chance.

The monster turned me loose, stomped into the house, and brought Sarsaparilla out. Grabbing her back feet, he slung her head into a metal stud pole that held up the front porch roof. Then, to make sure the dastardly deed was complete, he stomped her head until the skull broke open. "We can't have no damn dog-killing coon around here," the monster announced with great satisfaction. He slung her in the trash barrel, lit a cigarette, then flicked the match in with her—a sacrifice for the demons by the monster. "Rest in peace, Sarsaparilla," I sadly whispered as I fought back the tears.

CHAPTER TWO

THE HAPPENING

"YOU'RE THE DEVIL, SON. I'LL KILL YOU NOW, SO GET ON OUT of here. You are not going to take these kids. You're the Devil. I didn't raise you this away to treat these kids like this!" It was another night of the Devil's rampage. I was seven and Jill was eight. We'd run to our grandpa's house for safety.

Grandpa had just labeled him the Devil; it must be true. Grandpa was never wrong. That was why he was our savior, an angel. That was why God did not answer my prayers and kill the monster. God can't kill the Devil. It made perfect sense now. How did I miss this? The monster was not a monster at all. The Devil controlled and created demons. I had only attended church a few times, and it was all about the Old Testament. Grandpa was a warrior angel who was here to protect us.

The single-shot ten-gauge shotgun was aimed somewhere close to the Devil's midsection. Grandpa had grabbed the gun just seconds before the Devil stumbled into the bedroom. The Devil announced his arrival by ripping the front screen door off its hinges and then shouting, "Get up, motherfuckers!" With his red face and purple lips, the Devil stood his ground at the end of Grandpa's bed. The Devil's eyes were bugging out as he yelled obscenities and drew his fist back. My grandpa held fast as the Devil insisted on taking my sister and me away from Grandpa. I watched Grandpa's whole body tremble as he attempted to hold the gun steady and not allow the Devil close enough to take it away from him. His finger moved from the trigger guard to the trigger. He looked frail in the moonlight with his long, skinny, pale legs making his boxer underwear appear comically large. Could he—would he—squeeze the trigger and free Jill and me?

No curtains covered my grandpa's bedroom windows, so the moonlight filtered through dust-covered glass and softened the darkness with a fog-like glow. The ancient cloth window blinds had long ago dissolved into an ingredient for a recipe for dust balls, and all that remained were the wooden rollers attached to the window seal tops. I was so scared that I could not catch my breath. I concentrated on the shotgun. Would it fire? Could Grandpa kill him? The gun was called a Long Tom. Not sure why. Black tape held the butt to the rest of the gun. The blue finish had long ago been consumed by rust. Grandpa always said rust never sleeps, so I hoped this sleepless rust had not rendered the gun useless. Could a weapon even kill the Devil?

"You're motherfucking crazy, old man, if you think I am leaving without my kids," he screamed at the top of his lungs. The Devil appeared to change color. The angrier he became, and the louder he shouted, the more his skin turned a dark purple. He balled his hands into a throbbing fist. One punch might kill Grandpa.

That was the first time and last time I ever heard him call Jill and me "my kids." Until this moment, I had never thought about being the son of a monster or a devil. I used to tell Jill that she was truly the monster's child, as she had a somewhat darker complexion like him. I, on the other hand, was pasty white and looked like our mother. Now that Grandpa called him the Devil, what did that make me? This was a defining moment, and my only belief was that I would never survive this life for long.

I had been asleep in bed with Grandpa. Jill was in the next room, sleeping on a threadbare, rotting couch. The room I was afraid to sleep in, as I just knew it was haunted. I had slept in that room only once, but I remember it like it was yesterday. The hand came out of the closet and touched me. It scared me shitless. Sometimes, even today, I think about that ghostly encounter. After that, Jill and I would sometimes sleep in his bed. This ghost, could it have been another angel, maybe like Grandpa? I always believed it was my grandmother, who died before I was born and when the Devil was only twelve. I would consider anything, including ghosts, if it would make the Devil go away.

Jill and I had made the trek to Grandpa's house many times in the middle of the night. That time we escaped through my sister's front bedroom window. We decided not to take the gravel road but instead cut through the woods and creek. If the Devil discovered us missing, we could have been easily captured on the road. Plus, we had to pass a neighbor's house down the hill that had several vicious dogs that scared us. The full moon made our shadows tall and long. The only noise was our feet, stepping on leaves and twigs. Shadows from the trees raced along with us. Finally we crossed the creek, where the water was shallow. We saw a scattering of crawfish. We slid backward several times as we attempted to traverse the steepest and last creek embankment before reaching Grandpa's house. We ran across his garden to the back of the barn, and felt relief when we finally arrived on Grandpa's back porch. Besides numerous mosquito bites and thorn scratches, we'd made the journey in good shape.

His doors were never locked, so we walked in through the back. Holding hands, Jill and I crept into his bedroom. Grandpa was lying on his back with no covers and snoring with his mouth wide open. Jill stepped forward to wake him up, but I pulled her back. Witnessing the serenity of his sleep captivated me. This was the first time that I realized someone could sleep like this.

Jill broke my grip and quickly reached the bed. I followed but tripped over Grandpa's night piss pot. Luckily for us, he had not used it yet tonight. The white-and-red, chipped-painted bucket made a startling sound when it rolled across the wood floor. But Grandpa only slowly opened his grayish-blue eyes, squinting. Calmly he said, "What are you kids doing here?"

"We are afraid of the monster, Grandpa," Jill cried.

"Grandpa, he is going to kill us," I stammered.

"Now, now, settle down, kiddos," Grandpa softly encouraged. "How you get here?"

"We walked. Cut through the creeks," I responded with a fake gasping of air added to my voice.

He never asked questions about the monster. He knew; he always knew what his son was. He understood why we were scared. His voice calmed us, for he only had one volume and tone, kind of like elevator music. He pulled back the covers and motioned for me to come to bed. He then got up, grabbed a blanket and pillow, and made Jill a make-shift bed in the living room. My heartbeat finally relaxed, no longer a bass drum. Grandpa quickly fell back asleep. A slight breeze whispered through the bedroom window and scattered a host of dust balls out from under the bed. As they hurried across the floor, I pretended they were an army attacking all the darkness in my life.

Tranquility was interrupted by the sound of a truck engine that needed new pistons. The monster made his grand entrance by driving across the front lawn and crashing his truck on the side of the front porch.

I heard him stumbling and staggering onto the porch, the truck engine still running. I smelled the wretched odor of burned oil and gas fumes spewing blue smoke from the truck's tailpipe.

Grandpa's whole body trembled as he attempted to steady the long gun and not allow the Devil to grab it. Everything happened in slow motion. I felt dizzy, trying to focus on what was happening. I was trembling more than Grandpa. I felt my bladder ready to spill. Through the doorway of the bedroom, I could see Jill sitting up on the couch in a frozen position.

This night, Mom had left us at home while she went to work her night shift. The Devil had arrived at our house more agitated than most other times. He was screaming so loud that the windows rattled in our little prefabricated house. His fists were blasting through the sheetrock walls; dishes were thrown throughout the house with screaming threats of no tomorrow. "The truth hurts, and all you motherfuckers are going to rot in hell!" he declared. He stomped down the hardwood floors while scratching his crotch. His eyes bugged out like those of a giant bullfrog being squeezed. Blood veins popped out of his overheated face as he screamed every obscenity known to man. He stormed past my room and opened the front door, but not the screen. The piss splattered off the screen door and sprayed the living room furniture as he attempted to pee on the front porch. These episodes were getting worse, and this time we thought it was the end; he was going to kill us. That was when Jill and I ran for the creek to Grandpa's house.

"Son, you're crazy," my grandpa said. "You're drunk. Get on out of here now and leave us alone. I will shoot you." These words were neither a plea nor a threat; they were spoken as a factual statement. I would try in later years to replicate this type of simple, direct, and purposeful communication.

The Devil raised his massive fist and drew his arm back, preparing for the knockout. Grandpa held the gun steady. Still on the couch, Jill was now covered in a blanket, only her eyes peeking out.

After what felt like an eternity of screaming, cussing, and slinging spit from all corners of his mouth, the Devil backed down. It dawned on me the gun was the equalizer. It made all the difference. My grandpa may have been afraid too, but he held that gun steady on the Devil until he turned and staggered out the front door.

"Fuck all you motherfuckers! You'll all rot in hell. You'll damn sure pay for this. To hell with your fucking whore mother!" The Devil continued to scream obscenities as he crawled into his truck.

Grandpa sat on the side of the bed as the Devil peeled out and sped away, rubbing his bald head. The moonlight seemed to brighten, highlighting his snuff-stained sleeveless undershirt. Grandpa was 78 years old. He was still six feet three inches tall, a veteran of World War I, deployed as a mule skinner. He never went to school and could not read or write. His parents were sharecroppers, and he had always been a rancher and farmer. He had lived most of his life in extreme poverty and had survived everything life threw at him. Maybe that was why he now quickly calmed down. But he was my hero, having just come within seconds of killing his son to protect us.

Grandpa never tried to explain what happened. He was always a man of few words, but I wanted words this time. Reassurance that we would never have to run again. What I really wanted was for Grandpa to say, "Wait here. I'll finish this off so you kids will never have to see the Devil again."

In our childish brains, there was never any doubt that Grandpa would save us; he always did. We didn't know the word at the time, but he was our savior. His stability, consistency, and kindness were our only tangible model of humanity. He didn't hug or ever say "I love you." He didn't have to; we just knew it. I never understood how our savior, our angel, could have participated in the birth and creation of this Devil.

I thought of the times the Devil would awaken us with gunshots. For no reason, he would fire at the moon and stars. That was usually a precursor to him dragging me out at sunrise to hunt squirrels. My job was to circle the giant cottonwood trees, making noise to scare the little varmints to his side of the tree. He did shoot a lot of squirrels. He would make me clean them. I hated it, slicing the tail and pulling the entire skin over the squirrel's head. Several of the little varmints were always cleaned and in the icebox, waiting to be cooked. We ate them fried, boiled with dumplings, and grilled.

Grandpa was back asleep, loudly snoring, after his Devil confrontation. Death, cleaning squirrels, and shooting at mice seemed trivial compared to what I had just experienced. I had trapped possums and rabbits while trying to play like I was Daniel Boone, trying to be a future redneck. Observing one human about to kill another changed me that night. I didn't sleep. I watched the sunrise twinkle through the brittle, stained, and ragged front-room window blinds. Grandpa usually went to bed at five in the evening and was up by four in the morning. On this day, he slept in until almost five.

We didn't want to leave. The Devil would probably sleep until noon. There would still be hell to pay when we got home. Grandpa was on the front porch enjoying the early morning cool breeze. He always wore the same type of clothes: khaki pants, shirt, ranger boots, and a cowboy hat, straw in summer and felt for winter. I was hungry, but I knew Grandpa would only have a carton of milk in the icebox. I knew not to drink any, as he drank right out of it, leaving brown snuff around the opening as evidence.

I wandered around the house like a scared animal looking for the next place to hide. A grossly deteriorating fuzzy couch and one old broken-down rocking chair occupied the front room. Two chairs and a small red peeling Formica table from the 1940s in the middle room. One bed and dresser in the spare bedroom, which Grandpa rented out to an old bachelor merchant marine when he wasn't traveling the world's oceans. This man collected rocks from around the world, and I sometimes stole a few. This man also had parked an old Airstream trailer in the pasture but rarely used it. I would tell people that I was going to live in one of those when I grew up.

"Grandpa, I want to live with you," I pleaded.

"Boy, you can always come back. The Devil comes and goes. The Devil won't always be in him. He's gone now, so I'm taking you kids home this morning."

"Why didn't you shoot him? Why didn't you kill him? Were you going to if he grabbed us?"

"I don't know. What I do know is that if you pull a gun on someone, you need to be prepared to use it."

"He is the Devil, isn't he?" I asked.

"He is the Devil," Jill chimed in while wiping tears from her eyes. She stomped the floor and cried, "Let us stay! We want to live with you forever."

Grandpa didn't answer, and I took that as a yes.

Grandpa never gave clear answers unless he was speaking of tangible stuff like castrating calves or butchering hogs. But he said one last thing to me that morning, and I have never forgotten it: "Don't take life so serious, as no one ever gets out alive."

CHAPTER THREE

THE EXPERIMENT

WE HAD LIVED WITH MY GRANDPA UNTIL I WAS AROUND THREE years old. When I was older, I found photos of Grandpa standing with all of us, holding my sister. I was in a diaper and maybe was eighteen months old. Jill, fifteen months older, also appeared to be in a diaper. But the photos were old and faded, so that was my best guess. We were at my grandpa's house, but I didn't remember living there. Guess we lived there until he bought the prefabricated home and gave us ten acres of his 160.

Our house would be considered modern compared to his. We had an indoor toilet, though the sewage was piped under the house and into a trench that went nowhere. The septic tank about 40 yards away was continuously full or clogged. Our goat and milk cow always had some green grass to eat along the sewage trench. Once we got a washing machine, and a drainage hose was run to the outside of the house. This was an excellent attraction for frogs, who created tadpoles. Snakes followed the frogs, so a young boy like me had my own miniature Nile River.

More hours were spent on the solid concrete front porch than in the house. It served a lot of purposes. Here we had our first line of defense for killing flies before they invaded our home. We also had scorpion races. The porch had been painted many times, but it never seemed to stick too long. All that chipped paint, along with the blood of thousands of fat ticks we removed from our dogs and stomped to see how far the blood would splatter, was a concrete palette comparable to the best Pollock.

Our drinking water came from a shallow well. This caused many inconveniences, as did the small electric pump that drew the groundwater to the house. As a result, everyone used the same bathwater once the bathtub was filled. I was the youngest, so I bathed last, which meant the water was usually so dirty I could not see my feet. And the water was cold in the winter and hot in the summer, too.

Grandpa's house was about a mile from ours. It had no indoor toilet or running water. He had an old dirt cellar and several outhouses. One was a milking house, another a chicken house, and one was something like an old garage. The toilet was in there. He had an old fox hide nailed to the wall so you could warm your hands before sitting on a wooden plank with a hole cut in the middle. You never wanted to look into that hole while doing your business. Once I remembered asking my grandpa how I'd been potty-trained, since the toilet was so far away. He replied that butcher paper and newspaper were placed on the back porch floor, which I guessed sounded like solution enough to him.

Then there was Grandpa's barn: my sanctuary, my refuge from the Devil. Many a day and night, I would find solitude in that old barn. I hid my *Hit Parader* magazines among the hay bales. If I left them there too long, the rats took full advantage of them for nest building. The Devil prohibited anything that depicted long hair on males, so bands like The Beatles were often cursed as part of his indignation with the world. I was not allowed any hair to touch my forehead, so it was slicked back until I got on the school bus, when it would go its own messy way again.

I'm unsure how we guessed the purpose of the little yellow pills we found in the kitchen cabinet. Jill and I somehow figured out that they were dangerous. Maybe I'm wrong, but I can recall finding them and our mom screaming at us never to touch them again. That was a sign that they were very important or dangerous. We decided on danger. They'd been strategically placed at the highest shelf's back where supposedly no child could reach. Mothers always underestimate their children, while fathers don't pay attention.

During my later elementary years The Rolling Stones song "Mother's Little Helper" made the connection for me about little yellow pills and the ode to all the abused and beaten mothers out there.

Women my mother's age had generally married as teenagers to escape whatever they were running to escape, only to find themselves in a worse kind of prison. Then children started coming. Did Valium allow her to tolerate suffering? Were we part of this created hell? If so, could we fix it? Did God create Valium to keep a balance between evil and good?

Once chastised and threatened with corporal punishment by the Devil, we were motivated to determine those pills' purpose. There was no Google in those days, so the only thing to do was to ask the older kids in school. Seek out the thugs who would probably do drugs or know about such things. A different type of Oracle. Our dark web of information.

Jill and I were in elementary school at that time. I was in the third grade, and she was one grade higher. I remember the teacher leaving class after our atomic bomb exercise and then returning and announcing that President Kennedy had been assassinated. *Why would anyone kill a good person?* I wondered.

I had already started to develop my chameleon abilities and personality. Jill had a select circle of friends with none who would have the ability to advise us on the little yellow pills, but I knew someone. Javier.

Javier was several years older. He'd probably started smoking in the first grade. He was driving old tagless cars up and down the dirt road that ran by our house when we were in the third grade. His parents apparently allowed him to do whatever his heart desired. He had long hair and styled himself as a Mod with Beatle hats, hip-huggers, bell-bottoms, giant buckle super-wide belts, and karate sleeve shirts. He called the police *coppers*. He would walk around saying, "What's a penny made of?" We would all yell back, "Copper!" He would reply, "What's a dirty penny made from?" We would shout, "Dirty copper!" Javier always did this when the local police cruised by while we were on the school playground during recess. The cop would wave and laugh.

I envied Javier. I tried to emulate whatever he was doing. I was too poor to copy his clothing style or buy all the newest rock albums, but I did adopt his usage of foul language. Every other word out of his mouth was *fuck*, so I started saying it all the time. Then one day, the school bus driver asked me if I knew what it meant. I didn't know. Humbling myself, I couldn't ask anyone but Javier. He explained; then, I was baffled. How could you use a word that meant having sex in almost every sentence that came out of your mouth?

But Javier would be the most likely to know what the yellow pills were and what they were for. Jill and I decided that I would approach him. I held the Valium out to show him. Two were all I'd taken from the cabinet that morning before going to school.

"Man, what you got there?" Javier quickly snatched the pills from my hand. "Damn, boy, you can get into a shitload of trouble bringing these to school." He promptly placed them into his too-tight bell-bottom pants front pocket and motioned for me to follow. His choice of pants had no back pockets and were so tight that they appeared to be painted on him. He had to shift his genitals from one side to another to ease the pain or discomfort. All the kids joked about how he frequently touched himself, but nobody was brave enough to tell him.

"I got them from my mother," I said, once we were in the back alley across from the school.

"Yellow ones aren't as strong as blue ones," he said. "But I'll take these. How much you want for them?" A slight grin appeared. I think he realized he didn't have to pay for them. But if he took them from me, then this newfound source would not present itself another time.

"But what are they *for*?" I persisted.

"With some beer or a bottle of wine, you could get super high."

I must have looked confused, because he explained further. "They kind of chill you out. You know, slow things down. Not be so nervous." Then he looked at me again. "You little shit, you haven't taken any of these, have you?"

"No!" I said. "I just found them."

Javier shook his head at me. "Well, don't," he said. "You could get dizzy or sick, or even die. Especially with too much booze."

"So they can kill you?" I anxiously asked.

"Damn straight."

Armed with this much-needed knowledge, I thanked him.

"Hold on there. We not finished here. How much you want for them babies?" Javier squeezed his hand into his pocket and then held out his palm, showing the pills.

"They're not for sale," I responded, and quickly snatched them from him.

"Are we really going to do something?" Jill asked when I returned home from school.

To this day, I still cannot remember whose idea it was. My sister did ask the question, this much I do remember. From there, it gets fuzzy. I think the initial trial run was her idea. We discussed how many pills it might take. Of course, Javier's take on it was all we had to go on.

We didn't want to waste pills, as we weren't sure if our mother would realize some were missing. So, as nine- and ten-year-olds might do, we attempted an experiment. The next time the Devil came home and passed out, we'd pour some of his whiskey out and piss in the bottle. This way, we would know if he could taste the difference of something foreign mixed in. Jill turned her back so I could have privacy while I prepared to pee in the whiskey bottle. I was scared and anxious, and that probably affected my aim. It was not a pretty sight as my pee splattered the bottle and then my hand before it found its way inside. I showed Jill the finished product.

"Did you even get any in there?" Jill giggled while refusing to examine the bottle any closer. "I think you need to add more."

"I'm all out. Plus, it already looks more like pee than whiskey." He never took the whiskey bottle out of the sack, so we doubted he'd ever notice any discoloration.

The next morning, the sun was starting to rise. I counted the flies on the ceiling that had started buzzing when sunlight came through my east-facing window. Jill crept into my bedroom while rubbing the sleep from her eyes. We waited and watched. She glanced at me with a look of apprehension. Was she thinking it was all a mistake, and that we shouldn't have gone this far? The deed was done. Was it too much pee? We were excited but also very anxious. We would be the only suspects if we failed, and then the Devil would unleash his fury upon us.

On cue, he awoke and stumbled outside toward his pickup. After a hard-drinking night, he needed to rekindle the spirits with his guzzle of whiskey. Our hearts were pounding as we watched from my bedroom window. The whiskey sack rose to his lips.

"Goddamn!"

Whiskey splattered the windshield as he spewed it out. The bottle separated from the sack as it flew across the yard and crashed on the sidewalk. The Devil's face had never been more purple and red. He stormed out of the truck, leaving the door open. He tripped and fell over the uneven bricks of the homemade sidewalk.

"You little motherfuckers!"

Suffice to say that the beating we took that morning was of Olympic quality. But we didn't confess. I got some degree of satisfaction that no matter how bad the thrashing, this left doubt in the Devil's mind and was therefore a victory.

Jill and I disagreed on whether this was a successful test. Still stinging from the belt marks across her backside, Jill saw no silver lining in our endeavor. But I wanted to move forward with the Valium experiment.

"Let's try it and just make him sick. Maybe if he gets sick enough, he'll leave and never come back," I said.

"He'll never leave. Why would he? He does whatever he wants," Jill replied.

"I know. Mom's his minion," I said.

"What?"

"A minion. It's someone who takes care of vampires," I explained.

"I know what it is," Jill stated in her older-sister tone. We'd both read *Dracula Tales*, sharing the book when we borrowed it from the bookmobile.

Vampire or devil, we needed to decide what to do. I didn't want to go it alone. Jill didn't want to try again. But I continued to steal a Valium now and then, hiding them inside an old shoe in my closet in case she changed her mind.

CHAPTER FOUR

ANOTHER OPTION

OUR OLD BLACK-AND-WHITE TELEVISION RARELY WORKED. PLI-
ers were required to change channels, as the knob had been broken off for
years. The TV displayed only gray fuzz and made a hissing sound when
the wind blew. Jill and I took turns going outside to hold the tall TV
antenna steady or rotating it while the other one watched. On a good day,
we could get two channels. I don't recall any local news being on television. There was no crime beat. I do remember watching the FBI series.

The local news came from our fifteen-family telephone party line. I
am not sure at what age we got a phone, but it was pure unadulterated
entertainment. If another household was using the phone, the additional
fourteen couldn't call or receive calls. What we could do was listen in
on their conversations. Picking up the receiver without the other party
knowing it was an art form. There had to be total silence in the house
when you did it. If you needed to use the phone and some other family
was using it, you could kindly ask them to hurry up. Or you could be like
the Devil, and tell them to get the fuck off the phone or pick it up and
become part of the conversation.

In one of these eavesdropping sessions, we first heard of Tommy
Jaxs. He had been in jail for a few years for beating up and robbing old

men. Surprisingly, but maybe not for the 1960s, the area had many old widowers—men who lost their wives and never remarried. My grandpa was one of those. His wife died when she was only 38 years old. He had many friends who were in the same boat: farmers who occasionally got a mineral rights royalty check, sold off some cattle, or grew a good crop. Most couldn't read or write and didn't trust banks. They had fought in World War I and survived the Great Depression. Daily entertainment was playing dominoes at the local pool hall and hanging out at the only beer joint in town. At certain times of the year, many of them carried a lot of cash. Someone on the party line mentioned that my grandpa had been a target, but something had gone wrong. Tommy Jaxs's name was cited as the alleged culprit.

Howard Easley was every kid's favorite cop. He didn't look much older than your average high school student. With his disheveled, somewhat long blond hair, baggy uniform, one pants leg always stuck inside his boot, and goofy demeanor, Howard was the quintessential small-town cop. He worked the day shift and always made at least one drive around our grade school playground before that last bell rang to go home. He knew where we played hooky and would occasionally hang out with us to smoke cigarettes.

A creek separated our tiny town and the high school from the grade school. Under the creek's bridge, we would run and hide after getting off the morning school bus on days we planned to play hooky. There were usually five of us, and we would sit, smoke, and learn the facts of life from Javier and Mike. To say Javier was a thug is accurate; to say Mike was a thug is a colossal understatement. Mike transferred to our school from a big-city school, where he was kicked out. He smoked, drank, spewed cuss words we had never heard before, and taught us how to shoplift. Plus, Mike brought his mother's mink fur bra to show us, adding to his claim to fame. He was so genuine that Javier had to pick his game up a little.

I tried to smoke like the others, but inhaling made me sick. They must have known I was faking it but never teased me. I was coughing my head off one morning under our bridge when Officer Easley made his rounds.

"Any of you little shits have a light?" We hadn't noticed his arrival and were startled. Mike and Javier couldn't reach for their cigarette lighters fast enough. They competed to be in favor with him.

"Boys, you aren't planning to go shopping today, are you?" Officer Easley squatted and asked this while looking straight into Mike's eyes.

"Why, Officer, why would you ask such a thing?" Mike responded in his best Eddie Haskell flair from a *Leave It to Beaver* episode.

"Oh, I don't know. Just seems I've been seeing a few more shoplifting reports on the same days you kids are playing hooky under this rickety old bridge. Now, you wouldn't know anything about that, would you, guys?"

Officer Easley always asked rhetorical questions. Only Mike or Javier felt compelled to answer. I had my own inquiry on that day. What did he know about Tommy Jaxs?

"So, Officer Easley, I hear this Jaxs guy that robs old men is back in town?" I knew that Officer Easley kept no secrets and would exaggerate anything he knew. We were a captive audience and attentive to his every word.

"Yeah, that bastard is back. Didn't think we'd see him so soon. Guess he had lots of good behavior in prison, as he can always be a suck-up if it serves a purpose. I thought he'd come back around here come broom corn cutting time."

I hadn't cut broom corn yet, but when I did start at age thirteen, getting paid $13 in cash for a 12-hour day made me feel rich. We lived in broom corn country, and the migrant workers were called Johnnys. I was not sure why. Most were Native Americans. They would pitch their tents by the river after working in the fruit and vegetable fields in California, then go on up through the Midwest and end up in Florida during the winter. It made sense that Jaxs would prey on these people, as they were paid in cash daily, and no one banked their money.

"Luckily, we were able to catch him last time," Easley continued. "He'd planned on beating and robbing several more older men, but yours truly got him. Yeah, I got him good. He tried to put up a fight, but my little helper here took care of that. One slap upside the head with one of these was all he wanted." He placed his hand on a black-jack, a black leather spatula-looking thing with a flat hunk of lead in the end. A precursor to the modern-day police baton. None of us could picture Easley being cruel or even hurting anyone. Was he a small-town Columbo and truly smart behind that country bumpkin façade? Javier told me later that Easley wasn't even on the police force when Jaxs went to prison.

I needed more information. Had Jaxs planned on beating and robbing my grandpa? Was it true what my sister and I heard on the telephone party line? If something happened to Grandpa, there was no backup plan.

Before I could ask for a follow-up, Javier chimed in. "Like man, this guy supposed to be in prison forever or something?" This gave Easley another opportunity to rattle on.

"He's pretty smart. He knew not to use a weapon so the penalty wouldn't be as bad. But he's also damn lucky 'cause he could have killed one of them old codgers. Then he would have to dance with Old Sparky," he said with a laugh. He meant the electric chair. "Hell, Jaxs is a big man. He could have robbed them just by threatening them; he didn't have to beat the shit out of them. That's just pure meanness."

Easley made some sense to me. Why beat an old man if you didn't have to? I had an attraction to the underdog and the desire to lend a hand. War on the bullies would become a calling card for me.

Officer Easley continued, "We're keeping an eye on him. He's staying behind the beer joint in that ratty shack with old Charles Bowin. Charles is just nasty, and they make a good match. They both crazy as a bedbug."

I couldn't wait to tell Jill what I had learned. She was in a panic hearing that Jaxs was staying in town. She took being concerned about our grandpa to a whole different level.

The school bus ride took over an hour, but distance was not the only reason it took so long to get home. The bus was packed with kids, made frequent stops, and traveled over narrow dirt roads. Jill and I were the first ones on in the morning and the last to get off in the afternoon. No air-conditioning, so all windows stayed down, allowing the red dust of the dirt roads to twist and roll through the bus like a hive of bees.

"What are we going to do?" Jill asked. "Does Grandpa know Jaxs is back in town?"

I explained how I knew this Charles Bowin. There were many drunks in town, and Charles was at the top of the worst list. He would drink aftershave, vanilla extract—anything with alcohol in it. But he wasn't a demon. When you're ten years old, you think everybody is old; to me he was ancient. He looked like walking death and smelled worse. His face sank in like a skull with a thin layer of sun-drenched skin stretched over it. He was always unshaven and had a yellowish-red streak in his white hair from where he constantly ran his fingers through it to keep it off his forehead. Chain-smokers like him always had nicotine-stained fingers.

If I missed the school bus, I'd hitchhike home with my friend Randy. Randy's grandpa owned an auto mechanic shop of sorts next to the beer joint with assorted metal junk out front, a few used cars for sale, and a menagerie of whatever he'd negotiated for in exchange for whatever he was selling. He also had the corner on the town's loan-sharking. We'd go by there first to see if his grandpa would take us home. Charles Bowin was always hanging out there. Rarely did Randy's grandpa give us a ride, but Charles always offered. We made that mistake once. Charles told us he was taking the long scenic way to our homes, but we ended up on some unknown back road.

I don't think we knew what *scenic* meant, but that should have been a clue for us to beware. He started talking dirty to us and explained he could teach us a few things to help us with the ladies. Randy and I looked at each other and jumped out of the car at a four-way stop. Later, Randy said that Charles was a dirty nasty man who liked little boys but that he wasn't afraid of him. To prove he wasn't scared, he said he was ready to take another ride with Charles and that he'd beat him up next time.

I told Jill how Charles was forever bumming money, cigarettes, and alcohol. Randy always had a cigarette to give him. Several times we sold him alcohol. Randy and I would comb the bar ditches where all the drunks threw out their mostly empty whiskey bottles. There was always a little whiskey left in each bottle, and we'd combine it to make maybe a half-pint, then sell it to someone like Charles. Or we'd trade the whiskey for a favor. Charles rarely had money, so we'd give him the half-pint in exchange for him buying us beer. We usually had enough change for a quart of Coors.

So that was my plan, I explained. Since Charles and Jaxs lived together and were drunks, it made perfect logic that they would share a bottle. We could put as much Valium as we could get in a bottle of whiskey, sell it to Charles, and, hopefully, Jaxs would die. Problem solved. Jill and I used our favorite secret hiding place to conduct this planning session, the big elm tree. It was the largest tree on the property, surrounded by nature's obstacle course of at least a thousand thorny vines that no adult would attempt to navigate.

"But what if they both get sick and die?" Jill asked.

"Well then, they both just die," was my reply. I'd never told anyone about Charles trying to molest Randy and me. That would be too embarrassing, plus other kids would ridicule us. But I told Jill. She needed to be on my side, to understand that these men didn't deserve to live any longer. She bought it and was genuinely indignant.

"We'll get caught," she fretted. "Mom will miss the Valium. We just can't do it!"

"So you want Grandpa to die? How you going to feel when he gets killed by Jaxs?"

Jill bristled and stared at me. "Of course, I don't want Grandpa to get killed," she replied through grinding teeth.

"All you need to do is just don't tell," I insisted.

Eventually, she gave in. She would start stealing the Valium while I collected the whiskey. No way was I going to involve Randy, even though he undoubtedly would have welcomed the opportunity. I walked the bar ditches that paralleled every section of road and driveway in our rural area, searching for the needed whiskey. I would also need to steal half a pint from the Devil. Time was of the essence. The plan was in action.

CHAPTER FIVE

THE PLAN STARTED

JILL SECURED THE VALIUM. MY PART WAS TO GET THEM TO JAXS inside a whiskey bottle that he would drink. I needed Randy's help. I couldn't tell him what my sister and I were up to, but he wouldn't care. Randy was practically raising himself and could go anywhere at any time he chose. He was small for his age, but he'd fight anybody, any size, anytime. He had these long bangs that stayed in his eyes and made him look mean. His grandpa had that auto repair shop in front of where Jaxs was living; this was the only repair shop in town where old men would hang out when they had no other place to go. Many of these men could not climb the long stairs to the town's pool hall, so Old Duck's was the place to pass the time. I needed Randy to gain access to Jaxs.

I approached Randy about selling the whiskey or trading it to old Charles to buy us some beer. That way, Jaxs and Charles would probably drink from the same bottle. It wouldn't bother me if Charles got sick or died. I'd never had one of those sex talks or stay-away-from-stranger talks with my mother or anyone else, but I knew now Charles was a nasty human.

Randy explained that Jaxs was working as a mechanic for his grandpa, and we should sell it to Jaxs at the auto shop. He said Charles wouldn't have money to buy it. Jill thought that was the best option, because she was concerned that if the bottle was shared evenly, the Valium would not be enough to send Jaxs to hell.

The auto shop was a patchwork of old rusty and new sheet iron, skinned over a combination of wood and iron poles that made up its skeleton. I wasn't sure the overhead door could even shut. Not that it made any difference. No one locked their houses in those days. Randy's grandpa was a lot like Randy: mean, compulsive, and just downright ornery. And, like Randy, he'd fight anyone too, or, as the older men would say, at the drop of a hat.

Randy's grandpa greeted us by saying, "Well, what you little fuckers up to today?" Randy never called his grandpa anything other than Old Duck. I never knew why and never needed to ask, but his flat-footed reverse pigeon toe walk was distinctive. Old Duck was taking a piss right outside the entrance to the auto shop, which was at the end of the town's two-block-long main drag. The whole town was only four square blocks with one stop sign in the middle. He didn't even attempt to hide his penis from us. He shook it a few times, then said, "Boys, you still won't be able to do this when you're a man." He proceeded to bang his penis against a light pole. He then turned it toward us. "Yes, they call me Old Duck, and with most things, I just don't give a fuck."

"See this scar?" He pointed to his penis. "Got that scar there on the end in a damn knife fight back in 1955. Hell, it almost cut my dick plumb off." Neither one of us said a word. I thought Old Duck's candor caught even Randy off guard. He was bowlegged with darkened leathery skin and an intimidating gravel voice. Maybe that voice and willingness to pull his penis out in broad daylight were why nobody ever fucked with him. I wanted to grow old like that so even the Devil wouldn't fuck with me.

"You crazy old son-of-a-bitch," Randy shouted. Old Duck's best-running buddy, Folgers, had snuck up behind us and given Randy a wedgy. I never knew his real name, but we all called him Folgers because he drank that cheap-ass coffee all of his waking days. He looked like a bullfrog on steroids, as broad as he was tall and with no neck. He had been cut from ear to ear in a knife fight, but you couldn't see the scar unless he lifted his orangutan jaws to show you. His eyes bugged out, and he was always sweating. He was said to have wrestled the last bear ever found in the county—allegedly he settled in the area after a career traveling with small-town circuses. He was the only carney we had ever met and had a reputation for giving the hardest wedgies.

"I can sense you little fuckers are up to no good," Folgers growled. He had a raspy, irritating voice that could have put the famous DJ Wolfman Jack, the Wolfman, out of business. Folgers sounded and looked mean; it made sense that Old Duck used him to collect debts and be around for intimidation.

I had the whiskey bottle hidden in the front of my pants. Embarrassing as it was, I had to wear old hand-me-down pants. My mother had added elastic to the waistband so I could continue to grow into them. As I grew taller, she'd sew additional length to the legs from other worn-out denim pants. The result was multiple layers of different stages of faded denim. In the 1980s this look became fashionable, so Mom was way ahead of her time. But that day, the humiliating elastic that I was bullied about was serving a purpose. I pretended to scratch my crotch but rearranged the bottle in case a wedgy was in my future.

"Well, Old Duck, we just hanging out. Skipping school and looking for trouble," Randy replied. Randy never lied about anything, but his grin was a dead giveaway that he wasn't telling the whole story. He didn't know what I was really planning. We hung out and talked awhile and watched the drunks come out the side door of the beer joint to take a piss and then go back in. The beer joint had only a one-holer urinal, so going outside to piss was a necessity. As we continued making small talk, I witnessed an old drunk trying to hump some woman while sitting in a rocking chair out back of the beer joint. He was too drunk even to walk straight, much less to have sex.

"Hey, Jaxs," Randy shouted while kicking at this man's feet who was working underneath a car.

"What the fuck do you want?" Jaxs replied while rolling out from underneath an old '57 Chevy.

Oh shit, I thought to myself.

Jaxs was one of the biggest men I had ever seen. He rose from the car and looked to be about 6'5" or taller. I always measured height by my grandpa's size. Jaxs was bare-chested under his oil-stained overalls. His arms and shoulders were massive. He was cleanly shaven with a perfect Elvis Presley hairdo. His arms, chest, shoulders, and back were covered with hair like a gorilla. He scared me. Nothing scared Randy. Maybe if Randy knew what I had planned, he would be scared.

Jaxs grabbed an old used bar of oily Lava soap, washed his hands, and said, "Come over here." We walked over to the shop sink while Jaxs dried his hands on a dirty red shop rag.

"Don't you ever touch me again. I don't give a fuck that you are Old Duck's grandkid," he calmly stated to Randy.

"Just trying to make a little cigarette and beer money, you know," Randy replied.

"You little bitches, I ain't loaning you any money. Get the fuck out of here."

"We aren't asking for a loan. We got this here, good Kentucky bourbon," replied Randy as he motioned for me to show Jaxs what I had. "We want to sell it to you."

"Fuck that. Give me that damn bottle," demanded Jaxs.

Before I could contest his demand, he grabbed the bottle as I was taking it out of my elastic-waist pants. His hand was huge and engulfed the whole bottle like palming a basketball. Randy protested and started prancing around, clenching his fist as though he was going to whoop up on Jaxs. Old Duck was too busy shooting the shit with some oil field workers out front to pay any attention to what was going on with Randy and me.

"Really, you little shitheads. I swat flies off my ass bigger than you two." Jaxs took the bottle, took a small sip, and stuck it in the front pocket of his oversized overalls. "What the fuck is this nasty shit?" He held the bottle up close to his face and said, "Jim Beam, this here ain't no goddamn Jim Beam whiskey. The seal was broke, so what is this shit?"

I wasn't going to tell Jaxs, but he was spot-on. I recollected that I had included Old Crow, Old Rocking Chair, Ezra Brooks, Weller, and some that just said *corn whiskey* on the label. I only used the Jim Beam bottle because it was the newest, cleanest bottle I could find.

"Now get the fuck out of here. And, don't even think about telling Old Duck 'cause he will beat your ass for even having this shit."

That was enough for me. I was ready to get the hell out of there. My job was finished as Jaxs now had the tainted whiskey.

"Fuck you, man! Give it back or pay us," Randy demanded.

Jaxs pulled a large crescent wrench out of his back pocket. "Not now," Jaxs said as he pointed the wrench at us. "But if you don't get out of here, I'll come find you and beat the shit out of you guys. So fuck off now!"

I pulled Randy away as he kept yelling at Jaxs, "Fuck you, man, fuck you, man! What's the matter with you? Don't you want the money? We going to let this asshole do this to us?" Randy asked as we walked away.

"Randy, we tried. It didn't work out. We can get more whiskey. It ain't worth it. That man is huge. He could kill us."

"The motherfucker wouldn't touch us. Old Duck would kill him if he did. He could sic Folgers on his dumb ass," Randy explained.

Old Duck never struck me as someone who would defend anybody but himself. Perhaps he would protect his grandson. Maybe it was another reason to keep Folgers around. I wasn't sure that Randy knew the whole backstory on Jaxs; for all I knew, he might even have Old Duck on his potential hit list. Randy and I agreed to disagree, so off we went to collect more whiskey so Randy could get his quart of Coors.

I explained to Jill that the deal was now in play, and we just had to wait. She seemed somewhat shocked that I had completed my part. "This is real," I reminded her. "We're in this together." All Randy had done was go with me, and I assured her that he had no idea the whiskey had Valium mixed in it.

CHAPTER SIX

THE WAITING

JILL AND I LISTENED IN EVERY DAY ON THE PARTY-LINE CALLS,
hoping to hear some news of Jaxs. This was our only forum for updates
from the outside world of our Devil's den. No word would indicate that
he probably just got sick or something. If that were the case, he might figure out he got poisoned by our whiskey. I played with my old beat-up toy
Tonka Army jeep in between my turn to listen in on the party line. It was
made of heavy metal and was probably the only toy I had that could not
be destroyed. That jeep was my form of escapism. Jill had graduated from
dolls to reading Donna Parker mystery books. I couldn't understand why
anyone would read a book if it wasn't required in school.

Sleep was hard to find on hot summer nights. Jill and I would migrate
to the front porch, lying on the concrete and gazing at the stars. We waited
until almost midnight to do this, as the concrete needed to lose the
heat captured from the day's sun. We could only do this when the Devil
wasn't home. Even if we misjudged his arrival, we could hear the old
green Chevy pickup coming from a mile away. We sometimes referred
to it as the Devil's carriage—Jill's newfound love of reading added to
both of our vocabularies.

Lying on the porch, I felt like I could reach out and touch the stars.

There were no outdoor lights, close neighbors, and there was no glow from a distant city. Without starlight, total darkness. With Mom working the night shift at a nursing home, we had all this coveted peace and quiet until the Devil arrived. If he showed up unexpectedly, we could run through the woods to Grandpa's house.

Jill and I were pointing out patterns in the Milky Way one night when we were startled by the sound of someone walking up to our driveway. It was impossible to walk our driveway without making noise due to all the loose gravel.

"What y'all doing?" It was Denny, a new temporary neighbor, who was staying with his uncle up the road about two miles. It was not unusual for new people to show up and live with relatives during broom corn or other crop harvesting seasons. Everybody had to work, so if you had relatives along the seasonal farm work route, you moved in with them. The occasional rich kid from some big city would show up and live with a relative during the summer. They never worked. Usually, they were punished by being sent to a relative. Denny wasn't one of them. He was poorer than poor.

He appeared as a shadow walking toward us, a moon shadow. I didn't know him well, not like a friend. But everyone in this area was bonded by the commonality of poverty.

"Got any water? I been walking from the fields to home. My ride wouldn't wait on me. That there is a long walk to get to Uncle's."

I showed him the water hose and turned on the outdoor faucet for him. He drank for five minutes; then he squirted water all over his face and hands, shaking it off like a shaggy dog.

"You kids need to be careful out here these days," Denny advised.

Kids, I thought—hell, he wasn't old enough to call us that. He was 16 years old at the most.

"We doing okay. Our parents are inside," I lied. Undoubtedly he had already heard of where the Devil lived. Even these kids from other towns who came for the harvest seasons would listen to stories of the Devil's escapades.

"Well, all right then, but some people been missing. They say old Tommy Jaxs has gone missing with some broom corn Johnny named Sonny. I worked with Jaxs's son the last few days, and he say they're looking everywhere for his dad. I worked with Jaxs and Sonny some this season. Don't know them well; just know them when I see them. Sonny's boy worried about his dad too. Both them guys are real bastards. Bet somebody cut 'em, and they floating in the river somewhere."

Jill and I looked at each other. We were both thinking, *What have we done?* How could we have known Jaxs had any kids? It wasn't play anymore, if it ever had been. For our peace of mind, we concluded that Jaxs and Sonny were only drunks who were probably not missing at all. They were just out on an extended drunk escapade.

"You're right, Denny. They're just bastards, old drunk bastards," I responded.

"Well, you guys take it easy," said Denny as he tipped his ball cap at us and strolled away.

The Devil was on a roll for the next three days. Two nights in a row, Jill and I had to crawl out the front bedroom window and make the trek through the woods and across the creek to work our way to Grandpa's house. It never crossed our minds that we could be placing his life in danger. Maybe deep down we were hoping that Grandpa would pull the trigger on the Devil this time. The Devil became more active during full moons, and we never knew when those moons would arrive. We didn't have a calendar to check them.

On one of these nights, thinking maybe the Devil was following us, we took refuge in the trunk of an old 1961 Buick. It had been wrecked and parked in the pasture. We had a lot of land, so our old vehicles ended up in the pasture. The cows used them as something to lean and rub their backs against. Nature did its best by providing tall grass that grew unrestricted around the cars that would eventually offer camouflage to hide the unsightly rusting.

That night we saw what we thought was one of our cats running up the trail ahead of us. The moonlight presented just a shadow. But when we ran and caught up to it, a skunk sprayed us. When we arrived smelling of high heaven, all Grandpa said was, "You kids got to learn this stuff on your own. That's the best part of figuring things out." He put us in an old rusty metal water trough and scrubbed us down with his special recipe lye soap.

A week later, Randy and I did one of our four-mile night walks into town. He was waiting, hiding in the tall Johnson grass that lined the bar ditches. We cut through the woods to stay off the main roads. With all the migrant workers, local bullies, and the violent rural culture, it was always best for us to minimize our exposure. Our destination was the only burger joint in town, where all the cool older guys hung out. We planned to get a fountain Coke with lots of ice, which was a luxury, then walk to the pool hall down the street.

The burger joint was packed. The parking lot looked like a muscle car convention. There was a jacked-up GTO, a Road Runner, a souped-up 1963 Chevy Impala, two Z28 Camaros, and the meanest, fastest beast of them all, a 1962 Ford Falcon. It belonged to Leon Spottedhorse. Leon was the darkest-complexion Indian I knew. He was daring, mean, and rugged. He loved to rebuild and modify cars into hot rods, and his would always be the fastest. He'd already been in two wrecks, and his passenger was killed both times. Leon had those car wrecks' scars all over his body and face. Legend had it he'd been a star athlete, our town's version of Jim

Thorpe. But the crashes changed all of that. Now drugs and alcohol controlled his world. He was older than most who hung out in this small town, maybe in his early 20s.

"Randy, I don't want to go in," I said nervously. "Leon's in there. The last time we ran into him, he knocked the shit out of us."

"Come on, Jenkins, don't be a pussy. The place is packed; he won't even see us. Besides, you know he's just trolling for girls anyway," Randy said.

We were soaked in sweat from the walk into town; we must have smelled and looked pretty bad when we made our entrance. The crowd mostly ignored us when we sat down at the counter. This gathering wore the latest bell-bottoms, wide belts with colossal medallion-type buckles, karate-sleeved shirts, and Beatle hats. Not to mention those who wore knee-high moccasin boots, headbands, and tie-dyed shirts; they were the true hippies. Randy and I must have looked like country bumpkins.

The smell of char burgers and overused vats of grease gave our sweaty, smelly bodies some cover. The sign read, "Grease changed every Thursday." We ordered from the waitress, Kathy, and no sooner had we done so when I felt strong flexing arms wrap around my neck and pull me backward.

"Jenkins, you little fuck. Mommy give you a hall pass to come to town?" I could smell Leon's alcohol-soaked breath as he squeezed my neck harder. Maybe, I thought, Leon's bullying of me was his way of showing affection? Was he kidding around? If the older boys thought Leon liked me, maybe they wouldn't fuck with me.

Randy was taking all of this in stride. Even if he was smaller than me, nobody ever seemed to pick on him. Maybe it was because they were afraid of his grandpa or that crazy Folgers.

Leon proceeded to drag me off the counter stool toward the door. "Come on, you little shits, let's go for a ride."

"Oh, no," I yelled back. "I ain't getting in no fucking car with you."

Being his usual self, Randy always sided with the older bullies over me and immediately responded, "Hell yes, let's go."

"See, Randy ain't no pussy," Leon calmly stated. He never raised his voice. Leon didn't have any awkwardness around anybody; he just didn't give a shit.

With my heart pounding out of my chest, I stopped resisting. We went outside and Randy hopped in the front seat of Leon's hot rod Ford Falcon, and I hunkered down in the back. Leon fired up the engine. It sounded like a diesel truck with glasspacks, shaking and rattling with muscle.

"Where we going?" Randy asked. For the first time, he seemed a bit worried.

Leon just turned to look at him with a sinister smile and said, "Does it really fuckin' matter?"

He stomped the gas pedal so hard I thought it would go through the floorboard. He did two donuts in the burger joint's gravel parking lot while spraying gravel over its glass entrance. He shifted his pistol grip Hurst shifter into second gear and spun sideways as we hit the main road's pavement. He slammed it to third as he ran through the town's only stoplight. We were headed north. There was nothing north of town but a river and migrant worker campsites.

Leon took a whiskey bottle from under the seat and lit a joint while keeping the car steering straight by locking his knees on the steering wheel. We were cruising at 80 miles per hour, and this crazy dude was driving with his damn legs.

Randy and I shouted over the engine, "Leon, you can let us out now."

"Fuck that shit, you little fuckers. Get some hair on that chest and grow some big balls."

Leon slammed the brakes as we slid into a plowed field. He then gave it the gas, downshifted, hit the highway going back south, and hit the brakes again until we stopped. He pulled alongside a broken-down car with four people in it. Leon rolled his window down and, with the calmest of voice, said, "You fine-looking young men need some help?"

The men were apparently Mexican migrant workers, as they spoke no English. They exited their car and through rudimentary sign language, it was determined that they needed a push to get their car started.

"We're here to assist and please my south of the border brothers," Leon said. He motioned for the men to get into their car. He spun the Falcon around, laying rubber across the road, and pulled up behind theirs. The sign language that followed was simple. Leon would ease up on their back bumper and then push the car until it started. After that, we would be on our way to wherever Leon was taking us.

Everything started off well. Leon pushed the car onto the road even though his front bumper didn't match their old Fairlane's bumper well. At 20 miles per hour, the car started with a black smoke backfire that rose like a cloud over Leon's headlights. The men waved for Leon to back off and were probably saying thank you. However, Leon didn't stop. All he said was, "Watch this, motherfuckers, we going to have some shit fun now."

Leon downshifted, then banged it back into third, and within seconds we were doing almost 60. The Mexicans were hanging out the windows, yelling, "Ya, ya, ya, no mas, no mas, no mas, no mas." Leon let out a sinister laugh and gave the Falcon more gas. Randy and I were now on the floorboard, expecting to crash and die at any moment.

At 75 miles per hour, Leon hit the brakes and backed off. He flipped off the Mexicans and then turned onto a one-lane dirt road that followed the river. It was just two ruts with foot-high grass in the middle. A few miles down, he stopped alongside a migrant worker camp.

"Here we are, fellows. I want to see where they found old Jaxs's and

Sonny's bodies. I ain't buying that shit that dumbass sheriff said. He say they got into some kind of wood alcohol or some crazy moonshine shit. Sonny was my cousin, and he wouldn't drink that kind of shit. He had a little pride."

Migrant workers camped by the river backed up from their campfires into the shadow lines in front of the tents. Even they were afraid of this crazy Leon. The light flickered from the slight breeze fluffing the fire, creating an orange illusion across their eyes. They appeared as a pack of coyotes in the shadows, and all I could see was the orange of their eyes.

"Oh my God," I whispered under my breath. Denny, our new neighbor, had said Jaxs and Sonny were missing, and now Leon said they'd been found.

CHAPTER SEVEN

DOUBT

"I DON'T KNOW."

"What do you mean you don't know?" We were back at the big elm tree, and Jill was in a somber mood.

"Jill, I just don't know!"

"Did we kill them?"

"I guess maybe we did," I said. "Or maybe we didn't."

She chose denial. "Well, I don't think we did. Those pills and whiskey mix just couldn't have killed two men."

Part of me agreed. But I also felt a sense of power if I believed we did. It felt good, intoxicating. I'd never felt in control of anything before. Everything in my life had been dominated by the Devil's actions, directly or indirectly. I couldn't share that feeling of power with anyone. Our small town would create many versions of what happened to those two.

Our small town was the quintessential Americana rural haven. A three-block main street was separated by a stoplight that rarely operated. The traditional storefronts of the mid-1960s were there. The first two blocks included two Laundromats, a pharmacy, a clothing store, a variety store, a grocery market, a one-screen movie theater, and an ice locker dock and storage. The ice locker dock was essential to survival. This was where customers could rent freezer space to store butchered meat and buy ice to keep other items cold on the long trip back home. The last block contained a deteriorating old three-story red-brick boarding hotel. It mainly housed older men whose wives had died and they had no adult children to care for them. The hotel was a depressing place. One bathroom was at the end of each floor. No cookstoves were allowed, so residents used hot plates for cooking and stingers to heat their coffee. Room doors were always open, and every resident appeared to have false teeth soaking in a jar for cleaning. Charles Bowin, the local nasty man, had lived there until they kicked him out. Allegedly he would masturbate with his door open.

The three most vital businesses in town were on that last block: the *Weekly Democrat* newspaper, the pool hall, and the store belonging to old Salem Lowe. If we were going to find any news on the cause of death or anything related to Jaxs and Sonny's deaths, it would not be in the newspaper, which ran grocery ads and covered school activities, livestock sales, obituaries, and church news. For the real news and gossip, the pool hall and old Salem's store were the places to be.

The old pool hall was on the second floor of a timeworn building with peeling paint, exposed brick, cement blocks, and wood. No one ever knew what was on the bottom floor, which had no windows and no noticeable entry. The decaying wood stairs leading to the pool hall started on the sidewalk and went straight to the second floor. The stairs were always moist with snuff and tobacco spit. It was a steep climb. The pool hall was one open floor. Windows opened in summer, and there was one small open-flame gas heater in the winter. A urinal protruded from one corner wall. To take a piss, men just turned their back on the crowd. Women were not allowed, and I couldn't imagine any desiring to hang out there. Snooker was the main game for the younger crowd, but there were also two tables to play eight or nine ball at a quarter a game. The older men played dominoes on tables separated by tobacco spit cans that were always full. Every game had an ante, and the gambling wagers went up from there.

Salem Lowe's store didn't have a name. It had a solid glass storefront with no lettering at all, and Salem lived in the back. My grandpa would take me there to buy small animal traps and pocket knives. One never knew what Salem would have in his store from one visit to the next. It was the original bargain basement. He bought for resale what others couldn't sell. Some days he'd have cases of every type of marble a kid could wish for. Other days he might have crates of mousetraps.

Salem always greeted customers from the shadows of the back of the store by saying a very slow and drawn-out "Hello." He wore wire-rimmed glasses with the left eyeglass painted black, leather sandals with socks, and baggy khaki pants pulled up just under his chest while being too short to reach his ankles. He always wore a dingy paper-thin and torn sleeveless white T-shirt. No one ever knew where he came from or if he had family or relatives. What everyone did know was that he knew everything in town: the good stuff. His information and gossip were much better than the pool hall crowd.

I was on a mission to determine what people were saying about Jaxs and Sonny. Local culture dictated that I start at the pool hall first and work my way to Salem, who would never volunteer to create a line of gossip or rumor communication. You had to feed him the knowledge that you knew something about something, and then he'd correct you with more accurate information.

"Let's just leave it alone. Jenkins, this will all go away. I don't want to talk about this anymore. They died and we didn't do it," Jill shouted.

"All right, have it your way. So we didn't kill them. Everybody in town will have their own idea anyhow," I responded. I couldn't tell if she believed I was sincere; I wasn't.

CHAPTER EIGHT

INQUIRY

ONCE I GOT OFF THE SCHOOL BUS THE NEXT MORNING, I ducked around the back of the bus and hid behind a large blackjack tree. The final bell rang. I zigzagged from tree to house to hedge until I got to the single-person dirt trail; then I slid down to get under the hooky bridge. It must have been a good day to play hooky, because there sat Javier and Mike. Both were probably on their third cigarette by now. The twins were there also: Freddy and Neddy. These two could outsmoke anyone. The twins were in my grade but had been held back at least twice. Because of this, they were bigger and faster than the rest of us. They won all the blue ribbons at the grade school Olympics each year. We all came from poor families, but the twins were the most destitute. Since they were five they'd worked in the fields, but their claim to fame was cars. They were better mechanics than most adults.

"Want a smoke?" asked Neddy, the friendlier of the twins, as he handed a cigarette my way. I took it even though I didn't want it, trying to fit in. I did know that if you took a drag off one of the twins' smoke, you'd better not hand back a wet one, so I was careful to dry my lips before taking a drag. The twins would fight anyone over something like that.

Since Javier knew just about everything, he seemed disinterested when Mike started the show-and-tell with one of his mother's battery-operated dildos. I had no idea what the hell this torpedo-looking thing was. Needless to say, the hooky bridge could be very educational on some days.

All of a sudden Freddy blurted out, "I saw the bodies. They were lying by the riverbank. Eyes wide open. But no cuts. I assumed they would be stabbed."

"I saw them too," Neddy added. "It was like, you know like they were asleep with eyes open. Jaxs had one eye open. Sonny had both. I think that's what I saw. Right, that's what I saw."

"Come on now. How can you be dead and look like you're asleep at the same time? You can't fall asleep with your eyes open. You're making this shit up. Just because you guys are twins doesn't mean you have to tell the same bullshit," I said.

"I saw a dead body once behind this bar my mom worked at when we lived in the city," Mike said, not to be outdone. "My dead body was really buggered up. You know, like he had the shit beat out of him. One eye hanging out of the socket. Guess he fucked with the wrong man's girl." Mike laughed. We could never tell how much was truth with him and how much was fiction.

Being the coolest thug, Javier lit another cigarette while flicking the one he had just finished toward what little water was in the creek below the hooky bridge. "I've seen all kinds of dead bodies. Had a cousin shot in the head once down in Mexico. Saw that dead kid that died in Leon Spottedhorse's last wreck. The fucker's brains were just there hanging off that bridge where Leon missed the curve."

I hadn't seen the dead kid, but my mom had caught Randy and me drinking beer, so she drove me down to the wreck site and made me look at the brains that were dried on the bridge railing.

"Jaxs beat our dad up once for no reason," Freddy said. "I'm glad he's dead. I was going to whoop his ass someday anyway." He was always trying to act tough, so none of us responded. Freddy was strong as an ox but couldn't fight his way out of a paper bag. He had a super-hot temper that kept him from being disciplined enough to win.

I finally spoke up. "Jaxs was going to beat and rob my grandpa. Bad people like that need just to die. Guess God takes care of that type of stuff." Everyone looked at me. I couldn't believe it had come out of my mouth. I wasn't even thinking about God. Besides, if there was a God, I was still mad at him for not killing the Devil.

After that the conversation turned to girls and sex. Javier explained how he once almost had sex with a distant cousin. He enlightened us with a description of her private parts. He'd told me this before at the pool hall. Then Mike detailed his foray into the strip club where his mother worked. Apparently, he was supposed to stay asleep in the car while she finished her shift. He didn't say if he saw her dancing or not, but he hesitated just enough to make me believe that he did.

It was apparent that none of them had any real information I was seeking. I couldn't even believe Freddy, who usually lied about everything just to fit in. I stayed longer than I wanted to, hoping Officer Easley would come by and give up any information he knew on the deaths. Eventually I said I was going to go. It was too early to hitchhike home, so I went to the combination convenience store/gas station where the owner allowed kids to hang out and never asked questions. If you stayed long enough, he'd give you a soda pop and a candy bar. Even though he rarely initiated conversation, I thought he appreciated the company.

Being careful not to step on the fresh snuff and tobacco spit, I ascended the rickety wooden stairs to the pool hall. It was a hot day, so the door was open at the top of the stairs. It made no difference, since it was full of holes and cracks.

"Rack 'em up!" Leon Spottedhorse yelled for Jack to rack up for the next game on the first snooker table. Shirtless, standing there applying a little extra chalk to his cue stick, Leon commanded everyone's attention. The loose dust from the pool chalk powdered his scars from car wrecks and knife cuts that stretched across his chest and ever-growing beer belly. Most would concede that he was the best pool hustler in the region. From the stack of bills on the table, I knew Leon had been playing all night. The pool hall would sometimes stay open all night if people were playing and money could be made. Leon motioned for his next victim to step up while dangling a cigarette from the corner of his perpetual smile. He was playing against a rotation of three oil field roughnecks from out of town. Any local who knew Leon would not be playing for the kind of money lying on the table. Leon only lost when bets were low money, which was just to keep people interested.

"Give me a tight rack this time," Leon said. Everyone knew that Jack always gave an extra tight rack, and Leon requesting one was just another way to start psyching his opponent out. Jack slowly shuffled over to collect his fee.

The usual elder statesmen who practically lived in the pool hall were there. The iconic Pop Chevy, the lawnmower man, slammed the dominoes down whenever he won a game. He could fix any small engine. If Leon was the pool-playing king, Pop was the domino equivalent. Pop was playing a game of chicken foot dominoes with all the usual suspects. Red Farris was famous for allegedly once having a horse in the Kentucky Derby. Tom Paul, who claimed he was Steinbeck's inspiration for a character in *Grapes of Wrath*, was also at the table. It was true he had done hard time at the state penitentiary. Most of these men who played here had some claim to fame that couldn't ever be confirmed.

I chose a stool between the domino and pool tables, where I was situated to hear any gossip. With my ice-cold RC Cola in hand, I settled in.

Even a whisper could be heard across this large open room. Who knew why, but this place was like being able to listen in on a party-line call. And I was in no rush, because it would be four hours before I could sneak on the school bus to go home. Anyway, the people-watching was great.

"Jenkins, you little shit," Leon said, noticing me. "Make yourself useful and get me a Tab. I got to watch my figure." He winked as he spoke to me while quickly running his third table in a row. I could tell that the three opponents he was rotating through and whose money he was taking started showing discontent with Leon's bodacious presence. I slid the Tab through the maze of sodas in the old, rusty, chest-type pop machine. It had always been broken, so customers were on the honor system to either leave money on the lid or pay Jack.

"Jaxs was no dummy. He wouldn't have drunk no bad liquor. Hell, Sheriff Brown hasn't solved a major crime since he has been in office for the last 20 years. It's always an accident or some mystery he calls undetermined death. There's a lot of meanness going on around here, and people just look away from it and then come up with simple explanations," Red explained to Tom and Pop.

"What do you think happened then?" I asked without thinking. I had not planned on talking.

"Everybody knows Jaxs had a lot of enemies and was certainly not one of God's best creations," Pop responded. "Hell, we all know somebody did him in, and we all know we'll never know who did it. Damn sheriff's too stupid to solve where his own shit comes from."

"Nobody cares about those fuckers," responded one of the roughnecks playing against Leon.

"Now, that Sonny wasn't a bad guy. Hate to see that boy go. He always did right by me, and I paid his pool tickets 'cuz I always let him play on credit," Jack added.

"Shut the fuck up. Nobody asked or wants your fucking opinion," Leon retorted while marking up his score on the ragged chalkboard. "He was my damn cousin, so don't be talking any shit that you don't know." Like he always did, Jack kept his head down and shuffled off. While listening to the domino players talk about Jaxs, I missed the tension building on table one with Leon.

The violence came quickly. The taller, skinny roughneck swung at Leon, hitting him behind his left ear. Leon shook his head from side to side. Then, with a sinister smile, he broke his pool cue in half over his knee. "Motherfuckers want to play? Well, come on. I'll take all three of you."

The three roughnecks should have taken pool cues when they rushed Leon. Maybe Leon, having taken all their hard-earned money, contributed to the crescendo of violence. Fighting was a big part of the small-town culture.

He crotch-kicked the chubbiest of the three, then quickly rocked the other two with a pool cue across their faces. Two stumbled forward, pushing Leon against the chalkboard, breaking it in half. Some of the men playing dominoes never looked up. Others gave glancing looks at the fight. Nobody dared try to break it up. Even if there'd been a phone in the pool hall, nobody was going to call the police.

They kept coming at Leon, occasionally getting a good hit or kick in. Then they all fell to the floor with Leon on the bottom. "Let him up! Let him up!" screamed one of the attackers. "He's biting my nose off!"

Leon rolled out from under them when they stopped hitting him. He then presented a disturbing and bloody smile before spitting into his hand. He then threw the flesh and blood in his hand at them. "Here, you can have this back."

"You bit a piece of his fucking nose off!" The skinny one held his face as blood oozed between his fingers, while his friend yelled across the room. Blood dripped on the floor and mixed with the spit, sweat, and whatever else had fossilized on the old wooden boards.

With a bloody face surrounding that smile and pointing the broken pool cue at them, Leon calmly motioned for them to come at him again. He then finished removing a jaw tooth that was partially knocked out in the fight. He threw it at them.

"Fucker, you crazy," one of the assailants yelled. They quickly shuffled down the stairs, hailing insults along the way. Leon followed and threw the broken pool cue at them. It was over. The sound of dominoes being slammed on the tables meant business was back to normal.

Leon wiped the blood from his face and then smeared it over his bare chest. Some of his scars were so pronounced that the blood detoured around them like a river eyeing for new land to devour. "Want some war paint?" he said to me, still smiling. This was all good fun for him. I shook my head.

"Then either put money on the table or get the fuck out of here." Leon chalked his stick and motioned for anyone to come play. I got the fuck out of there. I didn't want to be around if the roughnecks returned with reinforcements, and I didn't want Leon to decide we should take another ride in his Falcon.

At Salem's store, I could hear voices in the shadows coming from the back. Out of the shadows, a slow-walking Salem appeared. "Well, there, Monty's grandboy. What can we do you for today?" He spoke while looking over round wire-rim glasses barely hanging on to the end of his nose. He always appeared to be analyzing every square inch of you with his one good eye.

A dust-covered thick glass display case served as a partial divider to separate what customers could shop for unassisted and those items only Salem was allowed to present. The case contained a sparse population of pocket knives, hand tools, and an assortment of used items. Animal traps, lawn tools, nails, and various other possessions found in hardware stores were located behind the counter.

"That's a good-looking Camillus knife there," I said nervously. I thought of him as an intelligent, nonviolent zombie. His mannerisms, like his walk and talk, were in slow motion.

"That's the only knife worth carrying in my store." He then explained the history of the brand and how a Jewish German immigrant had started the company in New York. "That's the only brand of knife your grand-dad will carry. Much better than Old Timers, tougher steel and easier to sharpen." Salem had a reputation for being a walking encyclopedia. In fact, he collected encyclopedias.

"I know. Grandpa always gives me his used ones," I replied. I pulled an old yellow three-blade Camillus from my pocket and showed him. It had deep groves in each blade from all the sharpening.

"Oh, yes, I remember selling him that one. That particular model was discontinued. I suggest you hold on to it. It'll be valuable someday."

I wasn't sure what his definition of value was, given that he had old newspapers stacked to the ceilings that he referred to as priceless.

"So I guess you saw that ruckus Leon got into at the pool hall?" Salem queried smoothly.

"Yeah," I answered. How did he know that? I'd just come straight from there.

The expression on my face must have shown my surprise. Salem said, "Tall feller came in bleeding and asking if I had any bandages. I bet you have a different account than his version. Think the man lost a part of his nose. Here, help me with this loose fan belt and tell me about it."

Salem held a ladder while I climbed it to reach the one rubber belt that turned all three of his ceiling fans. They were all on a cog-type pulley system. Sometimes the belt would slide off the main pulley. As we worked, I gave him my side of witnessing the Leon fight. Taking advantage of him wanting this information was a good segue to asking what he knew of Jaxs and Sonny.

"What's a youngster like you so interested in death for? Everyone has a theory or an opinion. It makes sense that speculation runs rampant."

"Just curious," I said, shrugging. "Met him a few times. Heard people talking about it."

"Seems to me somebody had it in for them boys. Didn't really know Sonny, but that Tommy Jaxs, I knew pretty well. He came here a lot to trade knives and buy ammo. Used to get mad 'cause I don't do credit with the likes of him. Now he's dead and owes everybody in town. I figure he welched on the wrong person or rolled the wrong victim. But then again, the type of people he associated with would have just shot, stabbed, or beat him to death. So therein lies the mystery, little Jenkins. Actually, two mysteries now. How did he die, and why you so interested? Or maybe there's no mystery at all. Could be death by stupidity, if in fact they poisoned themselves with tainted booze."

"It's big news around here, so I was just curious. That's all."

"You know a drunk thinks he can move about and among us unseen. They do things that they don't think others see—like drunk driving, cheating on cards, or beating their wife or children. He thinks nobody can see what he's doing. They end up making fools of themselves or get caught doing whatever they think others can't see. Now, if you mix arrogance in there, you got a true fool that will never get ahead in life. Understand?"

I looked down at the grimy wooden floor. I didn't wish to make any more eye contact with Salem. I wasn't quite sure what he was trying to tell me. Maybe no child my age at the time should have understood. My takeaway was, quit asking questions. It was time to make my exit.

"It'll always be a mystery until someone decides that it shouldn't be. Now, you be careful out there in this world." These were Salem's last words for me that day.

I still had two hours left to kill before catching the bus home, so I snuck in the side door of the movie theater across the street. *Viva Las Vegas* was the afternoon matinee, and it was about to end. Only an old retired school-teacher, Mrs. Tucker, and I were there. You couldn't miss her dyed white hair that had turned a pale blue. She sat up straight in the theater chair even though they were designed for reclining, her posture just like it used to be at the teacher's desk in school. I sat two rows behind her and studied the giant paintings on the side walls. They depicted a battle between cowboys and Indians. It was only fitting, since the theater was named the Redskin.

CHAPTER NINE

RINSE AND REPEAT

THAT NIGHT THE DEVIL ANNOUNCED HIS ARRIVAL BY KICKING our two dogs off the porch. Of course that wasn't necessary. It was never necessary. We'd heard the rumble of his old muffler-less pickup, but advance notice had no value. Chairs were kicked into the wall; dishes crashed against the floor, and then a fist came through the sheetrock.

Back under the bed for me. Lying on my back, I played with the torn and tattered decomposing mattress above me. It was an old feather mattress that had been a hand-me-down from some relative. It had two rutted-out indentions where someone had slept on it for years in the same spots. Large, yellow-stained circles were on both sides where I had often peed in the bed. The mattress was often flipped to the dry side and then flipped again when I had another accident. But they weren't accidents, at least not in the beginning. I was too afraid to get up and go to the bathroom many nights, afraid I might wake the Devil.

Under the bed, I whispered a prayer. "I'll do anything you ask. I can't take this anymore. Please, please, God. Help, help me. I'll never drink or get drunk. I'll go to church and like it. I'll do whatever you want if you just kill the Devil."

My heavy breath brought out the dust balls. I imagined each one was a planet where tiny creatures lived, and I was God expanding and moving their universe. I needed those balls of matter, those tiny masses of physical substance that occupied space but went unseen and uncared for. Coupled with my crazy imagination, dust balls became my escape, my alternative therapy.

"Jenkins, Jenkins! Help me! Get him off me!" Mom was screaming from the back bedroom where the Devil was yelling and they were slapping each other. She must have come home early from work; she didn't usually get home until seven in the morning. My imagination was engrossed with the micron-sized world of dust balls.

I was too afraid to come out from under the bed. She screamed again. I heard them hit the floor with a loud thud. Mom was always trying to lose weight, but she was at her biggest now. Had she gotten heavier so she could better fight the Devil? My mind was racing with a kaleidoscope of thoughts to distract me.

What could Jill or I do? The fight eventually ended, and the Devil screamed and cussed us all at the top of his lungs until the sun came up. In the morning, Mom got us ready and it was as if nothing had happened. We just went to school like we were a typical all-American family.

The transition from the scary, crazy world I lived in and pretending to be a normal kid at school became more complex. I couldn't sit still in class. Concentration to just read a book page was difficult. Teachers had resorted to just placing me in the back of the room and ignoring me. Paddling at school became an almost daily event. The two different people I had become were starting to run together.

Tetherball was the most popular game at school—so popular you had to stand in line all recess for a chance to play. This game became a defining moment for me. Terry was waiting in line to play several spots behind me. He was one of many school bullies. When my time came to play tetherball, Terry pushed me down and took my place. Usually, I would have just gotten back in line. One day, I snapped.

I got up, ran toward Terry from behind as he played, and tackled him to the ground. I grabbed the back of his head and started beating his face into the gravel. I rolled him over and began beating his face with my fist. He shouted that he had given up. I couldn't stop. "I'll kill you, I'll kill you!" I screamed, not caring that I had violated the number one rule of playground fights to stop when someone cried uncle.

I grabbed a handful of the small white gravel and stuffed it into his mouth. It was all spontaneous. I wasn't thinking about how to kill him; I just knew I wanted to. There was no cognitive process of eliminating other options, like being too weak and puny to strangle him.

The assigned recess teacher and two others pulled me off Terry. I tried to hurl myself back at him and one of the teachers picked me up, threw me over his shoulder, and carried me to the principal's office. I sat there shaking not from fear, but from a wave of unbridled anger.

The principal spoke to me carefully. "Do you know that we had to take Terry to the doctor? He swallowed a lot of gravel and also had it in his ears."

"I was going to kill him," I responded with great indignation that surprised me. I was honest, and I wasn't sure why. Usually I lied even if the truth was benign.

"Jenkins, listen up. You need to quit saying that you were going to kill him. That takes this incident to a whole different level. If you persist in saying this, we will need to call the police."

"But I was trying to kill him!" I glared at the principal.

"Okay, Jenkins." He frowned, ran his hand across his forehead and then down one side of his face. He looked frustrated. "I see that your grandfather is listed as the person to call in case of an emergency. Is that correct?"

"I don't know. I know he doesn't have a phone." My anger was dissipating. I now understood the gravity of what had occurred. I explained that I could find my grandpa at the pool hall or beer joint. I guess they probably wanted me out of their way quickly, because they sent me with a janitor to find and drop me off with Grandpa.

Alonso, the janitor, was a favorite of all the kids. He was an old farmer who said he only worked at the school to get insurance. He claimed to have been a professional boxer and always bragged about his scarred face and the number of times his nose had been broken. I figured he was chosen to escort me because he also frequented those two establishments where one might locate my grandpa.

"Boy, you need to stay busy," Alonso said to me. "I can sign you up to work with me as part of the Young Adult Conservation Corps. The old YACC. Then you can help me clean all these stopped-up toilets at the high school." This was nothing I wanted to do, so I just sulked.

We found my grandpa at the beer joint. Red, the owner, met me at the door. Minus the face mole, she looked just like Miss Kitty from *Gunsmoke*. Her harshly dyed red-orange hair was always styled like a beehive. Every inch of hair was in place. Everyone assumed she was Irish as she had named her establishment the Irish Inn. I waved off Alonso, who was watching from his truck. "Tell the truth now to your grandpa. Thataway he'll give you a righteous whipping," shouted Alonso. I could hear his laughter as he drove away.

"Looking for your grandpa?" Red asked. "He's at the table over there in the corner. I see no harm in you coming in." Of course, she always said that unless there was, as she called it, "rousness."

Grandpa's straw cowboy hat was pushed to the crown of his head, allowing light to reflect off his baldness. Now sagging with age, his once square jawline gave his stoic gaze a transcendent presence. The aroma of stale beer and smoldering cigarette smoke arrested this fleeting moment of tranquility. My grandpa, my savior, and my sanctuary never smoked or drank. Beer joints and pool halls were the only places where the old farmers and ranchers could gather, barter, and kill time as their usefulness diminished. Most didn't have families, so this was their daily socialization.

Red handed me an ice-cold Coke, my favorite kind in the smallest of bottles, and motioned for me to sit in the corner. She opened the bottle with the beer opener hanging around her neck like a necklace. She then used the other end of the opener to open several beer cans. Red knew the routine.

Grandpa had only two facial expressions: calmness and disappointment. That day I received both simultaneously. He didn't say a word to me until we climbed into his 1962 long-bed Chevy pickup. It was a three-speed on the column, but he never used first gear. He always took off in second gear, making the truck motor ping and rattle.

"Boy, what was it this time?" He was always a man of few words. As opposed to me, he could outlast anyone on a pregnant pause. I lied a lot in those days but never to him. I provided an honest account of what happened.

"So you wanted to kill this kid. I know his parents. They came up through the sharecropping system like many of us. They all got issues. But you can't go around telling people you were trying to kill someone, boy, or they'll lock you up. You got to learn to deal with your anger. When you show that kind of anger, you be showing your whole deck of cards. You giving your hand away."

Back at Grandpa's place, I went to my favorite hiding place again in the barn, pulled my forbidden *Hit Parader* magazine from under a bale of hay, and spent the rest of the day fantasizing about being a rock star, growing my hair like The Beatles, and thinking about not showing my proverbial deck of cards. I planned to start walking home in time to arrive a few minutes before the school bus. I'd done this so many times that I had it down to a fine science. Grandpa would never tell, but my sister might. She would know I wasn't on the bus, and if I didn't tell her why she would eventually find out.

Life was becoming a constant déjà vu, a perpetual purgatory. I would find myself once again breathing the dust balls to and fro while hiding under the bed and praying for God to kill our Devil. I tried to understand and implement what my grandpa told me about not showing my hand, but my anger grew. The beating of Terry had empowered me. I decided that I would no longer allow myself to be bullied. I'd given up on God coming to my rescue.

CHAPTER TEN

A NEW LEVEL

THE PALMS OF BOTH MY HANDS WERE BLEEDING. I HAD squeezed the coat hanger so hard it had cut into my hands. I didn't understand. How could this happen? The wire coat hanger wasn't sharp. I just stood and looked at my hands in disbelief. Had I actually squeezed it so hard it entrenched into my hand? It was another night, and the Devil had been beating my mom, who was screaming for help. My anger exploded. Coming out from under the bed, I grabbed the first thing I saw. Clenching the hanger, I ran and jumped on top of the Devil.

I yelled for him to shut the fuck up. I couldn't take it anymore. I hit him with the coat hanger until he knocked me off. Hitting the floor hurt, I was afraid. I ran and crawled back under my bed.

He didn't follow me. An eerie silence ensued. A wolf spider who sometimes shared my space stopped crawling and seemed to stare at me to ask what happened. Where was the noise? Maybe Mom and the Devil were in shock. I had never taken a direct attack approach before. Even if I'd wanted to kill him, here I was once again under the bed, shivering in fear.

I knew the beating was coming. There would be hell to pay for the coat hanger attack. I just didn't know when it would happen. Maybe the whipping would come when the Devil was sober. That would be bad, but not as bad as when he intoxicated himself with the demon whiskey. Time was of the essence.

Jill and I were dreading Sunday night, for that was when Mom would work a double shift. The Devil would have been on a whole week's drunk by then with only brief visits to the house for short periods of rest. We never knew where he went on his escapades. For whatever reason, he always came home on a Sunday night—maybe because the liquor stores were closed.

Our big plan was not to be at home on that Sunday night, which was a week after my coat hanger attack. There was an old pink 1958 Chrysler that my grandpa allowed one of his friends to park in his pasture, so we walked across the creeks and woods to get to the car before dark. We had played in it before but had never spent the night in it.

We moved into the abandoned car about sundown. We cleaned out a few spiderwebs and settled in for a hot, muggy night. A rat or mouse family seemed to have made a home in or around the engine. It was impossible to sleep between the noise they made and the night's heat. We had worn what we were going to wear to school the next day. That way, we could simply walk to a neighbor's house and catch the school bus.

I ended up spending most of the night lying on the hood and counting stars. With no light from any distant town or another source, it was as if I could reach up and touch the stars. The vastness of the star-filled sky made me feel even lonelier than usual and insignificant.

I didn't think about it then, but we must have reeked to high heaven when we got on the bus the following day. I had dried sweat rings across my shirt that resembled what a receding tide would leave on a beach. My hair was matted and stuck to my head. I blamed Jill for us forgetting to bring toothbrushes.

It was the last week of school before the summer break. I was exhausted from no sleep, plus I felt dirty, sticky, and embarrassed. I tried to stay away from others at recess. Keeping my distance in class was not much of an issue. Teachers weren't sure what to do with me. So they did the logical thing. Each year was the same: They placed my desk in the back of the classroom so my fidgeting and other systems would not bother the others.

I was hanging out in the restroom, trying to keep my tired self and stinking body away from the other kids. Terry walked in, still showing the results of the beating I had given him. My first thought was *Shit—here we go again.* But it didn't go like that.

"Hey, Jenkins. How you doin'?"

I just looked at him, not knowing how to respond.

"You look like shit, man."

"Rough night," I managed to mumble out.

"I get it. It's not like nobody doesn't know what your old man is."

Of course Terry was right. It was a small town and a sparsely populated rural county. Before I could get angry again, he surprised me.

"I get it. My old man is kind of the same way," Terry said.

I didn't know much about Terry or his family. He rode a different school bus and lived at the far end of the county from me. We'd never had a conversation. I didn't trust him. I was still angry with him and wasn't sure that I wouldn't try to kill him again if we were to fight.

"Look here. I'm good with you," he said. "I don't want any trouble. Got my own."

Suddenly Terry started to appear human to me. Maybe being a bully was just his coping mechanism. I had determined that birth was a lottery, and Terry and I didn't win. "Okay," I finally replied. "I don't want any trouble either."

"Hey, you want to see something?" he asked.

"Sure," I hesitantly replied.

He proceeded to drop his pants and showed me his butt. It was black and blue with bruises, overlaid with blisters, and crisscrossed with welts. It looked like a checkerboard that had melted while all the checkers were on it.

"Don't tell anyone," he said. "If my dad finds out he'll beat me some more."

I didn't want to, but I kept staring. Finally he pulled his pants back up.

"What the hell did you do?" I blurted out without thinking.

"He claimed I didn't feed the cattle all the bales of hay I was supposed to."

"That's all?" But I understood. One of my last beatings was when I was accused of not using enough clothespins on the laundry hanging on the clothesline. The wind had blown the laundry off in the dirt, and it had to be rewashed.

"Why would I make that up?" Terry said quickly.

Before I could say anything, he went on. "It was also for what you did. He was pissed you beat me up. I didn't tell him anything, but the principal sent him a letter. Plus, after he got the letter, I had to go to the doctor. Had some gravel removed from one of my ears. He say he coming to see you. Gonna teach you a lesson or something like that."

I was shocked. Grandpa had told me to stay away from that family because the dad was crazy calloused. I didn't know what to say.

Later, Jill told me that Grandpa would take care of Terry's dad if he came around.

"Well, that doesn't help me feel any better!" I said.

"Well, it should. Grandpa and I were at the feed store once and Terry's dad came up and talked to us, so he knows him."

For most kids, summer break from school is the start of fun. For Jill and me, summer was just relief from riding a school bus. We went to the creek and woods early in the mornings, played all day, and returned home by dark. Grandpa would sometimes pick us up and take us to cattle auctions, or just let us ride in the back of his pickup as he checked on his pasture and cattle.

August was always the hottest month, but it was crazy hot that year. It was scorching in the house, so Jill and I stayed outside almost every day. We had options for finding cooler places to play, such as the chicken house or the little shed built over our storm cellar. We also waded in the creek water. One place we did not want to play in during the summer was the smokehouse.

The smokehouse was constructed of triple-thick planks of wood. The door was even thicker, with multiple layers of plywood and two-by-fours added. The floor was built with redwood boards because they didn't rot like other woods. It had no windows. The smokehouse was for preserving meats by keeping them cool and dark. But for whatever reason, it was never cool in there. It rarely contained any meat, sugar-cured or otherwise, and it just became a quiet place to hide in the fall and winter. The Devil never explained why he'd built it.

There was no plan; it just happened. Jill and I were playing out by the hog pen on a hot August morning. We had already fed our three hogs and were throwing dirt clods in the hogs' mud-wallowing hole. Jill saw the pickup moving at a slow crawl up the hill toward our house. An old white rusty square-as-a-box International Harvester pickup. Smoke was rolling out of the tailpipe. "Terry's dad," Jill said.

We ran as fast as we could from the hog pen to a large cottonwood tree. "Do you think he saw us?" I asked.

He parked the pickup on the side of our hill next to the hog pen. We watched as he slowly maneuvered his stout body out of the truck.

His stained white T-shirt only covered the top of his hairy belly button. From the chest up, he still had the muscular body appearance of a much younger man. "I see you," he seemed to sing out.

Walking between us and the house, he yelled, "Hey, boy, your old man home?"

"Don't say anything," Jill whispered.

It was apparent he saw us. He lumbered toward our tree.

"I just want to talk to him about you trying to kill my boy. Does he know that his son is a crazy little retard that needs to be put away?"

His words didn't match his expression. Instead, he combed his fingers through his thick, greasy black hair and presented a crooked smile. Jill and I had learned how to read people, so we knew this was one of the disciples of the drunken realm. As he walked toward us, I could see the streams of sweat meandering around his fat cheeks and a double chin that created a waterfall over his fat-rolled neck.

He was situated between our usual escape route through the woods and creek to Grandpa's house. He moved like a slightly faster version of Frankenstein's creature. I kept expecting him to hold his arms straight out and start grunting. My heart was pounding so hard my chest hurt.

We had no choice: We had to run. And the only thing we could think of was the smokehouse. We dashed to it, but once inside, there was only a momentary sigh of relief. There was no lock on the inside; the deadbolt was on the outside. We knew this, but somehow all we'd thought of was how strong the smokehouse was.

"Is he coming?" Jill asked.

"I don't hear him," I whispered. I opened the door and saw Terry's dad lumbering around the hog pen and heading toward us.

"Come on!" I said, pulling Jill's arm but losing my grip. I ran outside to the north side of the smokehouse. With my back up against the wall and arms spread out, I felt as if my chest would explode. I took a deep breath and quickly crept back toward the front.

It all happened in a heartbeat, a split second. I saw Terry's dad open the smokehouse door as he said, "Kiddos, you in there?" I heard Jill scream. I grabbed the only possible weapon close, a grub hoe, as I ran around the smokehouse to the door. As I brought the hoe down on his head, I heard him say, "Now I ain't going to . . ." as he fell forward and landed with his body halfway through the entrance. Jill was still inside.

She jumped over his body and tried to slam the door shut. But his feet were in the doorway. We pushed his feet inside and forced the door shut. I had to use the hoe to hammer the deadbolt to a lock position.

Jill and I looked at each other, hearts pounding and breath heaving in our chests. Then we ran as fast as we could to the woods. After sitting on a large sandstone, Jill spoke first.

"What do we do now?" she asked.

"I don't know. I don't know," was all I could muster. I fiercely rubbed my hands around my temples until it hurt.

"How hard did you hit him?" Jill was shaking and started to tear up. She stuttered, "You think he's dead?" She was firing off questions so fast it made my brain spin.

"I don't think so. I saw his arm move when we shut the door," I responded.

"Well, what are we going to do now?"

I looked up at the sun coming through the trees. Its light flickered through the leaves as rays sprayed our sand rock, where we'd etched our names one day long ago. They were now half gone from the weathering. I tried to focus.

"It's around ten o'clock," I guessed from the sun's angle as I glanced at it through shielding hands. "So maybe let's not do anything right now.

We can check on him in a couple of hours and unlock the door so he can get out."

Jill just stared at me. "No," she said finally. "You do it. I'm going to go to Grandpa's."

"Why?" I asked her. I threw my arms in the air in frustration.

"This is your mess," she said. "We wouldn't be here if you hadn't beat up Terry and then told everybody you were trying to kill him. I'm really scared, Jenkins. I think I'm going to throw up. Leave me alone!" Jill stomped her feet.

"Calm down. We can't just not do nothing," I said. "Remember, I told you what Terry said. He said his dad was coming to get me. Me, not you." I stabbed my chest with a finger.

"I won't help you! Jaxs was enough. I'm not helping this time."

"If we let him out, he's always going to be after us," I insisted. "Please, I need you. If I get killed, what are you going to do? Do you want to be on your own with the Devil?" Jill kicked a pinecone and then covered her hands over her eyes.

"Okay, okay," she said. "I'll help."

"Okay, fine. Let's go let him out at noon," I said. "But if he kills Grandpa or me, it's on you!"

We spent the next two hours walking the creek banks and throwing rocks in the water. We didn't argue anymore and barely spoke to each other while we waited. I spent my time worrying about what may happen when we let him out. Jill drew horses in the dirt and occasionally looked up and aimlessly surveyed the surroundings.

At noon, we crept up to the smokehouse and placed our ears to the door. It was now scorching hot and humid, and we were soaked in sweat.

"I don't hear anything," Jill whispered.

"Me either." We looked at each other uncertainly.

"Hey, you in there," I shouted. Nothing.

Jill knocked gently on the door. "Hello, hello," she said.

"You promise not to hurt us and leave, and we'll let you out," I said.

"Did you hear that? I think I heard him grunt," whispered Jill.

"I don't hear anything."

I took the grub hoe and banged on the front door, then the sides of the smokehouse. Still no sound. I knocked again but harder. Chips of white paint flew into my face.

"You think he's asleep or passed out?" Jill asked.

I shrugged. "No. I think he's really hurt or dead. Wait, bet he's faking it."

"What are we going to do?"

I placed my ear to the door while Jill started walking backward while never taking her eyes off the door.

"I don't know!" I was getting impatient but also scared.

"Let's just unlock the door and run to the woods," Jill said.

So that was what we did.

A loud bang echoed through the trees as I unlocked the door with a big swing of the grub hoe. Then we ran back to the sandstone where we used Grandpa's hand-me-down Old Timer pocket knife to carve the date, August 4, 1967, with a giant question mark after it. Piss ants scurried about and across our carving as if to cover it up. Crows cawed and circled us as we made our way slowly back toward our house. At the creek, a cottonmouth hissed and opened his jaws, showing off his pure pearl-white mouth: his way of telling us to keep our distance. It was as if nature was chastising us. We stayed in the creek for almost an hour.

There was the truck, in the same place Terry's dad had parked it. We saw it as we cleared the last creek bank toward our house. Crouching, we moved slowly through the weeds and darted from tree to tree. Finally we got close enough to see that the smokehouse door was still unlocked, but also still closed.

After much discussion, I decided to open the door and look inside while Jill waited at the wood's edge. The rusted hinges squeaked as I slowly opened the door. There he was, lying face-up with his T-shirt unable to cover his protruding stomach. A ring of sweat outlined his body. Several flies were parked on his chin and lips. His lips were purple, and his skin gray.

I stared as if in a trance. I couldn't say anything was going through my mind. Maybe this was what shock was, an event where time stood still. Finally, I yelled at Jill and motioned her to come over. At first she didn't want to look at him. As soon as she saw the body she turned away and started muttering something about a plan.

It was simple and sounded good, and maybe the best two kids our age could conjure up. Jill's version of shock made her behave mechanically as she instructed me on what to do. Grandpa had allowed me to drive his pickup in the pastures to feed cattle, so I knew how to drive. We tied a rope around the dead man's feet and then the other end to the bumper of his pickup. The keys were in the ignition. Then I got in the pickup, put it in reverse, and pulled him out of the smokehouse. Surprisingly, there was no blood trail.

It still amazes me that we were able to do what came next. I had helped Grandpa build fencing many times, stretching barbed wire with a wire stretcher. I got the one hanging from our back porch and attached the wire stretcher rope to his hands and the pulley end hooked to our yard's old iron gate. Then I started cranking its lever. Each lever pull slowly dragged the body into the pickup from the driver's side to the passenger's. We both had to lift his head to get the body slightly elevated so the pulley would pull him onto the seat. The graveled driveway had torn his shirt and scratched his back. Once he lay across the seat's center, we could push his head inside and close the door. The idea was to back the pickup out of the driveway to the top of the road, take it out of gear, and let it coast to the hill's bottom. With just a little luck, the pickup would veer off the road and crash into the creek.

"It'll be like he had a heart attack or something," I hoped out loud. "Hopefully no one will ever ask."

"I don't care," Jill said. "Just get him out of here." She gave me a go-to-hell look and ran into the house.

It almost worked. I jumped out of the truck as it started to roll down the hill. At the bottom, it veered to the left and was hit by an oil tank truck just coming out of an oil lease. I ran into the house.

CHAPTER ELEVEN

THE ART OF LYING

"WHAT YOU KIDDOS UP TO?" ASKED GRANDPA. HE WAS TAKING his usual afternoon catnap. He had a highly worn roped-bottom rocker where he would lean back, place his feet on a porch pillar, pull his old straw hat down over his face, and drift into a snooze. He would occasionally wake just long enough to get a good spit of powdered snuff out across the yard. His spit trail stained the water-starved dead grass. No matter how hot the weather got, his front porch was always cool with a constant breeze. This added to my belief that his house was haunted.

Jill and I knew we had to go to Grandpa's house right away after what happened with Terry's dad. We needed our sanctuary, that sense of security that we felt there. Just being with him made the world seem right again.

"You guys didn't see old Tornado when you came across the creek, did you? Didn't see him this morning when I was feeding the cows." Tornado was Grandpa's prize Hereford bull. He got his name because he would twist and turn to break through the barbed-wire fences to get at other bulls in neighboring pastures. He was a fighter, and I was terrified of him. I'd make a quarter-mile loop around him to avoid contact whenever I saw him.

In the presence of Grandpa, we were kids again. We tried to forget about what had happened earlier and taunted a few scorpions coming out of the front porch cracks. But reality came crashing back in when Sheriff Brown walked around the corner of the house.

"Good day, all. Sorry to interrupt, but I was checking around to see if anyone had seen Cecil Lewis today. Seems he had a wreck down the road a ways. It didn't come out well for him, so we're just checking on a few things."

I froze while Jill pretended to play. She maneuvered around to the side of the house, out of sight of the sheriff. I stared at his polished black roach killers, not wanting to make eye contact.

"Sorry to hear that, Sheriff," Grandpa offered. "Didn't really know the man. He didn't stop by here."

"Young man, did you see Mr. Lewis today?"

"No, I ain't seen anyone today—just my grandpa."

"You seen any other kids up and down the road today? Seems the truck driver he ran into thinks he saw a couple of kids standing in the road right up the hill before the crash."

I just shrugged in a way that would indicate no. Grandpa gave me a look that let me know he knew I was lying. He always knew. Grandpa usually kept his thoughts and judgments to himself, and this was one of those times. He chose not to call me out on my lying.

Fortunately, the sheriff didn't seem to notice, and he departed as quickly as he had appeared. Tipping his hat, he bid us a good day.

Summer break came and went, and we were soon back in school. Two weeks in was my first hooky day under the bridge with the thugs. I had brought a package of my mother's Viceroy cigarettes. They were popular with the thugs for being a silly centimeter longer. I wasn't sure how long that was, but the cigarettes made me popular. They enhanced my chameleon development, which in reality was just an innovative way of lying in all you say and do.

It wasn't like we were well organized and planned these hooky days. Mike or Javier would meet us as we got off the bus and suggest it was a good day to be under the bridge. The twins, Freddy and Neddy, would see us sneak behind the bus and run down the sidewalk toward the bridge and follow us. Sometimes we would get a guest appearance of some new kid who wanted to hang with us, but they rarely returned.

That day, Mike announced that he had not enrolled in school but walked there each day so his parents wouldn't know. He just lived a few blocks away. They were moving to another city in a few weeks, and he didn't feel a need to waste his time. Of course we all lied about how he would be missed. Nobody would be missing Mike. He was a total asshole, and most of us were afraid of him. I laid it on heavy about how he was our leader and would be missed.

It was a given that Javier would be the new leader, even though he'd always been one informally. He was the strong, more silent type that nobody messed with. On the other hand, Mike was an extroverted bully who would fight anyone at the drop of a hat. For no reason, he'd walk up and slug any of us but Javier. Javier knew his own toughness but didn't need to prove it like Mike. I was glad to see Mike go.

There was a lot to catch up on. Except for Mike, we all lived in rural areas and didn't see each other much in the summer. Mike was the center of attention, for he knew all the gossip. His first bit of information was about Norman, who had been killed in a car wreck while trying to outrun the police. Norman had joined the Marines and would have been going to Vietnam. However, the draft had not started, so Mike added that Norman was stupid for enlisting. Mike's take was that Norman was outside the city limits of the state capital, but the city police continued the pursuit. Finally, they saw Norman lose control and crash down a ravine. They turned around and went back to town without notifying anyone of the crash.

"There's proof," Mike said. "The cop's footprints were right there, where they looked down the ravine at the crash. When a farmer found the body, he described how it appeared that Norman had tried to crawl up the embankment to the road. If the fuckin' cops hadn't chased him for speeding, then would have helped him after the crash, he would be alive today. The idiots." I thought to myself, *Stay away from big-city cops.*

Mike seemed genuinely pissed off about Norman. Maybe he could have real feelings, I thought. But unfortunately, we all had developed sociopathic symptoms out of the necessity to survive, and Mike was the poster child.

"How you know so damn much, Mike?" Javier asked.

"Man, remember my mom is a stripper, and all the cops come to the Organ Grinder and buy her drinks. They talk up a storm. I hear it all from her. We moving 'cause she got a better dance offer.

"You know Terry's dad was murdered, right?" Mike moved on to his following news.

I froze. *What did Mike know, and who was talking?* I'd tried to put it out of my mind after Sheriff Brown walked away from Grandpa's porch that day. It was a wreck. It couldn't be anything else in anyone's eyes.

"Seems the doctor say he died from something called hyperthermia or dehydration or something like that. Plus, they be saying he had rope marks around his wrist and scrapes on his back. So he was dead before hitting the oil tanker truck. Cops talking to everybody in the county."

I felt paranoid, which caused me to suspect Javier somehow noticed when he hastily chimed in and changed subjects. He had gotten a used Honda 90 motorcycle. Javier had been held back a year in school, so he was older than others in our group and was probably the only 12-year-old in the county driving a motorcycle on all the main highways. The year before, he'd gotten a 1942 Studebaker but was only allowed to drive it in pastures and on oil field roads. Naturally, we were envious. The twins interrupted with a proposal to steal pop bottles from the town's only convenience store. The bottles were stacked behind the store in a locked chicken-wired bin. Neddy said it was easy. "You have someone go into the store to distract the old guy at the cash register," he said. Meanwhile, the others would sneak around back and cut the wire. Bottles were selling for five cents each. We all agreed this was a great idea.

We could sell the bottles quickly at the only full-size grocery store in town. Then we'd use the money for beer and cigarettes. Mike suggested we use old Charles Bowin to buy the beer. I said nothing about that idea. The twins would be the stealers who would grab the bottles and run. They were the fastest of us all. Javier and Mike would be lookouts. Who were the rest of us to argue with that? I was picked to have the honor of walking in the store and keeping the old guy occupied. The other cocon-spirators appreciated my developing gift of gab. Our under-the-bridge hooky group had now morphed into a crime syndicate.

Valuable lessons were learned in at least my first and last foray into property crime. Lesson number one: Five preteens walking up to a store on a school day is advertising that something is amiss. Lesson number two: Other customers are more important to watch than the slight chance a cop shows up. Mike and Javier made very pitiful watchmen. Third lesson: The twins were fast compared to us, but not when Good Samaritans made citizens' arrests.

Aside from the twins, maybe the rest of us could have gotten away if we'd had a car. Once the shit hit the fan, there was no place to hide. The store had no close neighbors. I stayed in the store as I witnessed several customers herd the twins to the storefront. Javier was being his usual cool self and talking with his captor without trying to escape. On the other hand, Mike was trying to fight the huge oil field worker who had him in a body hug. Of course, Mike was yelling he was going to fuck everybody up and screaming his innocence. Three more lessons here: Limit your codefendants, or at least be more selective; staying at the crime scene and acting innocent doesn't work; and extensive planning is a necessity.

Officer Easley placed us all in his squad car. He only handcuffed Mike, who was still threatening to fuck everybody up. I could see Javier doing his best not to laugh. Javier and I had the pleasure of riding in the front seat.

All of us but Mike were allowed to sit around the dispatcher's reception area to await our retrievers. The twins' dad was the first to show up. He worked as a garbage collector for the town and was simply dispatched to the police station. He had a calm demeanor and said nothing to his sons. He signed the necessary paperwork, including no charges being filed if specific fees were paid and an apology to the victim. Javier's dad was next. He always had a perpetual grin, and it was on full display today. He seemed proud of his son as he patted him on the back. He only appeared displeased for having to take off work. His cap was worn backward as welders do to fit their welding helmets.

I finally got to see Mike's infamous mother in all her splendor. Her beehive hairdo must have required an entire can of Aqua Net hair spray—the kind of spray we'd light with a match and use as blowtorches. It had that much alcohol in it. I could see the outline of a full-length girdle under her skin-tight red ankle-hugging dress. It was a complement to the sparkling red stiletto-heeled shoes. She had a slender face and long nose that reminded me of Lassie. All I could think about was what she would look like in that mink fur bra Mike used for show-and-tell.

Officer Easley was much less business-like with Mike's mother. He appeared to know her rather well. I was sure he was a frequent visitor to her workplace. Mike was quickly released from the town's only jail cell.

His mother gently squeezed Easley's shoulder as she thanked him for taking such good care of her son. "Get your ass in the car, you little son-of-a-bitch," she yelled at Mike.

"Fuck, Mom; I didn't do anything. I was just walking down the road. Fuckin' cops got it in for me. They always harassing," bellowed Mike.

Easley's eyes locked on her ass as she grabbed Mike by the ear and dragged him outside. This was the last time any of us would ever see Mike. I sat there looking at naked natives on some island in an old *National Geographic*, awaiting my fate. Some misfortunate soul had left this little nugget, not knowing it would bring an erection to any boy my age.

Officer Easley asked me, "Jenkins, you going to keep saying you were just in the store and wasn't part of this laughable attempt at a crime? Guess it doesn't matter as the county ain't going to file no charges, and we only have city court on traffic citations. Like the rest of your little gang, you can just go home and hopefully get the beating you need and deserve." He rested his hands on his hips and tried to assert some type of authority.

"I keep telling you, yes, I didn't do nothing. Now, can I go?" Once I denied something, I was sticking to it and not changing my story.

"Well, it makes little difference, now does it? The county truancy officer will be here to see you and your little buddies, as I'm required to call them if the school hasn't already. Anyway, you're going to keep me company for a while. Sheriff Brown has been wanting to talk to you. Says you're hard to find. I called him, and he just happened to be close by."

My heartbeat quickened. For the first time, I felt claustrophobic. Surveying the room, I looked for exits. It wasn't until I focused on an open window and followed floating clouds that I was able to calm down enough to speak. "What, what does he want to talk to me about? I'm not hard to find. I never go anywhere."

"Jenkins, now that's his business, not mine. Who knows what you kids are up to when you are not in my city limits. You've probably been tipping cows or must have pissed somebody off. For all I know, you guys are growing pot or cooking moonshine."

"I haven't done anything."

"Look here. It's likely no big deal, plus you don't have to talk if you don't want to. It's not like the sheriff can call your mom or grandpa and get permission to speak to you. If your grandpa had a phone, I'd be snitching your ass off all the time. That party line you're on ain't worth the effort to keep calling and getting a damn busy signal. Look, Jenkins, don't talk to him if you don't feel like it. Hell, you're a juvee, and you got some rights."

I wasn't exactly sure why Easley was giving me this advice. My first thought was that Easley was trying to buddy up to me so that I might tell him something I wouldn't say to the sheriff.

"I don't have to talk to you if I don't want to," was my first comment to the sheriff. I just jumped out there and told him that as soon as he walked into the police station. He looked at me and smiled, pushed his cowboy hat back to show his receding hairline, and lit a Marlboro. He reached down to dust some sand off his boot but kept his eyes cut at me. He looked like Richard Boone as Paladin in *Have Gun—Will Travel*, one of my favorite Western shows.

"You don't know what I am going to ask, so settle down, son. Officer Easley, can I have a little privacy with Jenkins here?"

As the sheriff created an almost unbearable long pause, I thought, *The Lone Ranger wears white, the pope wears white, and nurses wear white. They were all good people, but this sheriff always wears black. Hmm, he must be a bad guy.* Later, I would realize he was just a Johnny Cash wannabe.

"Let's try this again, son—just a couple of questions. You can answer them or not." He turned a chair backward, straddled it, and pushed it up against the bench I was setting on. "Let's see here; it looks like we have a Good *Samaritan* who claims he saw Mr. Lewis's truck parked at your house on the day he ended up dead. Did you see him that day?"

"No," was all I said for each of the eleven times he asked me.

"Now, sure appears you're sure of that?"

I gave him his long pause right back at him. I didn't answer at all. I did want to ask what a Samaritan was, but I figured I could just look in a dictionary later.

"Now his son Terry says you and him had a little run-in at school, and his dad was furious with the outcome. Terry says his dad went to see you on the day; let's call it a tragic wreck for now. That will keep things simple."

"Nope, didn't see him." I stuck to my no. *Were they talking to Jill too?* I wondered. Then panic set in again; I needed to get to her before the sheriff did.

Sheriff Brown removed his hat, ran his fingers through his hair, exhaled, put his hat back on, then stood up and towered over me. I didn't look up; I just stared at the peeling yellow vinyl on the back of his chair. He rubbed his chin and kept staring down at me. "Now, Mr. Lewis would not win father of the year. I am sure he had enemies. Did you see anybody that day that seemed out of place?" He pushed his hat further back until it barely tilted on his head. I didn't say a word.

"Look, I'm just trying to find out one thing. Did you see Terry's dad that day? You say no, you didn't. Were you and your sister home that day?"

"We go to the creek every day and don't come back until Mom comes home and honks the car horn for us. That's our sign to head home." My response was a truthful answer, even though it was not a direct answer, and Jill would maybe answer the same way. This was all I was going to give the sheriff.

He called Easley back into the room. "Officer Easley, guess he's all yours. I take it you'll be calling the county truancy officer? I suggest you call State Child Services too, as it looks as if Jenkins here and his sister, Jill, run around unsupervised on most days. It seems they might fall into that category of children in need of supervision. Take care of that, will you?"

What a dumbass, I thought. Jill and I had been going to the creek by ourselves since I could remember. The sheriff wasn't so smart, or he would know that Mom had called the sheriff's office many a time to get them to come to arrest the Devil. No one ever came.

CHAPTER TWELVE

1969

MY TOOTH FLEW ACROSS THE ROOM AND BOUNCED FROM WALL to floor. Everything appeared in some sort of suspended stop-and-go motion. I got the first dozen punches in with my patented hay-bailer move that was fast and furious. The Devil fell to his knees. He'd asked me to stop. I did. I couldn't kill him this way. His death needed to be a mystery like the others. My anger had overloaded my planning, my logic. After I stopped at his request was when I saw his enormous fist coming, but it seemed like I was moving in slow motion and I couldn't get away from it fast enough. There went the tooth. I was the victim of a sneak attack.

I was now 12, and bigger. I'd watched the escalation of the Devil's anger. He'd come home on a rampage. He'd attempt to be intimate with Mom, who confronted him about where he had been, which heightened his rage. She'd claim she could smell another woman on him. The cursing Olympics would begin, and then the violence. If I entered the fray, it would have the same ending: The Devil would sober up for a few days, and he and Mom would behave as if nothing ever happened. We would be a pretend *Leave It to Beaver* episode for a passing moment. I never understood if this was a survival technique for my mother or some type of enabling mental illness. Whatever the case, I was the fall guy who would receive a belt lashing. If anyone was concerned about my mental state, no one showed or shared it.

I'm unsure that I will ever fully understand why Mom was the way she was or why she endured an adult lifetime of physical and mental abuse from her demonic husband. Jill and I were her only salvation; she loved us dearly but not enough to take us away from this hell, if she was even capable. My mother's father had apparently been a wife-beater too. Her mother had an affair and left him but ended up with another husband who also beat her. This man, my grandfather, my mother's father, was alive until I was around 17 years old. He worked on the railroad, was an alcoholic, rolled his own cigarettes, and loved to fight. I saw him maybe twice in my entire life. He had one empty eye socket from a flying beer can that had destroyed it during a bar fight.

I'd been preparing for the moment. That night the Devil was just drunk enough and I thought I could take him, but I knew I needed the element of surprise. I stepped out on the front porch. He hit Mom once and then again. His back was to me. It was my chance. I rushed him; my fist hit the back of his head. He spun around, and I put him on his knees with multiple punches. I may have lost a tooth, but I gained confidence. I was jacked up. Did I become a man that day? At the time, I thought so. The Devil could be hurt; he could be beaten.

I was now a teenager. I'd discovered weightlifting, and fell in love with any girl who would look at me. I did drawings of the school bus seating arrangement and pickup schedule to increase the odds of the prettiest girls only having one seating option: the one next to me.

It had been two years since Sheriff Brown questioned me. No one was talking or speculating on what happened in Terry's dad's death anymore. Jill was never interviewed. Placing that whole incident behind me seemed easy. As with Jaxs, it appeared that Terry's old man was in that same elite assemblage of demons who nobody cared enough about to investigate seriously. They were both worthless, so to my thinking, I'd done everyone a favor.

The weightlifting made me feel more threatening and stronger than I actually was. That was what I partly blamed for losing a front tooth. Jill was working on a plan for the Devil's demise, and I just needed to have patience. She was back to stealing and hiding Valium. But we needed to do something soon as the Devil was indeed possessed, taking evil and ensuing craziness to a whole new level. The numerous stays in secure mental health centers seemed to have made him more wicked. Every time we were ready to pull the trigger on our poison plan, he would do something stupid and crazy in town, end up in jail, and then be taken to one of the state's mental institutions. Jill and I called these places the crazy houses. Sometimes he would have misdemeanor charges filed against him, but they would be dropped by the time he got out.

Just when I would start to believe that the Devil was really not the Devil but just a drunk, violent, evil man with no soul, something would happen to reaffirm what I'd grown up believing. Days before the big fight, he was talking and screaming in tongues. His glossolalia sounded like some foreign language. It was crazy scary. That, coupled with the few times Mom dragged us to church and the preacher screaming about casting out demons and how the Devil was real, was all the confirmation I required to hang on to my belief.

Three months earlier, the Devil's clothes had been found by some fishermen on the dam of a local farm pond. Everyone thought he had gone swimming and drowned. Jill and I wished so hard for that scenario to be true. The pond was dragged for the body, but nothing was found. Three days later, a naked Devil flagged down a farmer plowing his fields. The

Devil's feet were cut to ribbons from having walked barefooted some 30 miles from where his clothes were found. Ticks covered his body, and a layer of mosquito bites encircled the ticks. He was hospitalized for several weeks at the county seat, which had the only hospital in the county, with around ten beds. This was more proof that the Devil was not invincible but authentic. Maybe he was getting weaker as he grew older.

Speculation was that he went into what was called an alcohol-induced blackout. I knew these blackouts resulted from the demon inside taking total control. After being taken to the hospital, he talked about how he had killed a family and buried them on my grandpa's farm. Even though there were no reports of a missing family, the sheriff brought a backhoe to Grandpa's and dug a few holes where the Devil said he had buried them. Grandpa told them the Devil was in his son. As a result, the Devil ended up in a court-ordered psychiatric ward. This was one reason that 1969 was my favorite year: We were going to have four months of no Devil. I also got a new dog that I named Attila. I guess someone didn't want him and had just dumped him off on the side of the road. I wasn't sure how many breeds of dogs were in him, but he had a mouth like an alligator, dachshund legs, a pit bull torso, and the temperament of a pissed-off Chihuahua.

That year, music became my escape and greatest love. The town pharmacy added *Creem*, *Rolling Stone*, and *Hit Parader* to its magazine rack. They would quickly sell out, so you had to figure out when the pharmacy stocked new editions. Next, I had to find a way to town before they sold out. Last, there was the matter of having enough money to purchase them. Sometimes I would walk to town, pick up pop bottles on the way, and then sell them. Randy and I continued to sell the whiskey we collected from discarded bottles thrown out along country roads. You had to be highly dedicated to rock and roll to go through all this shit. Fortunately, I also got some of them as hand-me-downs from Javier.

Of all my buddies, only Javier shared my love of music. He introduced me to four-track cassette tapes. He also had a collection of transistor radios. All of this was important if you were a wannabe rock star like me. A distant cousin gave me an old Montgomery Ward acoustic guitar that he was going to throw away.

Using a discarded guitar chord book from the school library, I learned the basic chords. Luckily for me, most rock and roll hits that summer were three- or four-chord sensations. The problem was learning a song; I had to repeatedly listen to the top 40 radio stations until they played the song in rotation. I would have to wait hours or even days to have enough listens to learn one.

Jill somehow got a record player—a game-changer for the summer of 1969. The pharmacy stocked a few of the latest singles and albums that were popular. They were 99 cents each, which was a lot of money for me. My first two purchases consisted of "Lady Madonna" and "Honky Tonk Women." I loved the cover sleeve to "Honky Tonk Women." It reminded me of freedom and doing whatever I wanted to do, even though I thought it was an ugly woman in the picture. That song became my anthem. The one-hit wonder of Zager and Evans's "In the Year 2525" also resonated with me.

Guitar didn't come easily to me, probably caused by my inability to focus. Javier, on the other hand, was a natural. Of course, his dad played guitar and taught him. He was soon playing in a band. We were dedicated rock fans, so to us it was unthinkable that the Archies could have a hit with "Sugar Sugar." What the fuck? Who were the people buying such shit disguised as music?

It was the summer of love and Woodstock. I was caught between being a rocker and wanting to dress like a Mod, trapped between peace-and-love flower child and revolution. My garb was a combination of both:

everything from headbands and peace sign necklaces to that John Kay of Steppenwolf look. I spent days playing songs such as "Get Together" by the Youngbloods; then I'd listen to *The Crazy World of Arthur Brown*, The God of Hellfire. The latter became my second anthem.

With the Devil on hiatus I didn't need to spend as much time with my savior, my grandpa. He came by our house more often, so I guess he appreciated the peace and lack of high drama. His sense of humor was always dry and unassuming, but it was more pronounced with the Devil's absence.

"Jenkins, my boy, guess you're old enough that it is time I taught you to hypnotize old Bitty here," Grandpa said with a sincere look and soft tone. Bitty was a pet chicken. We always had lots of chickens, but Bitty was different. She was the only survivor of a coyote intrusion into the hen house. So Bitty was raised with the dogs and gained house privileges once potty-trained. She followed Jill and me around like a dog. She knew when the school bus would bring us home and was always waiting on us on the side of the road.

"Look here. Take old Bitty here, hold her tight, and make her watch your finger like this." Grandpa took his index finger and made circular motions in front of her eyes. Her eyes stared at the fingers, and then they closed, and she was fast asleep. He then placed her head under a wing.

"Now look here, you can throw her in the air and toss her like a ball, and she won't wake up." I trusted Grandpa and had never seen him kill or hurt any harmless animal, so I was confident that Bitty would be fine. We tossed her back and forth a few times.

"Now, boy, we got to wake her up, and that's a secret that very few people know about. You can only learn it with your eyes closed." I was hooked, fascinated by this hypnotized chicken, and was all in. I closed my eyes.

"Keep them eyes closed. I'm taking your hand, and we'll wake this chicken up." He took his rough, calloused hands and wrapped them around my wrist as I felt him guide it along Bitty's feathers. "Now, don't open them eyes."

"What the fuck," I yelled. I quickly pulled my hand back while simultaneously opening my eyes and standing up. Grandpa's laughter was thunderous. Bitty was unquestionably awake, and she was flying around the living room, searching for an exit. Feathers flew everywhere. I had just had my hand stuck up Bitty's butt.

Seeing Grandpa laugh like that, I started to laugh too. We both felt free with the Devil gone. *Life could be good*, I thought while cleaning the chicken shit from under my fingernails.

My magazines no longer required hiding, and I could listen to the record player anytime I wished. I wore my hair with bangs on the forehead. I could play my favorite three-chord song, "Wild Thing," on the old Montgomery Ward guitar. I experienced freedom. However, the most significant revelation was the intoxicating effects of having peace and quiet for the first time. Searching for this tranquility and a dash of no drama would be a lifelong endeavor.

I heard the car door slam shut before I opened my eyes and saw the headlights of a car pulling out of the driveway and back onto the dirt road. It spun out, throwing gravel against the house. A long silence ensued as my heart went from hammering to a slower pounding. The screen door creaked opened, then slammed. Who was now in the house? I could always smell the Devil even if I couldn't hear or see him.

"Who let this fucking dog in the house?" I heard the yelp as my dog bounced off the front porch. It was the Devil. I had been marking off the days, and he was not supposed to return for another month. *How could this be?* I wondered. I'd fantasized that he would never return. I may have even started praying again, promising God that I would change my ways and live a life for him if he only kept the Devil away.

"Never any goddamn food in this fucking house. Shit going to change this time." The Devil was screaming and throwing pots and pans. He turned the refrigerator over. Jill came to my room, where we agreed it was time for the old cut through the creek to Grandpa routine. Mom was still working nights, so at least we didn't have to worry about her for now. We pushed the bedroom window open. It was a full moon, and the stars looked so close I could reach up and harvest them from the sky. On the front porch illuminated by the moon, we saw the disarrayed pile of feathers that used to be Bitty. The Devil had stomped her to death, for she always slept squatted on the front porch. We made the trek to Grandpa's house.

I don't think I ever experienced such despair. I'd had a taste of freedom for the first time in my life. The taste also had an aroma of freshness, like a dew-sprinkled morning with fresh linen hanging on a clothesline dancing in a dawdling breeze. A yearning for this type of euphoria never diminished. Nor did I ever lose the determination to elude that level of despair that comes with the complacency of happiness.

CHAPTER THIRTEEN

CRAZIER

MOM SAID THE TREATMENT FACILITY HAD CURED THE DEVIL. His traumatic entrance back into our lives was just an expected relapse. I wasn't buying this.

Jill said, "I'm going to get married as soon as I'm old enough and marry a man who won't beat me and get drunk." Mom's response was a look of confusion.

I didn't say anything. I was trying to understand. Who were these people who said he was cured? No one talked to Jill and me about it. We would have told them he needed an exorcism. Even if I didn't really believe in it, it would have at least bought us more time and more freedom. How was one born into purgatory? What from the womb were we required to be expiating? I was always searching for answers to why Jill and I had been born into hell. But clearly it was just the luck of the draw.

Jill found a Ouija board hidden at the top of the kitchen cabinets, where only old items such as hand-cranked meat grinders and an ice cream churn were stored. She had been looking for Valium but found none. We had no idea what a Ouija board was, but it looked strange enough and didn't have any dust or spiderwebs on it like all the other items stored there. Something new like this, having entered our bubble, warranted a thorough investigation. I went to Javier's house, as they were the only family we knew that had an encyclopedia set.

After an exhaustive investigation, Jill and I determined that we were right and that if anyone had ever doubted us, we were exonerated. This Devil, this man, was possessed by a demon. Grandpa must have known it also. That was why he didn't shoot him that night, for he knew a demon could not be killed just by a shotgun. Mom must have been using the Ouija board to do something with the Devil, but we weren't sure what.

But later I found the burned halves of the Ouija board in two old oil drums outside our fenced yard that were used for burning trash. *Why had Mom destroyed it? Or did the Devil find it and burn it?* We would never understand. The mystery began to thicken.

Jill decided that the disappearance of Valium was related to the Ouija board. But if the solace found in the Valium had been replaced somehow by the board, now what? Jill decided to salvage the board. She presented it to me with pride, this burned broken board now glued back together.

"What is the Devil's real name? What demon is in him?" I was convinced my sister was scamming me as she asked these questions while the patched-up board's plastic spelling token moved underneath our fingertips. Whatever it spelled out, we couldn't pronounce it. Plus, I was convinced Jill was moving it. *This is bullshit, I thought.* "Just ask it yes and no questions," I grunted. I played along for a while, recognizing that she needed hope in something.

Our delve into the supernatural world didn't last long. Mom found our recycled board and it disappeared for good. She wouldn't answer any questions we had about why it had showed up in the first place. It was business as usual. She always said she played the cards she was dealt, a motto that was reluctantly becoming mine. My life had to have some light, some hope, if I was going to emulate her philosophy. Only the thought of the Devil's death gave me genuine hope.

Maybe Mom was trying to give us hope when she dragged Jill and me to an elderly psychic's home. Perhaps it was for her own. She never told us why we were going or what to expect. We wondered if Mom had seen this woman before, or if it was just this one time for our benefit. We were afraid, and then petrified once we met the psychic. She was blind and wore no eye covering, so we could see her pupilless white clouded eyes. She had no fingernails. We could see her touching our hands but could not feel her touch. Afterward, Jill and I could not remember a thing this woman had said about our future. Maybe we were so traumatized we blocked it out. As with many happenings in our lives, it was never spoken of again.

Maybe the psychic had told Mom to lose weight, because after the visit we stopped at the grocery store, where she bought a gallon of Metrecal diet powder. She was going to try to get skinny again for the Devil. Anything to please him, thereby accepting some responsibility for his behavior. She tried dyeing her hair red too. Sometimes it looked so fake.

The Devil's behavior hadn't changed, despite any rehab. Things seemed worse after my first fistfight with him, even though I found pleasure in showing off my missing tooth to Randy and a few others. It was my war badge. One day the Devil accused me of cutting electrical cords in the house. Later, the Devil shot a giant rat who was obviously the cord-chewing culprit. Once again, Mom would come home, clean up all the mess and blood, and we'd never discuss what had happened.

After the beating I took for the rat, I remembered what Sheriff Brown had said to Officer Easley about contacting child services and called the agency to turn myself in as an abused child. They explained that I needed to call the sheriff and his office to investigate my situation before they could do anything. Well, that wasn't going to happen. There was no way I ever wanted to talk to Sheriff Brown again.

If the summer of 1969 had been the best time of my life so far, I was in advanced purgatory for the remainder of the year. I was now in high school, the seventh grade. It felt good to be out of the school building where first grade through sixth was under the same roof. Jill, one year ahead of me, had become more distant and spent several nights per week at new girlfriends' houses. It was her way out, at least now and then.

I didn't have friends who I could stay with. Randy lived with his grandpa. The twins lived in a two-room shanty and still shared one bed. Javier was an option, but he was older and starting to get into drugs. In addition, all of us had outgrown the under-the-bridge hooky days. We were all starting to go our separate ways, but I wasn't sure which way I was going.

With no direction to go, I decided to try all of them. But in a small town my reputation was joined with the Devil's, and some school friends said that they couldn't let their parents know that we were hanging out together. Then there were the girls. It seemed that everyone I liked and wanted to spend time with had parents with a different idea. The teachers knew about the Devil too, and they had no expectations for me either. My chair was always in the back of the classroom, and seldom was I engaged.

When Jill wasn't staying with friends, we'd still sleep in one of the abandoned cars in Grandpa's pasture when things got too bad. Conscious of Grandpa's age and his increasing frailty, we didn't want to draw him into our hell so frequently. Many a day, I was self-conscious and embarrassed by my dirty and old clothing when I went to school after one of those nights in the car.

Javier invited me to come to his house when his parents were gone. "I got some cousins coming in from Mexico," he said. "You want to come down and do some pot, peyote, and mescaline? They'll have anything you want." I didn't do drugs but had no problems with those who did. If I was going to take a page from Jill's playbook and establish relationships where I could also spend nights, I would have to compromise on some negatives.

I got off the school bus at Javier's house. He had not been to school for several days, so I had to yell at the bus driver to stop there. It was only a two-mile walk to the highway where I could catch a ride. Javier's house was a square box with a dirt yard and an array of old motorcycles and cars strung throughout.

"Down here," I heard Javier's voice call out. The storm cellar door was open, and smoke was barreling out. The air reeked of pot as Javier toked on a doobie.

"Come on in, Jenkins. You look a little sheepish. Time to grow up a little." I descended the stairs to find a room full of older teenagers and probably several others in their 20s. The cellar was damp and cold, with only a tiny kerosene lamp on a small rickety wooden table providing illumination. The walls were lined with shelves full of jars of pressured cooked vegetables.

"This here is my little buddy Jenkins," he said. "Known him since the first grade." Only one of the six in the room could apparently speak enough English to understand. He appeared to be the oldest, and his eyes stared right through me. I felt uncomfortable and sensed that he knew that instantly. I declined his offer of a doobie and a black molly, which I'd never heard of before. Then he explained what quaaludes were for, took my hand, and placed two in my palm.

Javier jokingly called me a pussy and stated it was time to grow up. The others just kept staring at me, and I wasn't sure they were watching to see if I would take drugs or trying to intimidate me into leaving. I was wrong on both counts.

"Methinks you need to be initiated into our little group," the older one said to me.

"I'm not doing any drugs," I said.

"No, no. We talking about the initiation . . . real initiation. It make you a man, bro."

I looked to Javier for relief. Apparently, he'd taken too many quaaludes. He looked like a zombie, just lying in a corner staring up at the ceiling like it was some type of kaleidoscope, eyes moving from one side to the other.

"Hey, man, don't touch me," I demanded when the one guy grabbed my wrist. His grip became tighter. I pulled away. It was time to leave. I attempted to go up the cellar stairs when he grasped me around the waist and pulled me back down.

"Amigo, my little compadre . . . initiation, it's just a little thing, you know." Again, I looked for Javier, but he was now totally out of it. All he could manage to do was try to introduce me to his cousin again: "Here's Mexico, cousin . . ." Then his words trailed off.

"Mexico" unbuttoned his pants and revealed he wasn't wearing any underwear. He took a long draw from his cigarette, causing an intense red glow. He started burning a small patch of his pubic hair with the cigarette. "That smell, such a wonderful smell. Nothing like a little burned pubes to set the mood. Initiation!"

All the others were watching and nudging closer to me. I was scared. I took another glance at Javier. He looked peaceful in his slumber, curled up on the cellar floor like a newborn. Two grabbed me. I jerked my arms to pull away. They momentarily lost their grip but quickly snatched a new hold.

Mexico was walking toward me while playing with his penis. "Get yourself a little taste of this. Initiation! My one-eyed monster is going to bite you. No helmet on this big old soldier," he said while pointing to his penis. The grabbers erupted into a burst of menacing laughter. My eyes were darting all over the cellar, comparable to someone with multiple laser lights searching for darkness.

"Let's get him," one of them yelled out. Mexico momentarily turned to show his agreement to the one who yelled. He nodded in agreement. This was no game, but my darting laser eyes spied two large rocks that were broken off the stairs.

"One-eyed monster, one-eyed monster, my one-eyed monster is going to initiate, initiate, initiate you, little one," Mexico sang out.

Laughing so hard, the two detaining me weakened their grip. I reached down, snatched a rock, and hit Mexico in the forehead with it. The blood splattering was instant. He backed into a shelf full of pickled beet jars. The jars shattered on the floor.

"What the fuck!" Mexico screamed.

I grabbed a large piece of broken glass in each hand and started slashing whoever was closest to me. Everyone backed away, and I found myself going forward after them. It was like the Terry fight at school all over again. I'd lost it and was going to kill them all or die trying. I was going to die, but that was okay. At least I'd be free from the Devil. The level of rage was comparable to when I was gripping the coat hanger.

"This motherfucker is crazy. Man, he lost his mind," one of them yelled. This snapped me out of my rage.

What was I doing? These guys were backing up. I needed to get the hell out of there, and I now had an opportunity. I turned to run out and slipped on what I initially thought was a pool of blood, but might have been beet juice too.

Mind over matter: My hands were cut, but I didn't even notice until I'd escaped well into the woods and hid in the creek. Then my hands hurt like hell.

No one followed me. I worked my way through three creek crossings and cut through several pastures until I got to my grandpa's property and then to his barn. The alfalfa hay in the barn made my eyes water and I kept sneezing, but having refuge was worth it. Once again, here I was, hiding in my favorite place. Some of my stash of *Creem* magazine were there, although rats had gotten to some of them. I used some of Grandpa's black smear to disinfect my wounds—the stuff he used on calves and hogs after castration.

I tried to calm down and analyze what had transpired. I looked at the women's underwear section of the Sears and Roebuck catalog that Grandpa used for toilet paper. As usual, they aroused me, all those models wearing nothing but underwear, smiling seductively from the pages at me. Even if Javier's cousins were joking or just trying to scare the shit out of me, one thing I knew for sure: I was damn tired of people showing me their dicks.

CHAPTER FOURTEEN

A GOOD DEED

JAVIER MADE A POINT OF SEEKING ME OUT TO REINFORCE HIS contention that his cousins had just been joking around. But he'd been pretty much comatose the whole time, so he hadn't seen the evil intent in their eyes or heard their sinister laughter, nor felt the strength in which they tried to hold me. Our relationship would never be the same.

Between the Devil's return and the Mexico cellar incident, anger and mistrust consumed me. I was fighting anyone who looked at me wrong. Randy became my encourager in all things bad: my informal manager, picking fights for me to finish and developing ideas for meanness that I would execute. He was Frankenstein and I was his monster, a creation of our environment. So it was not surprising that I agreed to assist in punishing old Charles Bowin.

Randy was fuming over a story he'd heard about Charles allegedly molesting a cousin of his, a fourth grader. He was also upset that the boy's dad would not call the police. The dad already believed his son was light in the pants. I suspected there was more to the story, but if so, Randy wasn't giving it up.

"Jenkins, let's just get him out here in the country somewhere and just shoot his sorry ass."

"Really? That's your plan? We'd get caught in a heartbeat," I responded. To my knowledge, all Randy had to shoot anyone with was a bolt action single-shot .22 caliber that was probably 50 years old. He named every somewhat valuable item he owned. He called it Baby Blue Rooster Dick and had those words burned on the gun's butt.

It was a scorching mid-August day, and the usual blistering robust wind was blowing up dust devils across the freshly plowed fields of red dirt. Most trees had a permanent lean from the constant south wind. Randy and I often met halfway between his house and mine. There was a sizable native pecan tree just off to the side of the road where the road graders couldn't hit it, in a no-man's-land between the bar ditch and a property line. Randy and I had claimed this tree and its pecans as our own and did our damnedest to keep others away. Anyone driving by would stop to pick up pecans. This was one of the few trees that produced every year. We'd hatched many a childish plan under that tree, but today was seriously different.

"Come on, Jenkins. The old fart needs to pay, and he ain't got that bully Jaxs to protect him anymore." Randy aimed a tightly squeezed fist at me.

"Man, I don't know. He lives right there in town behind your grandpa's shop. How we going to get in and out of there without being seen by somebody?" I asked Randy while picking grasshoppers off my pants leg and letting them spit their juice on my hand.

"Hell, Jenkins, you know he tried to pick us up once before. We just ask him for a ride home, and somewhere between there and here, we jump him. Easy."

I stared at Randy to determine if he was just bullshitting me or was dead serious. A line of sandy mud ran down the side of his face. Randy had long, straight hair, and I knew he didn't wash it often. The sweat reminded me of the smokehouse and how clammy and wet Terry's dad had been when Jill and I dragged his body out.

"What about punishing him and then warning him that we'll kill him next time?" I felt the anger, frustration, and resentment rise from my stomach through my neck to my head as I engaged in a different option. I felt like something of a protector, a savior of sorts. Maybe some of my grandpa's blood was in me. We knew nothing about the science of sex offenders. We just figured every town had one and old Charles was ours. People would say that they just weren't right or they were just like their uncle or someone else in the family, but nothing was ever done to fix them.

"So let me get this straight," Randy said. "We get Charles to take us to your house and coax him into the smokehouse with some whiskey or some shit. Then we lock him in, let him sweat awhile, then let him out when he promises to be good. Have you lost your pee-brain fuckin' mind, Jenkins? It's easier to shoot the motherfucker in the head, dump his ass in a pond, and be done with it. What if he has a gun and tries to get queer with us? What then, smartass?"

"Then you can shoot him," I said. "Get one of your grandpa's pistols and leave that Blue Dick rifle at home."

The debate went on for a long while. Then we decided we couldn't agree. Randy left mad, saying he would do it anyway. Randy had big balls, but I was sure he wouldn't do it himself. He'd probably just been testing me.

Then summer was over, and school started up again. It was back on the bus for the hour-long trek to school and another hour home in the afternoon. It was harder to bum rides home now that we were in the eighth grade. Older friends with cars preferred to take girls home after school. Javier had a car, but I wasn't about to ask him for rides. So Randy and I were relegated to the bus.

It happened on the third week of school. September was as hot as August, and the school had no air conditioner. Randy and I got off the bus at school that day and decided hanging out at the pool hall was a good idea. We were out of change for the pool tables by noon, hungry and bored. We decided to walk the back roads to Randy's house.

Our walk took us by the open fire pits where all the town's garbage was taken and burned. Anyone could dump anything there for free and start their own fire. The black smoke was constant. When the pits filled, our little town would dig new ones that created large dirt hills, perfect for hiding a car behind when one needed privacy with a girl.

On this day we saw Freddy and Neddy at the dump. They were pulling the back seat out of their 1960 Chevy Impala. They had driven by the police station the night before to throw a large package of fuse-lit firecrackers at the front door. They had been drinking, and to hear Freddy tell the story, Neddy forgot to roll down the window. The firecrackers bounced off the closed window and into the back seat, then went off. The seat was on fire as Officer Easley stepped outside and laughed his ass off. They were lucky that Easley was on duty. Easley knew they didn't have a driver's license and didn't even bother to ticket them for that.

We walked past Pop Chevy, the lawnmower man, who was making house calls a little farther down the road. He never offered anyone a ride and always justified it by saying all the bulbs and tube replacements he had to carry around for jobs were fragile, and riders might break them. In reality, he was just an asshole.

It was an average playing hooky day—until it wasn't. The road dust slowly crept forward and engulfed the car seconds after it stopped. The old rust bucket squeaked and rattled while just sitting there idling. An unshaven, homeless-smelling Charles Bowin blew cigar smoke as he leaned out the window and rested his chin on his elbow. His arm was decorated with a combination of age spots, freckles, and an assortment of other damage.

"Kind of hot. You boys need a drink? Got me some Coors on ice in the back." Charles spoke calmly in his soft and high-pitched voice.

Randy had that look that said, *Let's do this.* A gaze part sinister, with a dash of confidence and self-righteousness, and a malevolent smile.

"So you want to give us a ride to Jenkins's house?" Randy asked in a nonchalant tone. My heart thumped.

"Well, of course. I am always willing and able to help our young folks when in need." Charles motioned for us to come around to the car's passenger side. I started to get in the back, but Randy grabbed my arm and pushed me in next to Charles. Randy got the window seat. As we drove off, I focused on the rusted-out floorboard where I could see the dirt road pass underneath us at what seemed like hundreds of miles per hour. I didn't want to be here.

"You boys not in school today, I see. Lucky I came by. It's hot out there."

"Thanks for the ride. Really appreciate it," Randy said, for I had nothing to say to this man. I was thinking, *Is this just my vivid imagination, or is this it, and Randy is going to punish or kill this man?* I trusted Randy, but that wasn't the same as trusting Jill.

"What you up to out here today? You still live behind my grandpa's shop?" asked Randy.

"Sure, I got that place, but I also have a little place out this way. It used to be a sweet potato farm owned by my parents back in the day. I keep the old house clean and save a few things in the old root cellars where we store the potatoes to keep them from spoiling too fast. Just add some lime powder. Here, I'll take you boys by there." Charles reached into a small ice chest and pulled out three beers. He placed one between his legs and tossed one each to Randy and me. Randy opened his, but I just held mine, thinking I might need it as a weapon later.

"No time for that," I blurted out as quickly as Charles took a breath. Everybody knows everybody's business in a small town. But the flip side to that is if you're going to have a secret, you had to develop a PhD in how to protect and hide it. Who knew Charles had a country place? Probably only his victims, and they weren't going to talk. Telling someone an older man molested you would result in being labeled a queer. Or you'd be held responsible for not fighting hard enough, which meant you wanted it.

"We got some whiskey at Jenkins's house. Let's go get that; then we can go see your old potato farm," Randy chimed in. I was sure that if Charles had been looking at Randy when he said that he would have seen that sinister and enigmatic look on his face.

"Guess we can do that. Coors will make an excellent chaser for that whiskey. Now, Jenkins, anybody home at your house?"

Before I could answer, Randy replied, "Nah."

"That's a good thing as an old fellow could get into trouble drinking with a couple of young dudes like you two." Charles laughed and slapped his thigh, causing dust to escape from the denim.

"Well, we ain't going to tell," answered Randy with absolute confidence.

We didn't meet too many cars on the back roads to my house. Still, when Charles saw one coming, he leaned farther down in the seat and on two occasions turned at intersections so as not to meet the oncoming car. It felt like it took forever to go the final three miles to my house. We passed our pecan tree meeting place, and sure enough, there were two guys there picking green pecans.

Charles pulled the old rust bucket of a car to the side of the road by my house. The red dust followed. My dog Attila ran out barking but stopped as soon as he saw me.

Randy got out of the car and motioned for me to follow. About half-way between the smokehouse and car, he turned to me and said, "I'm doing this with or without you. You in?"

"Yes," was all I could say, which surprised me. I had planned on telling him no. I had planned on being the first to say something on the walk to the smokehouse. I was going to say to him to forget this shit.

Once in the smokehouse, I improvised. I walked inside with Randy and then quickly stepped out and yelled, "Hey, Charles, got a problem here. Damn bottle of whiskey fell down a crack in the floor, and I can't reach it. Bet that long skinny arm of yours can do it, and I won't have to spend time pulling the floor up."

Charles canvassed the whole area before saying, "Sure, let's get this done." He shuffled his skinny old body across the yard, looking in all directions as he walked toward us. Attila had run back to his summer cooling-off spot under the leaking outside faucet, where the ground was perpetually cool and damp. With his nose parked between his two out-reached front paws, his eyes followed our moves.

I was going to lead Charles into the smokehouse, where we'd push him down, run out, and then lock the door. At least, that was what I told myself would happen. I expected Randy to follow my lead. But he lacked the patience, and grabbed Charles's arm when he came to the smoke-house door.

We had underestimated Charles. He pulled away from Randy with ease and drew back a fist to hit him. Before he could do that I dove for his legs, wrapped my arms around them, and brought him down.

"You motherfuckers, I knew something was up."

"Motherfucker, motherfucker, motherfucker," Randy yelled while kicking at Charles's head. Charles covered up while yelling back, "Gonna kill both of you fuckers." Then he went from defiance to "Leave me alone; I'm an old man. Damn it, stop!"

Randy grabbed ahold of Charles's legs too, and we pulled him inside the smokehouse. Randy kicked him in the face as we ran out and closed the door. Charles groaned, then cussed, then groaned some more. He threatened us and then begged us to be let out while saying he would let bygones be bygones.

I started to feel sorry for him. Maybe not because of what we were doing and about to do, but because he was old. He'd spent his entire life in this rinky-dink small town. One day he must have realized he was old and wondered what had happened to the years that had passed. Between the begging and the defiance, what was he thinking while we had him trapped in there?

Randy's adrenaline was running high. He was walking in circles and randomly hitting the smokehouse door, yelling for Charles to shut the fuck up. He looked like a rooster in the thick of a fight.

"It's fucking hot in here," Charles yelled. "Let me out. I need help. Fuck man, you hurt me. I need a doctor. Let me the hell out!"

I looked at Randy, who was sweating profusely, his hair even dirtier than it had been. "What you going to do now?" I asked.

"Shit, you tell me. Sounds like you want to tell me how to do this," Randy replied.

"No. This is your gig. You just need to share with me how this is going to end."

"It was your fuckin' idea to use the smokehouse."

"You're the damn one that wanted to kill him. I was just humoring you with the smokehouse option. Fuck man, I didn't think you even liked the idea," I shouted.

"Yeah, and I'm going to finish him off with or without you," Randy barked back.

I looked away for a second toward Attila, who was barking at a slow car passing down the road. Randy was so quick I didn't see the initial move. All of a sudden the smokehouse door was opening, and the gunshot was almost simultaneous. Charles must have been standing by the door. The bullet hit him right between his eyes.

I screamed, "What the fuck, Randy?" Randy said nothing. He just stood there doing some type of jittery dance and looking at the blood-splattered back wall of the smokehouse. He didn't look down at the body.

After a long pause, Randy said, "You're going to have to clean that wall off." I stared at him as a small puff of blue smoke rose from the gun barrel and floated peacefully toward the ceiling. I smelled a combination of gun-powder and gun oil.

We went straight from shock to down to business. Randy decided to push the body away from the door to close it. That was when we saw the back of Charles's head. The bullet had entered and created a hole, but the back of the head was almost completely gone. One would have thought we would be grossed out or at least have puked from what we saw. Neither of us did. It was as if we were immune or had had some type of vaccination to ward it off.

"Randy, where did you get that gun?" I hadn't even known that he'd had it. He looked at me and placed the gun back in the front of his pants.

"It was your idea, so I kind of borrowed it from my grandpa. It was his sidearm in World War II." Randy pulled the gun out again. It was a military .45 caliber.

"Damn, Randy, damn," was all I could say. I started my jittery dance in a circle.

"We did a good deed today, Jenkins. A good deed."

Randy already knew about the Devil causing all the digging and looking for bodies on my grandpa's land when he claimed he'd killed and buried some unknown people. So he knew what I was talking about when I said we could use one of those spots the sheriff dug up to bury Charles. The dirt would be loose, plus it hadn't rained much. It would be easy digging, and we could go deep. We agreed that I'd bury the body and Randy would do something with the car. He said he knew a place in the hill country about 20 miles away called 40-foot hole where he could drive the car in, and it would sink to the bottom.

So Randy drove Charles's car and then hitchhiked back after ditching it. I, on the other hand, had to utilize a wheelbarrow, push an old dead man across almost 80 acres, and pull it up three creek banks to get to the burying spot. Fortunately, he wasn't as heavy as I'd imagined he'd be.

After that, Randy and I had had it. Even months after we did what we did, Randy and I only spoke to each other superficially and never about Charles. I was walking around with a wave of constant anger, and I suspected Randy also had this same post-homicide affliction.

One day when I got off the school bus I heard a gravelly voice say, "Jenkins, got a minute?" Folgers stepped out from the shadow of one of the giant oak trees in town. In front of the school, this tree was a prize parking place sought after by the bus drivers.

"Got to get inside," I said nervously. "See you later."

"One minute, Jenkins. Now!" That stopped me in my tracks. Folgers motioned me to come hither and be in the shadow with him—his enigmatic persona in full display. I obeyed.

"You seen Charles?"

"No."

"Let's ask this a different way. When was the last time you saw him?"

Folgers kept rubbing his neck as he looked at me. I didn't know if that was because it itched from his throat-cut scar, or he was trying to send me a message.

"Haven't seen him," I mumbled.

He leaned into me with hands in his overall pockets and whispered, "Guess I know more than you do. Now go to school, you little rat. The next time I'll want honest answers."

"What the fuck, Randy?" Even though we hadn't talked in a while, I immediately found him when I went inside the school building.

"I saw Folgers waiting on you. He did the same thing to me," Randy rattled. "I was going to warn you. I didn't tell him anything."

"What the fuck, Randy... Why is Folgers even asking about Charles?"

"I told you before; he rented from Grandpa. Hell, I guess Charles owed back rent or something. Who knows?"

"But it's Folgers. Don't you think it is something else? You think Old Duck sent Folgers? Folgers is like the baddest fucker in this whole county."

"At least it's only Old Duck and not the cops asking questions. Count your damn blessings, Jenkins."

There may have been tension between us, but I was convinced Randy would never tell anyone about that day. I suspected he had his own reasons about Charles. He'd been right that no one would care about him. To my knowledge, this was the first time anyone had even recognized that he was missing.

"I saw that old froggy-looking guy hanging out with Randy's grandpa and talking to you this morning," Jill mentioned as we got off the school bus that afternoon. "That's twice this week I've seen him. I saw him parked up by that pecan tree where you and Randy hang out. He's one weird-looking man."

I wanted to tell Jill about what we had done. I needed someone to talk with, but I didn't want to get her involved. So I changed the subject. "How's the Valium hunting going so far? I'm ready to give it another try."

"I thought you'd forgotten," she said. "The last couple of months, you haven't said much of anything to me."

"Well, you got all your fancy overnight friends, and you leave me to fend for myself."

"Two more years and I'm out of here," she replied without addressing my jab at her.

"Anyway," she continued, "Mom is back on Valium, and I've been getting a few here and there. Not really sure why, though. It's not like it would work anyhow. Honestly, it just doesn't seem like an option." She shrugged and placed her hands outward with the palms up.

We were changing, it was true. Maybe I would have left before, run away from home, if it hadn't been for needing to protect Jill and our mom. Now it seemed as if all Jill was looking forward to was abandoning me. I was angry, but I also understood. Then she gave me some hope.

"Well," she said, "if we are going to try again, we need to do it soon."

CHAPTER FIFTEEN
IT'S COMPLICATED

"OKAY, GUYS, LISTEN UP. I JUST HAVE A FEW QUESTIONS," OFFI-
cer Easley said while he motioned for Randy and me to get into the back
seat of his squad car. We were almost to the town limits and hopefully
catching a ride to my house.

"I hear that Folgers has been asking some questions around town
about Charles going missing. It seems he's asking questions about you
and Jenkins too. Don't get me wrong; I don't give a shit about where
Charles is or if something lousy happened to him. I do care what happens
to you little shits, however. Now talk to me about what's going on."

Neither of us said anything. I stared at the filthy cloth back seat of the
car and thought how many drunks had thrown up or pissed their pants
back there.

"Guys, it's like this. I've been lenient with you two since you were
little wannabe thugs hanging out under that bridge in grade school. I
looked the other way on a bunch of that juvenile shit you two have done
over the years. So now I'm just asking you to work with me a little bit
here. Understand?"

"Ask my grandpa if you want to know what Folgers is up to. He works for him." Randy sounded defiant, and it convinced me he wasn't going to give Easley anything.

Five minutes of silence felt like an hour. Easley lit a cigarette and blew smoke into the back seat. "I shouldn't tell you fuckers anything, but you need to know how deep the shit can get on this." I looked at Randy, who maintained a stern stare out the window.

"You see, I think some of these mysteries the last few years are not mysteries at all. They all connected."

I about shit my pants. I started sweating and felt like I needed to vomit. All I could venture was, "What mysteries?"

"Oh, now you want more information?" Easley said. "Though, Randy, you don't seem too interested."

"Damn straight, Sherlock," Randy said. He looked like he didn't want to put up with any of this for a single minute.

"Then get the fuck out. Jenkins, you stay right there."

I guess Randy didn't want to hear anything, because he got right out of the car and started walking toward home. I didn't know what I was going to hear, but I figured it was better to stay and find out.

Easley turned around in the front seat to look me in the eyes. "I haven't put all the pieces in place yet, but it starts with Jaxs and Charles. Hell, everyone knew about Charles's affinity for the youngsters, but Jaxs was a manly man. You know what I mean?" I nodded in agreement.

"Right, it was always weird that those two stayed in the same house. Then there's Sheriff Brown, who didn't seriously investigate Jaxs and Sonny's deaths. He isn't even looking into Charles missing anymore. Maybe he just goes for the easy wins. He should do the job he was elected to do. I'd run against him, but he's done too many favors for people already. I think this is some favor Brown's doing now. We all know Charles is dead somewhere. Somebody knows where he is, and it won't be centuries before he's found."

He went on. "Then there's Cecil Lewis. Allegedly he died in that wreck by your house. I'm not buying it. Then there's that poor old Norman who was headed to Vietnam. We all know he was mixed up in some heavy shit too. I'm not saying I believe the rumors about the cop running him off the road; I'm just saying I'm connecting the dots."

"I don't know nothing about dots, Officer Easley."

"Oh, I think you do. I believe you're culpable. If you know anything and aren't telling me, then you're an accessory after the fact. Hell, you might even be construed as a conspirator."

I gave Easley a hard stare. I was trying to buy time before I attempted to respond.

"And I think your old man is snarled up in all of this, and you know it," he said.

"I told you, I don't know anything!"

He gave me one last look. I knew he didn't believe me, but then he told me to get out of the car. He didn't need to ask me twice.

I caught up to Randy, who explained, "I don't like anyone talking about my grandpa. I know he does a lot of business under the table, so to speak. That's why he has Folgers, and if Folgers is looking into Charles, I'm laying low. I can't be seen in no damn police car."

"Whatever, Randy. I've never seen you afraid or back away from anything. Guess there's a first time for everything."

The next day after the Easley visit, I rode to town with my grandpa to get cattle feed. He decided to hit the pool hall for a few quick games of dominoes, so I stepped into Salem Lowe's. "One candy bar at a time. I'm saving the world one candy bar at a time," Salem announced as I stepped up on the sidewalk in front of his store.

"Salem, say what?"

He didn't explain. "Balance, Jenkins. 'What does man gain from all his labor at which he toils under the sun?' Ecclesiastes, you should take some time to read it."

I had no idea what he was talking about, so I asked to see a couple of new pocket knives he kept under lock and key. I told him I'd quit trapping. I didn't have the money for the pocket knife I was pointing at, but I wanted to have it.

It seemed like Salem was watching me carefully. He sat down in a worn-out wooden rocking chair behind me. I could feel his eyes on me. All of a sudden he said, "Folgers, now there's quite an unusual character. Now, don't get me wrong. Every town has one."

I didn't say anything. Then he started rocking.

"Folgers is good at what he does," Salem went on.

I turned around and looked at him. "Good at what?" I asked.

"He's an enforcer," Salem said. "I think you would agree that one would be a fool to even think about a tussle with a man resembling a bowling ball. He always kept that Jaxs character in check. That's not a bad thing. And it takes a bad man to deal with another bad man. No love lost there between those two. Guess that's why Folgers didn't care to delve into his death. I'm not saying Old Duck didn't ask him to; I'm just saying whatever Folgers did on that was superficial. Jaxs was expendable and easily replaceable. Such is not the circumstance with Charles. You know this, don't you, son?"

Salem's stare burned into my brain. I refused to give in and ask another question.

"Oh well. I can see you're curious. It might help to know that Folgers found Charles's billfold while snooping around your property. What else would you call it when someone knows no one is at home but looks around anyway? Some might wonder why Folgers didn't hand it over to the police. I am not one of them. You understand why, don't you, Jenkins?"

I had to ask then. "How do you know this?"

"As I said, Folgers is good at what he does. Who knows where the trail started. Maybe with just asking a few questions here and there. What I do know is his path came across the twins. They told Folgers they saw you and Randy get into a car with Charles. Now maybe Folgers coerced information out of them. Perhaps it isn't even true, but that doesn't matter now that Folgers believes it. Then, of course, there's the billfold."

I was scared shitless, but I asked no more questions.

"The question for him is, why was Charles's billfold on your property? You do understand he will eventually find out. The man is a bloodhound disguised as a human."

Now I was in a major panic attack mode. *I needed to tell Randy, I needed to tell Randy,* was all I could think. I stared at the floor as I started to shuffle out the door, not wanting to hear any more.

"Remember, Jenkins, one candy bar at a time. What's your candy bar?" Salem softly presented his parting advice as I left.

I found Randy at the pool hall and told him what Salem had said.

"Damn it, Jenkins! Who in the hell can't see a damn wallet laying on the ground!"

"Look, it's not my fault. You had the easy part. I had to drag that man and dig the fucking hole!"

Randy and I argued back and forth for over an hour. Then he surprised me by saying that his father had gotten out of prison about a month ago and wanted Randy to come live with him. I'd always thought his dad was dead, because he never spoke of him. Randy planned to leave town and give living with his dad a chance.

So that's his plan, I thought. *Leave me here to deal with this shit.*

Apparently, Randy's dad had gotten an oil field job in Texas, and they were moving somewhere outside of Odessa. We agreed we wouldn't talk to anyone about what we'd done to Charles. He said that Folgers had not spoken to him, which I felt was odd.

Randy moved away within a week, skipping his last week of school. I didn't want to talk to Jill about this, but I was worried Folgers might try to ask her questions. So I tried to stay close to her. If she rode the bus home, I did too. If she walked to Grandpa's house just for a visit, I tagged along. I wasn't sure what I'd do if Folgers pulled up on us. My only proper weapon was a cheap bowie knife, which I tied with a shoestring to my ankle and carried everywhere I went. I wouldn't have a knife if I had not convinced Mom to redeem her S&H Green Stamps for it.

One day Jill caught a ride home with one of her friends' mothers. When I got off the bus at our house I saw Jill sitting under the old elm tree with her back to the road. As I approached her, I could hear her uncontrollable crying.

"What's wrong?" I yelled. She just kept crying. Her face was red as a beet, and she was trembling. I helped her to her feet. She was trying to tell me something, but she was incoherent. "Jill, did Folgers talk to you? Is that what happened?" But her crying only worsened.

I looked toward the driveway. The Devil's pickup wasn't there. I asked Jill if the Devil had hurt her. She just motioned toward the house, where the front door stood open.

I walked onto the porch, where I could see the pickup parked behind the smokehouse. I reached for my knife as I entered. I slowly walked through the living room to the hallway entrance. As I peered around the corner, looking toward my bedroom, my eyes met the large bloodshot bugged-out eyes of the Devil.

I yelled, "What did you do to my sister?" I rushed him with my knife. He dodged and grabbed my arm, almost breaking it. I lost my grip on the knife when his fist hit my nose. I grabbed my long barbell that was always in the hall and rammed it into his gut. He staggered but didn't fall. I retreated into the living room. The Devil followed, and then all of a sudden I heard a loud hollow-sounding thud; he dropped to his knees. Jill stool there holding the large cast-iron skillet she'd used to hit him.

Jill and I ran out of the house. I yelled at her to stop: "Let's go finish this. Let's kill him now!" But she kept rushing toward the woods that led to Grandpa's house. When I caught up with her, she was in a state of shock, still unable to speak. I was gasping from adrenaline, and from running and sucking pollen into my lungs. I felt like I was going to throw up. I fell to the ground gagging and throwing up. While on all fours, I looked toward the house and decided the Devil had not followed us.

We were both panicking. I wiped the puke off my face with a fistful of leaves and compost from the wood's floor. I didn't care if the Devil was dead or alive, but I was concerned that Jill was not snapping out of her delirium. We obviously couldn't go back home. Holding hands, we attempted to forge ahead but stopped, exhausted.

We sat with our backs against a large cottonwood. The tree's large rough bark was soothing as I focused on calming my breathing. Jill's crying eventually stopped, but she still wouldn't answer my questions. "What did he do to you?" I must have asked that at least 20 times. Eventually, nature's symphony induced us to sleep.

We were up with the sunrise when we saw the reflection of Mom's car lights through the woods as she turned into the driveway. The Devil's truck was gone, so we ran to meet her. We told her what had happened. She took Jill inside the house and asked me to wait outside on the porch.

Whatever Jill told her, all I knew was that Mom had us packed and moved into a small house in town that very day. It was one of the prefab track houses used by one of the oil companies.

Mom told us that we were not moving back to the country. It was nice not to have to ride the school bus or bum rides home. It was also a lost time for me. Jill was still traumatized by whatever had happened (and I hated to think about it), and I started drinking the whiskey I salvaged from the throwaways in the bar ditch.

I'd found the Devil's rifle and brought it with me. I kept it hidden from Mom. I intended to shoot the Devil if he tried to break in on us. I'd never shot a gun that used an ammo clip before, but I had shot Randy's single-shot bolt action rifle several times.

Our city house was just a block from school and maybe four blocks from the town center. Old Duck's operation was close to the middle of town, so I always took the long way to avoid encountering Folgers. I also now lived in Officer Easley's jurisdiction. He took full advantage of that by doing daily drive-bys. I wasn't sure if he was trying to intimidate me or waiting for me to come out of the house and talk. Sometimes he would pull up and sit in front of the house for an hour. Since there was only one cop per shift, he could do whatever he wanted unless he received an emergency dispatch.

The middle of town was where the two major county highways crossed. It was the only four-way stop sign in town, where each corner had a competing full-service gas station. It was an ideal location to hang out after hours. Those with hot rods would park and raise their car hoods so everyone could gawk at the engine modifications. Someone would make a challenge, and then there would be a drag race at the dump ground road. It was also the place where everyone went to finish fights.

I spent my time trying to live up to everyone's low expectations of me. One Saturday night I walked to the crossroads after having drunk as much whiskey as I could hold without getting sick. The hot-rod crowd was large that evening. Hanging out with all the smokers, druggies, and town badasses was a treat for me, because I could stay as long as I wanted and walk four blocks home.

An immaculate black low-rider Mercury slowly circled the gas station on each corner. Eventually it pulled into and stopped where my crowd had assembled. It was the first time I had seen a car with tinted windows. The car had New Mexico plates. Six guys unfolded themselves out of the vehicle. Most of them seemed to be in their mid-20s.

The driver was obviously the leader. He stepped forward and methodically surveyed the crowd. He had a face of stone and penetrating eyes. His cold black hair was combed back, and he wore sunglasses. He then focused on Dakota. Maybe he zeroed in on him because Dakota was the largest of all of us, at about 6'5" and 250 pounds. People used to say that Dakota was half Indian and half bear. He was attending a small state college on a football scholarship. He could walk on his hands and was the most agile big man I had ever seen.

"How's it going tonight," the driver said to him in a baritone voice, while scraping his foot over the concrete.

"Same old, same old," responded Dakota.

The driver flicked his silver cigarette lighter open and lit a baby cigar all in one motion with one hand. His riding partners were standing by the Mercury. I noticed that no one was leaning or sitting on it.

"No thanks, I don't smoke," Dakota stated without being asked.

"Okay, then. Here's the deal. See, we don't want any trouble. You see Little Joe over there. Well, he has an issue with one of your local baby thugs," the driver offered.

"What's your name?" asked Dakota.

"They call me Man."

"Well then, Man, lay it on us."

I slowly worked my way toward the imaginary front line. This looked like it could be exciting, and I wanted to make sure I could hear and see all of it.

"Seems one of yours has been fucking with Little Joe's girlfriend," Man said. "You know that's wrong in anybody's book. It's simple if you want it to be." Man was tall and skinny. He wore a black leather jacket even though it was hot. It was night, but he slowly took a pair of dark wraparound sunglasses, referred to as bug glasses, and covered his intense stare.

"Simple. Is it?" Dakota said with a smirk. But then he cocked an eye at Man and asked, "So who you think is fuckin' around with Little Joe's sweetie?"

"Some little runt by the name of Jenkins."

What the fuck? I held my breath, not moving.

"How old is Little Joe there?" Dakota asked.

"Little Joe there is 15."

"He doesn't look little. He seems like a rather normal size for 15. Why you call him Little Joe? He got a big brother or something like that?"

"Naw, he just likes to watch *Bonanza* all the damn time. What's it to you?"

Everyone laughed, and some of the tension fluttered into the night sky. I started to slowly step back and blend into the back of the group. I'd never seen these people before, but if they were asking about me, I wasn't taking any chances.

Then Dakota was standing before me. "Jenkins, you know anything about these dudes? You messing with Little Joe's girl?" he asked.

"I swear, Dakota. Never seen these guys and for sure don't even know who his girlfriend is."

"Well. We can't let them come into our town and get away with this.

You got protection here, and I won't let anyone jump in, so go out there and whoop his ass." Dakota could back up all he was saying as he was a big man, well over six feet tall, and had the largest biceps in town.

"What the hell you talking about? I ain't done nothing to no Little Joe or anyone else," I complained.

"Makes no difference. We talking about respect here now. You got to step to the plate and represent your self-respect and this town. You're not a pussy, are you?"

That did it. I had to fight.

In a loud voice, Dakota announced there would be a fight. As the crowd parted to create a human boundary boxing ring, I decided I needed to take a piss first. I'd had several beers in addition to some whiskey. As I opened the bathroom door at the gas station, I felt a crushing blow to the back of my head. It was too fast for Dakota to stop it.

The bathroom was a tiny one-staller with hardly any room to maneuver, much less have a decent fight. I grabbed Little Joe's head and smashed it into the back of the commode. Somehow a water line broke loose. Water was spewing everywhere. Neither one of us could see, but we kept swinging and hitting. We slipped and fell on the floor. The toilet had been clogged and not flushed in a while.

Dakota and Man pulled us out of the toilet. Dakota took command, separated the crowd, and stated, "Now, let's have a fair fight."

Little Joe took his shirt off and started dancing around me like some jackrabbit. The crowd yelled and laughed, "It's Bruce Lee!"

I heard Dakota's voice yell, "Motherfucker thinks he knows karate or some shit."

Just then Little Joe slipped from the shit on his shoes. I went for it.

I lowered my head and bull-rushed him. He grabbed a double fist of my hair and we hit the ground. I heard the crowd cheering and then, when I was sitting on top of Little Joe, I went crazy and couldn't stop trying to kill. My ears were ringing. I wanted to kill him . . . I was going to kill him. Left-right, left-right, my fist pounded his face while he tried to roll away from under me.

Suddenly I was pulled off. It was Dakota. "Jenkins, look at me, man. What in the fuck is wrong with you, you little crazy son-of-a-bitch?" He slapped my face and poured a beer over my head.

"Motherfucker is off the chain crazy," Man yelled.

Dakota handed me over to some other big dude and walked over and stuck his finger in Man's chest. "You're outnumbered here. Our boy fought; that's what you wanted, and now it's over."

"Your boy tried to snuff him," Man said. He sounded pissed.

"I said it's over."

They must really have thought I was crazy, because it didn't take much more convincing for them to shove a bleeding Little Joe back into their car and drive off. Our crowd dispersed too.

"Might want to put some ice on that," Dakota said to me. He offered me a ride home, but I said no.

I made it about a block before Officer Easley pulled up alongside me.

"I don't need a ride," I said.

"I'm not offering one, Jenkins."

"Leave me alone," I said.

"Got the call about the fight. It took me a while to get there."

I didn't have anything to say to him. He slowly drove beside me with his arm hanging out the window while I walked.

"Fortunately no one's pressing charges," Easley said. "Though of course I could still get a county warrant for the destruction of property and pay you a visit at school."

"I don't care. Do whatever turns you on," was my response.

"Well, dipshit, you better care. Who do you think sent those hood-lums your way? Can you say Folgers? You better start talking, or I won't be able to keep protecting you."

I kept walking, and Easley made a U-turn. I slowly limped the last two blocks to our rental, taking a moment to lie in the road for a few min-utes to get lost in the stars above. As I walked up to the front porch, my heart stopped. There was the Devil in all his glory, curled up and passed out on the steps.

CHAPTER SIXTEEN

LORD ON MY SIDE

ALL APPEARED TO BE FORGIVEN. WHEN I LEARNED THAT WE were moving back to the country house, I decided that I would never forgive anyone who had hurt me in any form or fashion. I was bewildered, outraged, and scared. Where was my life, one candy bar at a time?

The house in town came with used furniture, but it was much better than what we had in the country. Everything was just as we'd left it as I stood at the entry of our old home. The green plastic couch with cigarette burns and stuffing hanging out of the armrests greeted me with a sinister "welcome back, fool." I moved back into my room, put sheets on the bed, and hung the few clothes I had in the closet. My lone dresser had acquired new residents: A nest of hairless newborn mice inhabited the top drawer. I left them there and placed clothes in the other two.

The Devil had gained weight while on his last sabbatical. His eyes also bugged out even more than usual. Jill and I agreed he looked like Jackie Gleason. As always, there were no conversations. Mom acted as if nothing had happened, and there was never a conversation about why we had moved in the first place.

Mom was now on a religious kick, dragging Jill and me to church three times a week: Wednesdays, Sunday mornings, and Sunday nights.

The pastor was charismatic, a cross between the coolness of Steve McQueen and the riskiness of Peter O'Toole. He combed his blond curly hair straight back and always wore tight slacks, a pullover shirt, and the shiniest shoes I had ever seen. Our small-town church was his first assignment. I didn't know where he came from, but I was sure it was from some big city, maybe even another state. In less than six months he had tripled church attendance. Pastor Wayne was the talk of the town.

There was constant pressure to get baptized because that was what Baptists did. Plus, who could resist this movie-star pastor? I thought that if I got baptized, then maybe there wouldn't be as much constant pressure about attending church, so I'd just get it done.

I sang lines from the *Beggars Banquet* album in the song "Dear Doctor" while I walked down the aisle to baptism, though I took them out of sequence. Another song to add to the soundtrack of my life, and The Rolling Stones were dominating it. Since I prided myself in being the ultimate chameleon, I was surprised that the goody-two-shoes, go-to-church-since-birth crowd from school didn't embrace me afterward. Apparently baptism did not wash away my reputation.

The assistant pastor directed me into the changing room. There the pastor was in his underwear, combing his hair and preparing to baptize me. He handed me a robe and told me to put it on, so I did. He then instructed me to take my clothes off first and put the baptism robe on. I think he laughed at me. I'd never been naked in front of a grown man before, and I was not inclined to start that day. Plus, my underwear had holes and was dingy from swimming in dirty ponds. I refused to take my clothes off, and I put the robe back on. "You sure you want to do that?" he asked with a laugh. He then explained how this baptism thing would go down. I was scared shitless. He asked me to pray, and I asked him if I was to pray to God or Jesus. He looked at me funny and asked why I was being baptized. I told the truth, for it was for sure a straight ticket to hell for lying to a preacher. He seemed to accept this, and we proceeded.

I didn't realize that after the baptism the pastor required the newly baptized to sit on the front row, and after the service, the congregation strolled by and blessed you for your dedication. So there I squatted, wringing wet, dripping on the red carpet with a pool of holy water at my feet. My wet underwear was making my ass raw. I could sense the laughter behind the smiles and congratulations of my fellow classmates as they passed.

I didn't go to church for two weeks after that, and this brought the pastor out searching for me. Apparently there was some attendance requirement and there would be hell to pay if I violated it. Whenever I saw the pastor's bright blue Road Runner in our driveway, it was a simple avoidance maneuver to just stay on the bus until the next stop. Hadn't he heard me when I told him why I was being dunked in that Baptist water?

But this pastor was dedicated to the mission of me. I don't know how many times he tried to contact me. He gave up on trying to catch me by synchronizing with my school bus arrival. He saw Jill at home several times, and I was sure they had great conversations. She continued to attend church and seemed to enjoy the socialization offered there.

Then the pastor made a mistake. It was early Friday afternoon, and Jill had just left to attend a football game. School always let out early on a home football game night. The twins were supposed to pick me up later if they could get brake shoes back on their old Chevy. I heard the rumble of the glasspacks that Pastor Wayne had installed on his Road Runner. I guessed he added these loud noise enhancers to his tailpipes to be cool and announce his saintly arrival. I didn't want to miss the twins if they did show up, so I decided to let Pastor Wayne have his say.

I met him at the door and welcomed him. He appeared hesitant to sit on our old green plastic dirty sofa. He was very perceptive, and between all the patched holes in the walls, cigarette-burned floor décor, and taped-up broken windows, he probably figured the whole house needed a christening. He chose to stand.

"Mr. Jenkins, we have missed you at church. We would love to see you back this Sunday."

"I might be able to make it." I reckoned if I gave him a little hope, he'd quickly leave and not wear out his welcome. Very few people outside of family had ever seen the inside of the Devil's den. He should feel special, I thought.

"Well then, that sounds promising. Have there been any issues or concerns that kept you from attending? If so, I'm here to listen and work through it with you."

"I got baptized, so I thought I needed a little break. That being dunked was mentally exhausting." I wasn't trying to be funny, but this caused the pastor to laugh.

"Oh, Jenkins. It doesn't work that way. You caught fire, and now we got to keep it burning!" He produced a small Bible from his back pocket and started reading. He was reading too fast and spitting too much, in full-blown sermon mode.

I was starting to enjoy this entertainment. He placed his left hand on my head while clutching the Bible in the other. "God help this lost child who has reached out to you but now has doubts. The Devil is at work here, causing him to disbelieve. We are all sinners, and the Devil blinds us to this sin. The Devil doesn't want you to believe in God or him, for to believe in the Devil, one must also believe in God. The forces of good and evil are at work here."

The sentence about believing in the Devil made sense to me. Pastor Wayne was busy bringing his sermon to a crescendo, and I started to pay attention earnestly. I guess that was why neither one of us saw the Devil approach until we heard the screen door slam shut.

The Devil's face was red, and he reeked as usual. "Preacher, I like what I hear. Fuck that damn Devil. You kick that Devil's fucking ass!" He flipped his lit Camel over to the sofa so this vinyl shrine could bestow another burned offering.

"Mr. Jackson, it's a pleasure to meet you. I have heard so much about you," Pastor Wayne said to the Devil.

"What the fuck have you heard?" This question by the Devil seemed to stump the pastor. He probably wanted to take back what he'd said. Of course he couldn't have heard anything good. Maybe that was why he was so persistent in finding me and trying to get me back in church.

When the pastor didn't immediately answer, the Devil spread his arms out like a crucifix. "Exorcise me, motherfucker, exorcise me!" he screamed. He had yet to even acknowledge I was in the room.

"Come on, give me your best fuckin' shot!" I sat in a corner chair, crossed my legs, and prepared for the show. The pastor appeared perplexed and afraid. I wasn't. I was less fearful of the Devil and just angrier as I grew older.

"The truth will set you free. Now tell the truth, preacher. The truth will set you free, you rotten son-of-a-bitch. What do you know about anything? Bet you got a pencil dick!"

Pastor Wayne was starting to get that faraway look in his eyes indicative of retreatment. "Sir, I can see you are agitated and appear to be in a somewhat inebriated condition. So maybe this is not a good time to continue the Lord's work here."

"Listen here, you bastard, I don't drink, and what would ever give you the idea I was drunk? The Lord's work is never done, so lay it on me, motherfucker."

"You have an open invitation to come by the church anytime," replied Pastor Wayne as he gingerly stepped back toward the front door. The Devil proceeded to follow.

"Hey, preach, don't leave. Aren't you going to say a prayer? What about my soul, preach? Don't you want to save it, you fuckin' idiot?" The Devil followed Pastor Wayne to his car, continuing his yelling along the way. He stumbled twice on the loose red bricks representing a makeshift walkway to the drive. I couldn't hear all that was being said, but both of them appeared to become highly animated. They seemed to be using sign language, with the Devil pointing at the car and the pastor waving him off like a referee with a penalty flag.

Whatever was happening outside, it could only be bad for me. With the Devil so agitated, there would be hell to pay when he came back into the house. I went out the back door and started walking down the road, the debate still going on behind me.

"Oh, shit! That's Folgers's pickup," I said out loud. No one could mistake that 1969 orange El Camino for anything else. I turned away and saw the pastor pulling out of our drive. The Devil was just standing there looking my way. I looked back toward the pecan tree. Behind where Folgers was parked was a plume of red dust racing in my direction created by a metallic green Nova Super Sport. It flew past me, then locked its brakes up and spun around. I could hear the driver missing and grinding gears as he downshifted. I shielded my eyes and waited for the dust to settle.

"Jenkins, you little fucker, get in." I cleared my eyes of red dust, and there was Leon Spottedhorse.

"Jump in. Get the fuck in, Jenkins." I looked toward Folgers, who was now standing beside his ride, looking my way. I could hear the Devil yelling at me. *Could this shit get any worse?* I thought. I got in. Leon spun out while I was still closing the door.

"You like my new car?" Leon asked while hurtling past Folgers and giving him another dose of red dirt. "Bought it off some Vietnam vet who spent all his combat pay and needed to sell it. Got a hell of a deal."

"That's really going to piss him off," I predicted.

"Well, fuck that old son-of-a-bitch Folgers. I ain't scared of his stupid ass. He's not as tough as he thinks he is. Here, want a beer?"

"No, man. Can you just drop me off at my grandpa's house?"

"No can do, little buddy," Leon responded while reaching over and frogging my thigh.

"I'm headed over to pick up Dakota," he added.

"Just let me out anywhere then."

Leon started to fishtail the car intentionally from one bar ditch edge to the other. I kept trying to look behind us to see if Folgers was following.

"Relax, Jenkins. He ain't following." Leon pulled off into an old oil field road.

"Listen up, Jenkins. Hell, anybody in the know knows Folgers has a beef with you. Lots of rumors and bullshit out there about you two. So now you going to tell this Indian what the fuck is going on."

"Why you so damn interested in my shit, Leon?"

"This ain't some kid shit you playing around with this time, you stupid fucker."

I gave it a long thought before I responded. "Folgers thinks I might know something about where Charles Bowin is."

"Well, fuck. Everybody knows that someone killed that crazy old fucking child diddler. Hell, the world's a better place now. We ought to give a medal to whoever snuffed his ass. It was just a matter of time. Good fuckin' riddance! Now, what in the fuck would you know about any of this shit?"

I just stared out the window, watching the rusty old oil pumping unit go up and down, up and down, pushing that oil on down the pipeline. I wasn't going to talk, and Leon probably knew that.

"Well, then, Jenkins, it's your neck on the line and not mine, and don't think you aren't really pissing me off here." He slammed the Nova in gear, spun onto the road, and fishtailed each time he hit the next gear. We flew into town and then skidded to a stop at the crossroads where I'd had my infamous fight with Little Joe. Leon reached over, opened the passenger car door, and pointed south down Highway 18.

"Get your ass home, and don't let me see you back in town for a month. That should be time enough for this Charles shit to calm down. If I see you back here on the streets after dark, I'll kick your ass into next week."

Taking a deep breath and sarcastically thanking Leon for the ride to nowhere, I shuffled off down the road. I made it about a mile before Pastor Wayne's car came flying over a hill. He hit the brakes, then put it in reverse, and backed up to where I was still walking.

"Need a ride?"

"No, sir, I'd rather walk."

"You going to be okay?" he asked while pulling the car to the side of the road. He got out and walked over to me. "Sure would like to see you back in church."

I thought, *Will this nightmare ever end and people just leave me alone?*

"You know I have a few books that your family can read. Codependency, enablers, Al-Anon, and Alateen are all things you guys need to know about and look into," the pastor continued.

I could hear him continue to preach at me as I kept walking. I picked up bits and pieces of what he was saying until his voice faded in the wind. I had two ride offers as I walked home down Highway 18, but I waved them off. I was in no mood to talk to anyone.

When I reached my grandpa's house, I went inside and hung out for a while, and killed a scorpion lazily zigzagging across the living room floor. It was starting to get dark, and I wasn't sure when Grandpa would be back. It was unusual that he wasn't home before dark. I decided to walk home and take my chances there.

I was relieved not to see the Devil's faded green pickup. Jill wouldn't be in until late due to the ball game. My dog greeted me as I walked up. I was starving, so I went straight for the icebox. There was some leftover fried round steak and some fried squash. I fixed myself a plate and headed to the bedroom so I'd have a good exit window if the Devil returned.

I flipped on the light switch and immediately dropped my plate. Folgers was sitting in the dark on the dusty floor in the corner of my room.

"Don't run. I just want to talk," Folgers said, raising the palm of his hand toward me as he spoke.

I was sure my heart reverberated throughout our old wooden house.

"Now, now, take a deep breath." He used my dresser to help him stand. He looked menacing in his too-tight overalls and a white T-shirt that barely covered his bulging biceps. He was wearing an orange Mack Trucks ball cap with oily stains. A broom straw was dangling from his lips where he chewed on it when he spoke.

"Go ahead, pick up your dinner, and have a seat here." He patted the side of my squeaky bed.

I did as he told me. I couldn't have spoken even if I'd had something to say. I looked out the window and wondered if I was quick enough to move past him and escape before he could get those meat-hook hands on me.

"Jenkins, you seem like a tough little character and one that can keep his mouth shut. So let's take a calculated risk here and see if you can indeed keep your mouth shut on a few things."

I didn't say anything. Folgers pulled up an old sewing machine stool that I kept in my room to hide my whiskey gatherings.

"Looky here, yes, Charles was a molester, and I am sure he's in hell by now, but he served other purposes. He was so nasty that people just left him alone, which was good for my people, the people I work for. You see, I'm a broker of some unsavory services. It's a good business, and I don't have to bust too many heads. Are you following me?"

I heard him, but I wasn't sure I understood.

"Okay then. Let's continue," Folgers said.

Was he reading me, or was he just laying some kind of old-school, country gang shit on me? I looked at him as he went on.

"There's a lot of coin in pornography, and the younger they are, the more coin. Charles not only creates this porn; he distributes it to my clients. These same so-called clients, well, they like dog food too. I'm talking high-quality dog food here. Them rich folk around the county seat like some porn and good high-grade dog food. Them lawyers and business folks."

It came out before I could think. "Dog food? What the hell?"

Folgers let out a deep, dark chuckling sound. "You know, *dog food*, heroin—the excellent stuff. We could always trust old Charles. He was such a damn pervert if he didn't play ball with us we could just set him up and turn his ass in. Of course nobody would give a flying fuck if he turned up dead either. Guess that's what happened, which is why you and I are having this little powwow. So tell me: Did you kill Charles? I bet he tried something with you, and I know you're capable."

"No," I responded. "I couldn't kill anybody." I now had my heart slowing down and was beginning to believe that my fate was coming. Folgers was going to kill me.

"Okay then, let me lay it out for you more precisely. Charles was the holder, the keeper if you will, of all of our money. Oh, yes, he also had our dog food supply and some new porn film, the complete stash. It's about the money. It's always about the money."

"Why would you trust your stuff to that old, depraved mother-fucker?" I asked.

"Jenkins, I'm not sure where life will take you, but I guess not very far if you don't wise up."

"Who's this 'our' you keep referring to?" I asked, gaining more nerve. I couldn't believe I was having this conversation with Folgers, and clearly it didn't sit too well with him.

"You think I'm stupid or something? Here's the deal. I don't give a flying fuck whether you killed Charles or not. But you'll eventually tell me. You ever stopped and exercised that pea brain of yours to think why Charles was never busted? Whoever killed him did the world a favor, but not me."

"Why you so sure he's dead?" I interrupted. "Maybe he took your money and ran off."

Folgers grabbed my throat with one hand and lifted me off the floor. "I'm through here. I thought you might have some sense, but you crazy and dumb, just like your old man. You got two days to think about our visit. I'll be back, and you better have some answers." He dropped me and I fell to the floor, coughing.

As he stomped out of the house I wanted to yell, *You don't know who you are fucking with.* But only I knew that if I took credit for Jaxs and Sonny, I'd be involved in killing four people.

CHAPTER SEVENTEEN

IT THICKENS

THE DEVIL DID NOT SHOW HIMSELF THAT NIGHT. I DIDN'T EVEN get out of bed when Jill came home. I debated whether I should tell her about all this mess. We needed to get back to our actual mission of ridding the world of the Devil. I wasn't even sure Jill and I were on the same sheet of music anymore. Fortunately, it was a Saturday, and I would hopefully have plenty of time to think things out. Should I try to find Randy?

The morning dew glistened off the grass as sun rays struck. There was no way to hide your trail, for each step left an imprint waiting to be followed, at least until the dew escaped back into the sky. I sat on the creek bank, throwing rocks at the bass in the water.

I was beginning to understand that everything in nature had a purpose, and somehow it all appeared to be synchronized. Hell, even Folgers and Charles had a reason for existing. Grandpa would say to live and let live. Maybe I was just a part of nature that had no purpose.

I had a headache, one of those I'd get when I refused to cry. Sitting there, I couldn't remember the last time I did cry. Maybe it was the last time my grandpa had switched me. I couldn't have been more than seven years old. I'd been practicing with my slingshot and using his game roosters as targets. Two roosters were circling each other as they do before fighting. Grandpa must have forgotten to take the fighting spurs off of one from the last time he fought him. That was the one I targeted. I'd never hit anything I ever aimed at before, but on that day, I smashed his prizefighting rooster in the head and killed it instantly. Grandpa singled out a willow tree and told me to go and cut a switch. I did as I was told. He said it was the wrong switch: It was either too short, too long, or didn't bend enough. I finally cut one that he would accept. He spanked me hard, and I cried. He said, "Son, why you crying? Crying is for when you're sick or hungry, and you are neither, so shut up and take it like a man." Then he said, "Thanks for trimming my tree."

Carl Gordon's dad had died when we were in the fourth grade. He was a friend who was not a thug and not embarrassed to hang with me in front of all the undesirables. When his father died Carl took at least a month off from school. When he returned, he'd break into a cry for no reason. He'd say how much he missed his father when asked why. I never understood that. Why would anyone cry a month after? Why would anyone cry like that when their dad died?

Sitting on the creek bank, I doubted my anger. Was it only acting? Was I an emotional vampire, sucking other people's feelings out but giving none?

"The Devil did it. The Devil did it!" I said out loud. I could just tell Folgers the Devil had done it. That could solve everything.

"Let's finish what we started." That was what Jill kept repeating to me. I decided to share my predicament with Folgers and Charles. Carefully, I explained what went down with Charles and emphasized numerous times that it was Randy who'd pulled the trigger. But this made no difference to Jill. She was angry that I'd been involved at all. I pushed back and put some fault back on her.

"Finish what we started? That's all you got to say? We could have killed the Devil if you hadn't decided to be some type of social butterfly hanging out with all the goody-two-shoes in town."

"Jenkins, goddamn it, you need to grow up," she said. "We aren't kids anymore. Get a life and quit being so moronic!"

"Well if I'm so damn moronic, you probably don't want to hear my plan."

"What are you talking about? What is it? Don't try to bait me," Jill shot back.

"I tell Folgers that the Devil did Charles in. It's simple. He goes after the Devil; they get into it, and Folgers kills him."

Jill rolled her eyes and smiled. "That's the plan? Really? You can't just go and say the Devil did it. Folgers will want to know how you know and why you haven't told anyone yet. I don't think it will work." Jill quit smiling and placed her hands on her hips.

I crossed my arms and said, "You just don't want to do it. You're just thinking about getting out of this hellhole before me. I'll be here on my own, and you won't care!"

"What difference does it make? You don't need me. Do whatever you're going to do."

"I do need you, or at least I might. As a backup. You might have to tell Folgers you saw it too if he asks."

"Well," she said, "just be careful not to get carried away. If I have to back you up, you're going to owe me for the rest of your life."

With Jill's lukewarm consent, I could now proceed with a plan to engage Folgers. I needed to find Randy and talk to him. If he ever talked and told a different story, my ass would be grass. Randy would probably stick with saying he knew nothing, but I couldn't take a chance that Folgers would trace a link to Randy and crack him.

The plan was to walk the backroads into town and dodge being seen by what few passing cars I encountered. This entailed diving into the bar ditch several times before I got to town.

From across the street from Old Duck's place, peeking out from a stack of shingles at the lumberyard, I could see Folgers in his usual place, always watching out for his boss. There was never much traffic in town during the week, but I waited until I saw none before crossing the street. Just as I got to the other side, Old Duck came out of the garage.

"Jenkins, you little peckerwood, why ain't your dumb ass in school?" Old Duck laughed hard enough to make his stomach shake. Guess he thought his greeting was funny. "Heard from Randy?" I asked.

"That dickhead down there getting him some Texas pussy, 'cause we haven't heard a word from him since he left."

Folgers wasn't fooling me. I could see him leaning forward from that old straw bottom chair he was sitting on. He was trying to eavesdrop. I looked back at Old Duck, who was scratching his crotch. As he satisfied his itch, I could see the outline of his snub nose .38 in the front pocket of his overalls. Randy had said he always carried it there, and someday he would shoot his dick off accidentally.

"Here, let me introduce you to my new Cajun auto mechanic. We call him Gumbo, but you should address him as Mr. Hayley." Another stupid laugh bellowed out of Old Duck, who apparently thought he was a comedian. Gumbo didn't look like a mechanic. He was well groomed, wearing too-tight welder's coveralls. There was no hair out of place on his heavily oiled comb-backed tight curly hair. His biceps were huge, too disproportionately big for the rest of his body. He extended his hand to welcome me. I shook it and noticed how smooth it was, and I saw no grease or oil under his manicured fingernails.

"Gumbo here brings us those hurricane-flooded cars from Louisiana, and we refurbish, then sell them. Got a nice little '67 Mustang

Fastback for you we working on. We grind a little rust off, new paint job . . . make you a great deal on it, Jenkins. I'll tell your old man to buy it for you."

He knew I didn't have any money and wasn't old enough to drive legally. He was teasing me, and that part about my old man buying me anything was cruel. "I saw you here and thought I'd ask about Randy. Not interested in a car. Thanks anyway."

Old Duck and Gumbo opened the garage door, and I could see the Mustang all taped up, ready for a new paint job. Once they went inside, Folgers motioned for me to come hither. I took a deep breath and secured my bravery, then moved forward.

"I knew you were smarter than you looked. Smart move on your part to not wait for me to come find your lazy ass."

"Here?" I asked.

"Sure, why not? There's no echoes outdoors. Do you want to be inside somewhere alone with me again? I take that back what I said about you being smarter. Here's a lesson for you. Never lay heavy shit on someone without exits. I'm not talking about just one exit; you need several. Outside visits are always the best. Never get caught in a bucket."

"A bucket?" I quietly asked.

"In the old days, bars had only one entrance and exit, and it was the same door. That's a bucket, only one way to pour in and pour out. Don't ever get trapped, boy. That's your lesson for today, so pay me with what you know."

I presented my most timid, humble guise. I described how I witnessed the Devil and Charles sharing a bottle of whiskey in our driveway. "There was an argument," I said, "and my old man hit him and they drove off toward the east." It was hard for me to refer to the Devil as my old man, and I knew it came out awkwardly.

Folgers just stared at me with a neutral expression. After what seemed like an eternity, he asked, "Is that it?"

I nodded to signal the affirmative. His sigh was louder than his last question. The expression morphed to disgust as I was sure he was contemplating my honesty. Finally, he spoke again. "I'm not saying that I believe you, but let's pretend for a moment that I do. Money, have you seen any money lying around?"

I shook my head no. I was convinced that my performance was adequate and satisfied him that the story was true. I wanted him to think that now that I had told the truth, I was afraid that I'd suffer consequences from the Devil if he discovered what I'd done.

"They must have been in on the steal together," Folgers mused. "Never did figure him for a customer though. Where would your old man have hidden the money? Come on now, think."

"I never had any idea of what he does with his money."

"I need that money bad. So let's say you go find it, understand?"

"I wouldn't know where to start."

"You stalling for some kind of finder's fee?" Folgers asked in a tone of increasing anger.

"Sure, I can look around," I nervously responded.

"Well, you better do better than that! Your life depends on it. Hell, my life depends on it," he added, with the first hint of panic.

"How much am I trying to find?"

"Enough to get half of this town pushing up daisies," he replied with an anxious but evil voice. "Two days! You got two damn days. If I don't see you by then, me and you are going to have a come to Jesus meeting with your old man. Comprende?"

How many were tied to Charles and this money? I wondered. These and other thoughts of what to do next dashed through my mind. As I walked away, I only looked back once toward Folgers. I was surprised to see Gumbo go toe to toe and punch his finger in Folgers's chest. He then pointed his index finger at me and made a gun trigger motion. I quickened my pace.

I laid out the entire exchange to Jill. She wasn't happy, for it hadn't gone as she'd hoped. "Why didn't you straight-out tell him you saw the Devil do Charles in? He would have gone directly to him, and we'd be out of this mess. Now what are you going to do?"

"Maybe we don't need to wait on Folgers and go ahead and make our move," I responded in frustration. "Why don't you come up with a plan then? Apparently I just fuck things up." Jill stormed off in one direction, and I stomped away in another.

Three days later, I still hadn't heard from Folgers and the Devil had not been home. Jill went about her business like she didn't know anything about what we were waiting on. She'd taken her coping mechanisms for surviving our environment to a new level: Her strategy seemed to be to ignore it and take it one day at a time.

Mom asked me to stop by the pool hall and get some money from Grandpa, so I walked that way during school lunch break. Because we hadn't seen the Devil in a while, I assumed he had taken Mom's money and we were broke again. It was an excellent excuse to take the longer route past Salem's place and maybe get needed updates.

"Word is that Old Duck fired Folgers. Now, do you believe that?" Salem Lowe stood at his storefront door, unwrapping a package of Wrigley's gum and telling those who passed by to have a good day. "If you're headed to the pool hall, I would take a detour home if I were you."

"Say what?" I gave a soprano response while slowing down but continued walking.

"The biggest secret in these parts is that no one knows that the big one is a cluster of small mysteries," Salem softly offered while switching his straw to the left side of his mouth.

I stopped and turned toward him. "What are you talking about?"

"*War and Peace.* 'We can know only that we know nothing. And that is the highest degree of human wisdom.' You should read it, Jenkins."

"Why do you always speak in riddles?" I asked.

"Interesting that this small town has so many characters who pass through; then sometimes, poof, they're gone. Disappeared in thin air." Salem arched his hands skyward as he expelled the continuation of today's riddle.

I shrugged and bit my bottom lip. "Why shouldn't I go to the pool hall?" I asked.

"I think you know Mr. Gumbo. Fascinating that he arrives in town, and Folgers is fired. Now, no one can ask Folgers about that. It's hard to ask when no one can find him. Folgers is one of them there 'poof' characters. He just stayed longer than most. Let's see: Charles disappears; Folgers seems to be the only one that cares to be looking for Charles. Folgers vanishes after Gumbo comes to town. It's all a mystery, isn't it, Jenkins? Gumbo likes to play pool."

That riddle was enough for me. I wasn't going to see Grandpa now, and Mom could wait on the money. We never had any money anyhow. I gave Salem a thumbs-up to acknowledge what he had said, and that I understood the riddle.

"Sheriff Brown, now he isn't looking to find anyone. That's your disadvantage, Jenkins. Oh, yes, another mystery here that I haven't quite figured out. Where you at in the bigger mystery?" Salem's departing words were presented with an air of genuine concern.

Back home, Jill said, "Maybe Folgers did kill the Devil. It's been seven days now, and we haven't seen him."

After the talk with Salem I stayed after school, walked by Old Duck's and Salem's place, and frequented the pool hall. Of course, I never went up the stairs without ensuring Gumbo was not there. Leon knew something was up when I asked him if Gumbo had been in the pool hall. I was always nervous to talk to Leon, afraid he would force me into another suicidal car ride.

I shouldn't have been astonished that no one was speaking about Folgers. People had always kept their distance from him. I was going crazy, waiting on any information to help me determine what to do. Jill and I hadn't spoken about planning to kill the Devil in a while. Now we were sidetracked from our true mission. I hoped that Jill was right and that maybe Folgers had killed the Devil and then split. *That would mean the Devil did have the money and was involved with Charles*, I thought.

CHAPTER EIGHTEEN

GRIM REAPER

THE AMBULANCE PASSED US AT THE INTERSECTION WHERE WE turned for the final mile to our house. Mom had taken Jill and me to the county seat to pick up a Sears order because they did not deliver as far out as we lived. Jill and I turned our heads and watched the ambulance slowly drive toward town. One single gumball light on top. Mom said that since it didn't seem to be in a big hurry, it was probably a false alarm.

We pulled into our driveway, and I yelled out, "Oh shit." There was the Devil's truck. He was back. Grandpa's truck was also there. At least with Grandpa around, the Devil might not be in one of his demonic states. If he had been, Grandpa would have left. I felt a little less stressed for the first time since Folgers gave me my last notice. I'd been so busy snooping around, among other things, that I had neglected my visits with Grandpa.

There were no lights on, and the television was off. Ever since we'd gotten a TV, Grandpa would come over on most Saturday mornings and watch John Wayne and other assorted Western movies, many of which were silent. But Grandpa wasn't there, only the Devil, sitting in a dark corner of the kitchen. Then I saw what appeared to be puke and piss on the living room floor. Mom shooed us out of the house.

Jill and I waited on the front steps. Neither of us said a word. We knew something awful had happened. Our survival instincts would not allow our minds to conclude the worst-case scenario. We didn't talk. I focused on three red ants pulling a dead dragonfly across the sidewalk. I was about to storm inside and demand to know what was going on when our mom came back out.

"Grandpa is gone. His heart gave out. He was watching TV," she stuttered out in fragmented sentences. She didn't have to say anything else. From her swollen eyes and runny nose, I could tell that the worst scenario was now a reality.

"Heart giving out, what the hell does that mean?" I yelled back, surprising myself. It was as if I had no control over what I was saying. I ran into the house and demanded that the Devil tell me where Grandpa was. I lost control. "You killed him, you motherfucker, you killed him," I screamed. The Devil stared at the floor. I punched him in the head. He didn't move.

I ran through the 40 acres of cotton toward the creek. I needed to be alone. *Heart attack. How could that be? Mom said Grandpa was watching TV and just fell over dead, and there was nothing that could have been done. What the hell does that mean?* I was trying to figure it out.

Grandpa had never been sick a day in his life. He had no teeth, so he never went to a dentist. Hauling cows to the auction two weeks ago was the last time I'd seen him, and he was perfectly healthy then. We'd scraped the dry cow diarrhea off his pickup truck's back fenders so no one would think he was hauling a sick cow. Now he was dead from a heart attack?

Possums were noisily digging through leaves and clawing at tree trunks. They came out to search for food when darkness arrived. Along with other nocturnal animals, they delivered an exacting type of musical curtain call, applauding the falling of night. This was my cue to move toward home.

Mom must have gone to work, and Jill probably was spending the night with a friend. No one was home when I went back. Fortunately, the Devil was also gone. I might have just gone ahead and killed him without any pretense of an accident or cover-up in my state of mind. Sleep was elusive. My dog, Attila, as always, could sense the mood I was in. He lay across my chest and nuzzled his cold nose to my neck. Watching a methodically crawling daddy longlegs cross the ceiling kept me distracted until I remembered Grandpa's advice about them. He would say, "Boy, don't kill them; they're your best friend to have around." He told me how they ate insects we didn't want around.

Grandpa had never attended church, but I could sense he was conscious of the higher supremacy revealed in nature. He taught me a lot about Mother Nature in an unconventional way. Like the times he would come by the house and challenge me to find a terrapin, and offer five dollars for each one. Terrapins were plentiful, but I could never find one. Eventually he told me that terrapins went to bed after five in the evening. I tried to outsmart him by capturing as many terrapins as possible and keeping them in a box until his next challenge. Of course, he anticipated that.

The sun was rising. I usually crawled over the old covered wagon shell with wooden wheels next to the barbed-wire fence at Grandpa's house, preferring to jump off the wagon over the barrier instead of climbing through the wire. But now the wagon was gone. The four-person crosscut saw, the mule yokes, and all the stacked antiques around the house were missing. These were items that his parents, my great-grandparents, had used to sharecrop their way across the south. I ran to the house to see what else was missing.

Burglars, I thought, *someone had robbed his place. Word must be out that he's dead.* I hustled inside to find the house in disarray. Drawers were opened, and a mattress hung halfway off his bed. The shotgun was not in its sentinel corner, the same one he had almost used to shoot his son. Then it hit me like running into a brick wall: My savior, our protector, Grandpa, was gone forever.

Knowing Grandpa was dead made the house feel so much smaller—the living room where I used to play appeared no larger than a sandbox. The dingy, old faded white radio that we used to listen to *Dragnet* and *Sam Spade* episodes seemed miniature. The once sizable black battery acid stain that had streamed down the old round-top oak table that the radio sat on now presented as a trickle. At least whoever plundered the place didn't take the unopened half-gallon milk carton from the icebox. I sat on the side of his bed and drank most of it. Sitting there, I noticed the glass doorknobs were missing. I never thought they could be valuable, but apparently somebody did.

Cows were bellowing, hungry, waiting for Grandpa to feed them. They surrounded the barn where they knew he would throw hay from the loft opening. The chickens and fighting roosters waited impatiently at the house's back door for feed. When Grandpa drew his last breath, the world changed instantly for all of us. I fed the chickens and then moved to the barn to satisfy the hungry cattle. The hay bales stored there to make it through the winter were also missing.

Then I remembered Grandpa's World War I stuff. There was the old helmet and canteen I used for play. I found them in the ghost room's trim, somewhat hidden closet. I saw something lying on the top shelf above the clothes rack as I removed them. It was a bayonet. I guess it had been up there all these years, and I could see why he hadn't shown it to me when I was younger. It was over a foot long with a razor-sharp point. It was mine now. I needed something, a memento, before all was pilfered.

Grandpa's old friends came by our house to offer condolences the next day. Most were older men who had survived World War I, the flu pandemic, the Great Depression, and the hardships of living from one crop season to another. Some, like my grandpa, grew up in a sharecropper family and were able to emerge as landowners. None had ever had an eight-to-five job or worked for a steady paycheck. The Devil showed up in new clothes and an expensive felt Stetson hat. He also wore a new pair of alligator skin cowboy boots. He presented a smile and happy demeanor, but I could see the malevolence behind it all. *Why hadn't I figured this out earlier?* The Devil had robbed Grandpa's entire estate.

Since Grandpa had outlived all his other relatives, the funeral was held two days after his death. I was in utter despair. Jill and I sat on the church's second row behind Mom and the Devil. The casket remained open for the entire funeral. Pastor Wayne presided over the service, and I wondered what he was going to say. Grandpa had never attended church and couldn't read. It didn't matter, for I only heard a few words he preached that day. I cued in on the preacher only once when he mentioned Ecclesiastes. I guess that passage was the old standby for folks like Grandpa. Was it the vanity of human life he was using it for? If so, then was he wrong to use it? Grandpa exemplified a vanity-free life. My focus turned back to the Devil and how quickly he'd robbed from the dead.

I never understood why pastors felt the need to do a call to come down front to be saved at a funeral. Was it ego, or a sincere belief this was an excellent time to make the family wait even longer to bury their loved one? Maybe it was because people are weak, and their defenses are down during grief. Perhaps an evangelical preacher's success is determined by his savings and baptisms. Whatever the case, Pastor Wayne was all in with a blistering call to be saved.

The only interlude that interrupted my thoughts of hating the Devil was when Red, the beer joint operator and owner, broke from the viewing procession and flung herself into the casket to hug and kiss Grandpa's body. Red and Grandpa had been good friends for as long as I could remember. I felt a kinship with her. When she hugged my grandpa I wondered just how close they might have been. It visibly upset Mom. As for the Devil, he looked penetratingly pissed. I got bundles of satisfaction from that. Maybe Red truly loved Grandpa, and I was the only one who accepted and respected that love.

After the funeral, the pillaging continued. A semi truck drove up to Grandpa's barn and started loading his cattle the next day. The Devil must have sold them. When the truck arrived I was in the barn loft, avoiding people and trying to get my head together. By the time I decided to show myself, my Santa Gertrudis cow was already packed in the back of the trailer. That was mine. I must have been around nine years old when I saw that young cow. I had never seen a Santa Gertrudis before, and Grandpa had never bought one. He saw I was enamored with it, so he said it was mine. It was the most beautiful animal I had ever seen. I named her Suzy. I don't think he ever dreamed I'd build a small pen and herd that calf into it. I remembered that amazed yet bewildered look on Grandpa's face when he discovered what I had done. It was the same look when he found I had cut down a row of bodark trees and made bows and arrows out of them, impressed but not happy. By the time he found that Suzy was in my rickety pen, she was already tamed and eating out of my hand.

I went up to the truck driver and instructed him that the only non-Hereford in his trailer was mine, and he needed to let it out. "Fuck off, kid," he said. "I paid for that one like all the rest." He turned around as the noise of his front tire deflating startled him. I looked him in the eye and stabbed a second tire with my newfound World War I bayonet. It turned into a standoff.

Lucky for me and the truck driver, Pop Chevy pulled up. I wasn't backing down until I got my cow. Pop grabbed me from behind, picked me up, and carried me over to his pickup. I was shocked that this old codger was so strong. His grip on me felt like a steel vise.

"Now settle down there, you young whippersnapper. This is how these things here go now. You can't go around puncturing tires and shit like that. They'll lock you up," Pop Chevy said calmly, to defuse the situation.

I continued to try to wiggle from his tightening grip, but I soon felt drained of strength and emotions. Pop must have detected this as he turned me loose. He then walked to the truck driver, and they started talking. I could not make out what was being said, but I could see Pop hand some money over to him. Then he reached in his pocket and gave him more bills. Pop walked back toward me while using his thumb to dislodge and then throw a huge wad of tobacco out of his jaw.

"Look here now. You stay away from that man. He has legally bought them there cattle, and you can't do nothin' about that," Pop said with his country wisdom.

He placed his foot on the bottom row of barbed wire that separated the pasture from Grandpa's yard and, with one hand, rolled a cigarette. "You use these for anything?" he asked while handing me an empty can of tobacco.

"Not anymore, Pop. I used to keep marbles in them."

"I paid that man for the damage you put upon him. He was going to have you arrested, saying you assaulted him or something like that. He's not from around here, or he'd know that stabbing a tire is not an assault. He thinks you're crazy, boy." He smiled and blew a smoke ring.

"I bought your grandpa's lawn mower from your dad. I came by to get it, and you lucky I did 'cause that old boy was fixing to lay some whoop-ass on you," Pop continued.

I walked back through the woods, found a good spot to sit, and cried my eyes out. That would be the last time I ever cried. I thought, *When I die, I want a good death like Grandpa. He didn't see it coming.* I never knew him to be sick. He worked his farm and cattle until he died, with no suffering and no prolonged hospital stay. No nursing home.

I don't recall Jill and I ever discussing Grandpa's death or precisely how his death would change our lives. In this case, we were very similar; we moved on and put the tragedy behind us. Sure, we grew up and dealt with things differently, but the Devil was still here, and Grandpa was not. The balance of good and evil had tilted in favor of evil.

CHAPTER NINETEEN

CHIT-CHAT

THE TELEPHONE PARTY LINE WAS ABLAZE WITH THE NEWS. JILL and I took turns listening in, placing a washrag over the mouthpiece to be stealthier. Anyone using the party line always assumed they would have eavesdroppers and chose their words accordingly. Gumbo and Leon Spottedhorse had gotten into a fight over a snooker game at the pool hall. The word was that Gumbo pulled a switchblade and sliced Leon's guts open. Leon was hospitalized in critical condition, and Gumbo was on the run. Officer Easley had wrecked his police car giving pursuit. Easley was sent to the hospital but released after resetting his broken nose.

"Jenkins, is that you?" someone asked on the party line. In my eagerness or impatience with listening to this breaking news and related gossip, I had spontaneously jumped in on the call and asked if anyone else had been hurt.

"Get off the damn line!" someone else yelled. I stayed silent. They knew it was me, so why bother saying anything?

"Knives, well back in my day, it was all about the knuckles. Hit them hard and fast. These kiddos nowadays got to pull knives and shit. If I were younger, I'd kick this Gumbo's ass," Beatrice spouted out in her scratchy prehistoric voice. No one would ever mistake her voice for anyone else. She lived on the phone and listened to calls all day long. We all knew that her bedtime was six p.m. because she never interrupted calls after that hour.

The party line stayed hot for hours, folks embellishing the day's events. It probably would have gone into the night, but old man Abernathy chimed in with, "You son-of-a-bitches, I need to make a call, and if you don't get off this phone, I'm going to cut the damn lines." Everybody was aware that he meant business: Once Beatrice had called his bluff, and old Abernathy not only cut the phone line to her house but also knocked the telephone pole down that serviced the whole mile section. Her neighbors visited her and implored her never to challenge Abernathy again. It must have worked, for we could hear over a dozen hang-ups.

Was my name going to enter the party-line gossip? I'd been in a haze for the last two weeks since Grandpa died. *Javier would know things*, I thought. I had intentionally stayed away from him, but I figured we were still on good terms. I even ran my potential visit with him by Jill. She told me to be careful, reminding me about Javier's heavy drug usage. He'd already dropped out of school and was trying to earn a living playing guitar.

But Javier wasn't the older man he wanted to be, alone in his bedroom in his parents' house practicing a Led Zeppelin tune. He'd progressed from the more uncomplicated three-chord bands he turned me on to, such as The Troggs and Them, to Zeppelin and Hendrix. His family was poor, so I assumed he must have been selling drugs to buy enough albums to have more inventory than the music store at the county seat. He also had two new stackable Marshall amps.

The day I went to see him he was dressed like the lead singer of the one-hit wonders The Strawberry Alarm Clock. He wore an oversized Nehru jacket, colossal bell-bottoms, and enough medallion necklaces to weigh down his neck in a perpetual tilt. He sat on the side of his bed and played bits of every song on the top 40 radio while we talked. Scented candles were burning, and incense sticks were smoldering in three ashtrays. His chain-smoking had gotten worse.

"Man, it's been a long time, Jenkins. You been playing any guitar?" he asked while offering his cherry-red wide-bodied Gibson Les Paul. I only knew a few chords, and wasn't about to embarrass myself.

"Yeah, it's been a while," he said. "How you doing? Man, you got that 'Good Times Bad Times' Zeppelin tune down." I was uncomfortable. After more small talk, I asked what he knew about Leon's stabbing.

He pulled out a cigarette, lit it with the one he was preparing to snuff out, then grinned and said, "Let's take a walk." We walked out of his backyard, snaking our way around an assortment of junk tractors, rusted pipes, piles of brace fittings, and an array of old cars. His father never threw anything away and as an oil field worker, he had access to discarded materials of the trade. We pushed our way through head-tall grass, cockleburs, and assorted bushes. Javier had to take a smoke break on a dam of an old abandoned slush pit. The oil companies just left them full and open when they moved on. This one had two dead whooping cranes stuck in it. Cranes often landed on the oil slush, not knowing it wasn't water.

I hadn't realized that Javier's extended family of uncles, aunts, and cousins owned so much land, though it was worthless for farming or ranching with all the canyons, alkaline soil, and heavy forest. We scooted down a ravine bank, getting sticker burrs in our butts. "So, what do you think?" asked Javier while waving his hand across the horizon.

With the backdrop of deep red dirt and clay on the opposite ravine side, green plants almost ten feet tall rose from the bottom. "Easy as shit; throw out a few seeds and, look, magic," Javier proudly proclaimed. "The best weed in the county, Jenkins, if I don't say so myself. I'm fucking Jack and the Beanstalk."

I hadn't seen a marijuana plant before, and now there appeared to be thousands in front of me. I looked in all directions, then responded, "Guess this place would be surely hard to find."

"Bet your sweet ass it is," Javier smugly announced.

"So about Leon. Now that was a bad thing. My uncle was right there when it went down. Most people think they were fighting over whether one of Leon's shots was legal. Gumbo accused him of not keeping both feet on the floor. Everybody knows that old rule. And Leon can bend over and take any shot he wants and not take his feet off the floor. That was just an excuse for Gumbo to start something. Leon had already pissed him off by asking him too many questions about Folgers. Leon knew what he was doing by pushing Gumbo's buttons. He didn't care 'cause he ain't afraid of nothin'. Here, let's do a little work while we talk."

Javier showed me how to pick buds without damaging the plant. He pulled some plastic baggies out of his pocket, used his fingers to measure about three inches around, and stated that was about a lid. "I mix my lids a little bigger to beat the competition down," he explained. He then added some leaves. "We can't give them all good buds, now can we?"

I realized I'd just had a quick entrepreneurial lesson in the basics of the backcountry weed business. It was difficult at best to keep Javier focused. "So back to Leon, Folgers," I said. "What about all that caused this fight?"

"It was crazy, man. They say when Leon got cut across his stomach, he just looked surprised and yelled, 'What the fuck.' Even cut like that, they say Leon went on fighting him some more."

I persisted. "Javier, what about what led up to all this? You know, Folgers and that stuff."

"Oh, yeah, that gets confusing. My uncle didn't hear all of it. He say Gumbo asked about you and how you knew old Charles. Leon said something about you selling whiskey to Charles. Then Gumbo say something; then Leon says something; then Gumbo gets louder; Leon gets pissed and yells at him to leave you alone. Leon asked where Folgers was. Then all hell breaks loose. Man, wish I was there. Had to be one hell of a fight."

Javier went back to telling me about his pot business. He suggested that since he had to go to the county seat for deliveries, I should go with him. We could drop by the hospital and check on Leon. I agreed and soon found myself on the back of his Honda 90 motorcycle, blazing down the road. It was my job to hold the duffel bag full of premeasured pot. I almost fell off trying not to drop our precious cargo.

Deliveries of the freshly harvested pot were made to an assortment of unsavory individuals. One lady who must have been in her 30s offered both of us sex in exchange for her payment. Javier explained that he dated her 15-year-old daughter, then met the mother and dated her. Then there was the man in his early 20s who lived like a hermit in a room at a flea-bag old long-term motel. I could see a large chalkboard with chemistry symbols and mathematical equations spattered all over it. The guy was tiny, with a head of hair that would keep him from passing through most doorways.

We could hear Leon complaining as we walked toward his hospital room. He was demanding a cigarette. We had just left the waiting room where everyone was allowed to smoke, so I didn't get it that Leon wasn't allowed a smoke too. The last time I went to the doctor, he'd dropped cigarette ashes on me from the stogie locked to the corner of his mouth. "About damn time I got some visitors," Leon coughed out when we came in, while trying to get up from the bed.

Javier stuck two joints under Leon's pillow. It was my first time in a hospital room, and I was distracted by all the medical apparatuses connected to Leon. There were two tubes on either side of his exposed stomach. He pulled back a bandage to reveal the numerous metal clamps that meandered from his lower chest across the belly and ended on his left hip. The new scars crisscrossed over old ones.

"I think this new scar will match up well with all the others. What do you guys think?" He then pointed to various scars and proudly identified the year and specific car wrecks that had created them.

Javier and I glanced at each other and then back at Leon. In unison, we responded, "Looks great, man."

"What are people saying? They saying I got beat down or shit like that? 'Cause that didn't happen. I had the motherfucker until he swings that switchblade out. Should've known that Cajun motherfucker would pull some kind of shit like that. I'll fuck him up when I get out of here." Leon coughed his words out.

I handed Leon water from his serving tray. "Food really sucks in here. Javier, go get me a burger and fries from that Hamburger Haven joint around the block. Best burgers in the county."

"No problem, man," said Javier.

After he left, Leon motioned for me to sit beside his bed. "Look, Jenkins, this Gumbo is not someone you want to mess around with. I don't think Folgers would just walk away from a nest on the ground like he got with Old Duck. All he had to do was hang out, collect a few debts, and keep somebody from kicking the shit out of the Duck. I'm not saying Gumbo snuffed Folgers out, but something sure ain't right around there. The fucker asked if I had seen you, and I said, 'You seen Folgers?' Crazy fucker then starts acting all Neanderthal on my ass. I think that boy don't like you." Leon chuckled.

I felt a closeness to Leon, but I was still going to stick to my main rule of never talking about what I'd done. Then Javier returned with Leon's food, and Leon ate it like he was starving to death. Fried onions, mustard, and grease splattered his sheets.

"I'll look you kiddos up when I get out of here," he said. "Now scram." He coughed and motioned us toward the door, grinning and flaring his nostrils.

I had Javier drop me off back in town. Salem called out to me when I passed by his store. "People keep disappearing in these parts," he said. I was intentionally walking toward the Cattle Creek Grill from the opposite direction. The grill was right next door. Jill had started working there a week before, for a few hours after school and on Saturdays. I figured I could hang out and catch a ride home with Jill and a boy she liked, who worked there too and had given her rides home before. I waved at Salem and he motioned me over.

"You have a guardian angel, my friend," he said. "It would appear your buddy Gumbo is on the lam, absconded if you will. Unlike other missing persons, the law took an interest in finding him because it's difficult to ignore the stabbing of Leon. But alas, he won't be found."

"What do you mean, 'he won't be found'?" I asked.

But Salem was speaking in riddles again. "It's simply stated as I said it. He won't be found. Now, why he can't be located is and will always be a mystery. To know the future, one has to know the history. You, my young friend, need to contemplate what your future holds if you don't change your life's trajectory."

As I rode home with Jill and her boyfriend, I tried to make some sense of what Salem was telling me. But my mind wandered, too. Now that Jill had a job, I wanted one too, and I didn't want to do farm labor. At 14, I found my options were limited. There was an opening for a combo grocery sacker and butcher at the local grocery store. Still, transportation to and from work would be an obstacle.

No one appeared to be home when we arrived. While Jill was saying her private goodbye to her boyfriend, I lumbered into the house and smelled something burning. Smoke was drifting from the back bedroom, the Devil's den. I ran into the room. The Devil was lying flat on his back, passed out with one hand on his crotch and the other hanging off the bed with only his knuckles touching the floor. He'd fallen asleep while smoking. Fortunately, the mattress was cotton, and the burning cigarette had only caused it to smolder so far. When this happened usually Jill would sneak into his room and pour water on the cigarette to extinguish it.

The smoke got thicker, and I hoped the Devil would suffocate. "Damn it, Jenkins," Jill shouted while running past me to throw water on the mattress. The Devil didn't move. He kept snoring like a freight train. He finally scratched his crotch but didn't wake up. "Do you want to be homeless?"

"Hell, it wasn't going to burn the house down. Breathing all that smoke would hopefully kill him," I said.

Back in the living room, Jill and I argued. She could see daylight at the end of her tunnel; a little over two years and she'd graduate from high school and leave. She was spending more nights staying with friends than ever before. I challenged her lack of commitment to rid the world of the Devil. I accused her of complacency, like a prisoner who'd gotten comfortable with a routine. She denied this, and told me that while I was running around with my thug friends and getting tangled up in other nefarious actions, she'd stayed focused and now had 51 Valium.

Mom needed our help. How much longer could she endure this erratic life? Even if Jill and I could survive a few more years and then leave, how would she survive? What would happen if we weren't there? Why did she stay? By that point, we thought that foster homes would have been better than our reality. We were poor as dirt, and if it hadn't been for

Grandpa giving us a house, we probably would have been permanently homeless. With Grandpa gone, things could get much worse.

Our argument was painful. Many of our emotional scars were visible. Maybe we weren't as afraid of the Devil as we'd been when we were younger, but we both suffered from anxiety and depression. We were surviving, but at what cost? We held Mom accountable, because we felt that if she'd stopped sustaining his hedonistic lifestyle by leaving him, he surely would have died years ago. Jill pointed out that even those outside our family who had witnessed the Devil's episodes wouldn't believe the almost daily madness of our world.

We had to do something, and the Valium in the whiskey bottle trick remained the most plausible option. And the sooner the better.

In the Devil's truck, I found an empty fifth of whiskey under the seat. It wasn't enough to mix with all the Valium Jill had collected. We were taking no chances. If we tried and failed, he would kill us.

CHAPTER TWENTY

BURIED TREASURE

GUMBO WAS A BIGGER CROOK THAN I IMAGINED. WHY ELSE would the State Bureau of Investigation become involved in searching for him? If they were going to be stealthy in their investigation, they had come to the wrong town. Office Easley, now clearly the winner of Andy Griffith's Deputy Barney Fife award, told anyone who would listen that he was working hand in hand with the state investigators. It was difficult to ascertain how much was true and what was bullshit. Then the big news broke.

Human bones were found at Charles's old sweet potato farm. For some reason they were looking for Charles, or maybe something led them to believe Gumbo was hiding there. The bones were located in a shallow grave at the bottom of an old dirt root cellar. Between party-line chatter, gossip, and Easley, I was able to piece it together: The bones belonged to two children, probably from migrant workers' families. Officials suspected that maybe Gumbo killed Charles or at least knew what happened to him. Folgers was also a suspect, but he could just as likely be a victim of Gumbo too. The digging around the old sweet potato farm expanded.

Two weeks later, not too far downstream from my hooky bridge,

Folgers was discovered stuck in the mud in someone's garden. He had cement blocks tied to his arms and feet, and he was also gutted. Cattle Creek got its name from cows drowning when it would flood. The flooding had washed up poor old Folgers right into someone's backyard garden, and he had become compost. Given that locals would know how often Cattle Creek flooded, I thought that a local killer wouldn't have chosen that as a method of disposal. But Gumbo probably would not have known this.

In addition to the warrant for cutting Leon, Gumbo was now wanted as a suspect in the murder of Folgers. I was relieved that I didn't have to worry about Folgers's ultimatum to me. Then again, Gumbo was still at large. He was a wild card, whereas I'd known more about Folgers. Maybe Gumbo was back in Louisiana, hiding in a swamp. I hoped that wherever he was, he'd gotten what he wanted and wouldn't be coming around to look for me or anyone else.

It was back to normal for Jill and I; the Devil was on the rampage again. One night he threw all the dishes through the kitchen window. He kicked a hole in the television. We tried to wait him out, assuming he'd eventually pass out. But every time we thought he was asleep, we'd hear the flicking of his lighter. If he heard us, he'd get up and come after us. Once again, we found ourselves having to sneak out of the house in the middle of the night. We walked to Grandpa's house, which had been locked up since his death. Jill wanted to break in and sleep there. I refused but didn't give her the real reason: I was still scared of that ghost I had experienced. We stayed in the barn but didn't sleep.

The wind was ferocious as we cut through the creek the following day, heading home. We had our first frost a few days before, and now the wind was whipping the dead leaves from the tree limbs. Leaves twirled, danced, and twisted skyward. The weather in our parts was very unpredictable. It went from a frost to an 80-degree day, but you could smell fall in the air. We decided to wait a few hours before completing the walk home. With luck, the Devil might be gone by then. The wind died down, and the leaves spun and flickered to earth, looking for a place to decay. A particular type of peacefulness spread over me while watching the leaves finish their dance.

Jill pointed to a fresh mound of red dirt that the blowing leaves had exposed. "That looks like a grave," I said. She walked over to the mound and kicked at it. An armadillo had already claimed part of the dirt pile as a new home, and a new tunnel had been dug out.

"It's been here since the last rain," Jill commented while showing me the dirt clogs stuck to the toe of her shoe. She waited while I went back to Grandpa's barn and retrieved a shovel.

"Maybe it's buried money or some treasure," Jill said, partly joking.

"Probably Javier hiding some of his precious weed stashes," I countered.

We took turns digging. Whatever was buried there, it was buried deep. The shovel finally struck something metal, making a clinking sound. I stabbed the shovel around but didn't hit metal again. Sweat was running down my face, and I was close to deciding that whatever was buried here wasn't worth all this work.

"That's god-awful. Do you smell that?" Jill asked, holding her nose. I hadn't noticed a smell until she mentioned it. My shovel stuck into something at the bottom of the dig about that same time. I was now almost ten feet deep, and we were both concerned the sides could cave in. It was not too far from the creek bank, so the dirt was looser and easy to dig. I speared the shovel multiple times into the soft area. "Look! Look!" Jill pointed and screamed. The end of the shovel had what appeared to be blood and hair stuck to it.

"Holy shit," I softly muttered as I examined the shovel. I used exposed tree roots to help me climb out of the hole.

"Get back in there. You can't quit now," Jill argued.

"There's a damn decaying body down there. You go down there; it's your turn to do some work anyway," I countered. She surprised me by gingerly lowering herself into the hole. I warily viewed each area of dirt she brushed off to the side of the hole's bottom. "Stop," I shouted.

"What, what is it?" she yelled up to me.

"I recognize that shirt. And that belt buckle, a scorpion in amber framed with pewter, I know that buckle," I screeched. "That's Gumbo down there!" It was the belt buckle I'd hit that made that metal-on-metal sound.

Without discussing anything about what we had just discovered, Jill and I kicked, pushed, and shoveled the dirt back on top of Gumbo to cover him up again. It wasn't until we had filled his resting place in that we even looked at each other.

"You better not lie to me, Jenkins. Do you know anything about this? Is Randy back? Did you two guys do this?"

"Stop it, Jill! I don't know shit about this. I am surprised as you. I can only think of Leon." Even if Leon and I were some kind of friends, if he knew we'd found Gumbo's body, that might change things. "We'd better get out of here."

Jill and I quickly turned away from the grave, ran down the creek bank, splashed through what little water streamed through it, and didn't slow down until we reached our smokehouse. We ducked inside as soon as we saw the sheriff's car.

"What do you think they're doing here?" asked Jill while trying to catch her breath.

"Man, I don't know." I opened the door a tiny crack and saw a county sheriff's car back out of our driveway. The Devil was in the back seat.

"They've got the Devil!" I whispered to her anxiously. "They're leaving. Shit, man, maybe he killed Gumbo."

"Then they'll be back looking for the body," Jill said with certainty. For a few moments we were excited. With Gumbo dead and the Devil going to jail for it, the future was looking brighter. We wouldn't have to kill him after all. Peace and quiet and tranquility were at last in our future.

Our future lasted maybe two hours, because when Mom got home, reality trumped our fantasies. She explained that the Devil was in the county jail for a hit-and-run. He had left the scene of an accident. A witness had written down his tag number and described him to the police as a staggering drunk man. So it was back to the drawing board. After hearing what Mom had to say, I thought about everyone involved in this fiasco. Who was alive, who was dead, who knew who, and who knew what?

I no longer cared how all these fools were connected and that it all seemed to start when Randy made Charles disappear. Maybe it had started with Jaxs's death. There was a strong possibility that Leon got his payback on Gumbo.

The court decided the Devil was too sick to be held in the county jail, so he was transferred to one of the state's mental health facilities. Déjà vu all over again. Mom said it was a court order for a secure facility. She believed the Devil was truthful when he screamed at the jailers that demons were after him, and he saw Jesus in his cell. He kept yelling to see Pastor Wayne. They called the fine young pastor, but he refused to see him.

Jill and I had an intense discussion about what to do next. We agreed that it wasn't likely the Devil would be gone very long. No one had been hurt in the wreck, and he wasn't a suspect for anything else. We agreed that as soon as the Devil came home, we'd dump our whole Valium supply in his bottle and be done with it. We also decided we could never tell anyone that we'd found Gumbo.

Jill also gave me a royal chewing out and told me how lucky I was that Folgers and Gumbo were dead. She didn't care who killed who, just that my luck would run out if I didn't change my ways. She didn't have any idea what she was talking about.

I didn't know what was worse, knowing that the Devil was a free-roaming evil that would be home at any time or that he was detained and would return with a vengeance. He was gone for a month. I kept waking up multiple times per night at the slightest sound, in sweat-soaked sheets.

Leon was discharged from the hospital and immediately went back to the business of being the cool dude nobody wanted to emulate. He sincerely believed that Gumbo ran off because he was afraid of him, and he would tell that to anyone who would listen. Leon clearly wanted revenge on Gumbo, so this blew my theory that Leon had snuck out of the hospital and killed him. Either that or Leon deserved an Oscar for best actor. I wanted to tell him that someone else had already taken his revenge and that Gumbo was pushing up daisies on my grandpa's old farm. Even though Leon might be trusted, I didn't wish to bond with him over our mutual dead nemesis.

Javier kept coming around, trying to restore the type of friendship we'd had in our earlier years. Or maybe he wanted me to help with his pot business, as he kept trying to engage me to help him sell it. Apparently he had a bumper crop. I made the mistake of allowing him to convince me to try his so-called unique reserve buds. It made me dizzy, sick, and stupid for almost four hours. The one positive note from the experience was that I never wanted to put anything else in my body that caused me to lose control. It made me realize how much I needed to be in control.

"No words of wisdom today?" I asked Salem one day on my way to the pool hall.

He just smiled and then responded, "Not today, my friend. Seems you're the one with all the knowledge. Cherish that pot of gold, my friend."

"What?" I asked, turning.

"The luck of the Irish, my little leprechaun," Salem said as he tipped his hat.

I thought, *What the fuck? Is he some kind of mystic, or has he just learned how to mind-fuck people, and he plays along, not really knowing anything?* I didn't have time to engage him any further. I'd heard Randy was in town visiting Old Duck, so I was headed to the pool hall to find him. The last thing I wanted to do was go by Old Duck's place.

Randy had become a pool shark himself. I sat watching as he played Leon the best out of three snooker games, for $20. He won, which didn't sit too well with Leon. Maybe Leon was rusty from his hospital stay. He was playing without a shirt on, showing off his new scars. He wasn't as lean and mean-looking as in past years. He was starting to develop a classic beer belly, and the definition in his arms was becoming flabby—the results of a hard and fast life.

"You baby butthole buddies growing up on me." Leon smirked as he leaned over the pool table and called the five ball in the corner pocket. Randy and I shrugged. Neither one of us would allow Leon to pull us into one of his graphic and gross tit-for-tat shakedowns.

"Rack 'em, Jack," Randy called out. Jack brought his well-worn handled wooden brush and cleaned Leon's fallen cigarette ashes off the pool table felt.

"Guess you boys need a ride home, like the good old days. That old Ford Falcon is long gone. Wrecked the Nova but got me a Road Runner with a six-pack under the hood. Three deuces now that there's a six-barrel carburetor. The motherfucker can fly, fastest car I've ever had. Fuckin' orange, so need to get that black paint job. It's all about the image. Just fuckin' with you. I ain't got no image."

I waited out the pool games as Leon's rusty play improved and he won all his money back from Randy. Leon left after one more try to get us to take a ride in his new set of wheels. Randy and I switched to an eight-ball table, because I was no good at snooker.

"Old Duck didn't want me to come back for a visit. Don't want me hanging out with you. Says you're a lousy influence," Randy said, laughing while running the table.

"Well, hell, my mom has always said the same about you. You're a bad influence on me." We agreed that we were both corrupt influencers and fuck everybody else. "Randy, so what the hell is going on?" I asked him. "You leave, now you're back but leaving again. What gives, man?"

"Old Duck says it was getting too dangerous around here, and I needed to start over, so he sent me to Texas. I thought for a while he suspected I had something to do with that old creep Charles disappearing. Of course, no one knows what happened to that old monster." Randy winked and scratched on the eight ball. "Unless you say otherwise, I assume Charles is still missing."

Randy hinted that his grandpa had a criminal history as a young man but wasn't sure exactly what it was. Said he had found an old photo where Old Duck was holding a numbers board to his chest with the words "State Reformatory" painted on the wall behind him. He said that Old Duck had told him Charles had served time but never mentioned that he had too. I speculated that maybe that was how they met, in prison. Randy thought that was a possibility, then warned me to stay clear of his grandpa.

We spent the next two days catching up. He had a girlfriend, and was looking forward to getting back to her. He'd been like me, with most girls' families not wanting their daughters to associate with us. I was envious and thought I'd probably need to leave our stomping grounds to find a girlfriend too. Randy said he was going to join the Army as soon as he graduated high school. He told a recruiter he wanted to sign up when he became a senior. Now that the draft ended, joining the Army wasn't such a big deal anymore. What we did to Charles never came up again, and I didn't tell him about Gumbo.

CHAPTER TWENTY-ONE

ANSWERS

LEON'S MOTHER LEFT A MESSAGE WITH THE SCHOOL SECRE-
tary for me to call her. If you wanted to get in touch with one of us
country boys, that was what you did. Everyone had heard that Leon had
totaled out his Road Runner and was pretty banged up. If there was any,
the good news was that he'd been alone and hit a tree, so no one was
killed. I decided to drop by after school.

They lived in a small shack close to the banks of Cattle Creek. Their
house had never flooded, which led many to believe that Leon's mother was
a witch who could harness nature's powers. Leon was Bella's only child. His
father, Peter, was a disabled World War II veteran who seemed to drink an
infinite supply of Schlitz. People said that his dad wasn't right in the head.

"Jenkins, glad to see you. Guess you got my message," Bella said when
she greeted me through the rusty screen door. "Come on in." She gave me
a big hug, which was unusual. She was not the hugging type. The house
was dark, with only a small end-table lamp providing a dim light. The
once white lampshade was now a deep dingy yellow, giving the room a
hazy appearance. Peter watched a Cardinals game on TV and laughed
at Dizzy Dean's commentary. He was rolling a Prince Albert but had

difficulty holding the tobacco tin. He tried to tap tobacco out in just the right amount to fill the rolling paper evenly. His shaking hands would not allow this, so I cupped his hands in mine and assisted.

Bella said thank you, and once again explained that the shaky hands resulted from a war injury. She walked into another room and I went to find Leon.

Leon was lying on his back in his room wearing nothing but pearl-white boxer shorts, smoking, and rearranging his manhood. He had a new flat-top haircut. He never wore his hair longer than an inch.

"Jenkins, you fucker. How's the little country bumpkin doing these days?" He smiled and greeted me. My eyes were fixated on his stomach. It was swollen, vast and disproportionate in comparison to the rest of his body.

"I'm doing okay, just trying to survive so I can get out of this town someday," I responded.

"So, what do you think?" Leon rubbed his stomach and kept that wide grin. "I put a lot of work into this belly." He took a long hard draw of his smoke.

"What's up, Leon? You going to be okay?" I asked, trying to sound upbeat.

"Between a lacerated liver—I think that was wreck number three—and this last damn wreck, I'm pretty fucked up. The damn doctor says I have liver cirrhosis. Oh, yeah, I also had my spleen removed."

I had never heard of cirrhosis until then.

"Well, Jenkins, it's fucked up. I've had too much of the good life. Alcohol, my man. Too much, I guess, will give you one of these." Leon patted his belly. I heard what he said, but as I stared at all his scars, I wondered how he had been profoundly lucky so far. He was indestructible. If he had this cirrhosis, why didn't the Devil have it?

Changing the subject, I asked, "What kind of car are you going to get next?"

"A hearse, a damn good-looking black hearse," he replied while lighting a new smoke from the old one he was getting ready to snub out. I thought he was joking. His dark eyes grew narrow as he clarified, "Death Mobile, with only factory stock options."

Leon was the only person I knew who could be serious and funny in the same sentence. "What the hell, Leon? You saying you can't beat this? You the toughest man in the damn county."

He changed the subject. "You got any relatives that live way off somewhere?" I had a few, but our extended family wasn't close at all. There were never family reunions, and I only knew my cousins by name.

"No," I said. I knew he knew better, but he didn't follow up.

"Well then, you need to find some. I can't be protecting your ass around here anymore. I don't know how a poor little shithead like you can get so mixed up in the damn country mafia. You flunky turd, you been able to wiggle out of shit, but that ain't going to work forever. Do you have the dough? Don't look at me like I'm stupid, boy; you got the money?"

"I don't know what you're talking about," I said.

"Guess it makes no difference if you got the money or not. If the wrong people think you got it, you're fucked."

"Leon, what you talking about?"

"Keep playing stupid and I'm going to get out of this bed and slap the shit out of you."

I held out the palm to let him know I got it. "I know some people think I know what happened to old Charles," I said.

"Did some mule kick you in the head? It's more than you think; you the number one suspect, my man. Little Jenkins Jackson got the old country mafia searching for the cash of their ill-begotten gains."

I pulled up a chair and sat down by his bed. "Leon, I'm all ears, so what you trying to say?"

"It starts with Jaxs. You see, this little nest of heathens we have here are feeding a longer pipeline that ends at the county seat. You know, those rich people that want to have cake and eat it all year long. The big boys thought Charles had something to do with the death of Jaxs. The local boys, not so much. They knew Charles for what he was. They also knew Charles wasn't capable of killing a big man like Jaxs. Old Charles might slap a youngster around, but that was about it. Even I was stunned when they found those kids' bones out at his old place. Now that's some twisted shit right there. No matter what the police say, Jaxs was killed, and they snuffed Sonny 'cause you can't leave a witness."

"Jaxs had my grandpa on his to-do list for robbing." I'd remembered it all of a sudden.

"Yeah, and that was a problem. Jaxs had twisted off on his own, robbing those poor old men. Guess he wasn't satisfied with the crumbs the old country mafia boys were paying him. Because of that they didn't dig too deep to find out why he was done in. The man was a liability."

I still wasn't sure where Leon was going with this. Was he going to point the finger at me? I handed him his glass of water from the bedside table.

"Cat got your tongue? Guess I got your attention, huh?" Leon laughed.

"No, just trying to figure all this out," I said.

"Two people knew that you and Randy brought whiskey to Jaxs. Me and Old Duck. Me, because I do some work for them, and Jaxs told me how he stiffed you two. Old Duck knew 'cause Jaxs told him you were a bad influence on his grandson. Go figure that. Old Duck started planning to send Randy off to other relatives even before Jaxs died. And it wasn't because he was afraid you might turn old Randy bad."

"So why did he send Randy to Texas?"

"Protection, boy, protection. Old Duck didn't want Randy caught up in his business. Duck's business is to make money and funnel money to and from those bigger bastards. He collected people like Charles, Jaxs, and Folgers to carry out the dastardly deeds. If you could make money from it, they were into it. Chop shop, drugs, moonshine, porn; you name it, they were into it."

"How you know all of this?" I tried to breathe naturally.

"You don't listen," Leon said. "I said I did some work for them. Read between the lines. How you think I can get all these hot rods? You ever see me hold down a job? Hustling pool games don't pay all the rent, boy."

He didn't give me details, but I started reading between the lines.

"All right, so Old Duck brings in this real sorry motherfucking Cajun dude Gumbo to replace Jaxs. Plus, Gumbo was like the king of chopping stolen cars. Folgers was sent on the hunt for the missing cash once everybody decided Charles hadn't hidden it. Folgers sniffs the trail toward you, not solely because Old Duck may have told him about the whiskey, but exactly why, I just don't know. I just know he was hot on your trail. Then that fucker beaches up like some bloated mudcat. Hell, some thought I'd killed Folgers. That's some stupid shit. Now Gumbo with that foolish-ass belt buckle is missing. I'll kiss your white ass if he ain't dead, kemosabe. Fuckers probably think I did him in too. I ain't no killer. Funny that the three fuckers who kill are all gone themselves."

He started up with a brutal coughing spell. Bella stepped in to check on us. She chastised Leon for talking and smoking too much, and then left and returned shortly with a syringe in hand.

"Mom is an LPN, but that doesn't make her worth a damn in giving shots. Damn, horse medicine supposed to make me pee some of this swelling off," Leon fussed as he turned his butt up for the shot.

His mom left, and Leon looked at me with the most serious face I had ever seen him present. In fact, it was the first serious look he'd ever given me. "If this doesn't get better, I can't live like this," he said. "I've covered your ass a few times, so do me a favor if the time comes. Take one of these big beautiful pillows and give me a good send-off. Don't you fucking look at me like you don't know what I'm talking about."

I'd heard him all right. Maybe he'd killed Gumbo and Folgers to protect me. Surely he wasn't serious about the pillow euthanasia.

Back home, I shared all the Leon information with Jill. She took it all in, but being the more pragmatic, she was skeptical at best. She wasn't accepting an organized crime network right here in our small town. She couldn't believe a central bank for money laundering and deposits for ill-begotten gains was right here under everybody's noses at an old sex offender's house.

I tried my best to explain that it all made perfect sense with selective and incompetent law enforcement in an unremarkable rural county. What better shield for a criminal enterprise? Jill countered by pointing out that none of these thugs were smart. "Yes, dumb as foxes," I told her. I explained my theory that it didn't take real smarts if you surrounded yourself with dumbasses.

"So you're saying Old Duck is the smart one. Jenkins, you can't buy all that stuff Leon threw out there," Jill said in disgust.

It was apparent I wasn't going to convince her that Leon's story was plausible. Jill started firing a list of questions at me that she wanted me to share with Leon the next time I saw him. "Tell him we found Gumbo's body on our grandpa's land? Are you crazy, Jill?" I yelled out.

"This is for you, Jenkins. You're the one that got yourself tied up in all of this. You and that delinquent Randy. Do you want to know if Leon is pulling your leg or not?"

"It's you, too. Leon's no fool. We ask these questions, and he might just figure out what we've done. Don't forget Jaxs and Sonny," I countered sarcastically.

"We did nothing, understand? Our Valium didn't kill them, so quit saying that!" Jill gritted her teeth while squeezing her hands together.

"Whatever. And I guess we don't know anything about Terry's dad, the now deceased Cecil Lewis, either?"

"I'll go with you and ask him myself," Jill said.

I agreed, then started to change the subject to our plan for the Devil's demise. I still felt that her commitment to finishing what we'd started wasn't as strong as mine.

Before we could get into it, the phone rang. It was Bella. Straight to the point, when I answered the phone she said, "Jenkins, my baby boy has died." Leon. I wouldn't need to do the pillow euthanasia after all.

CHAPTER TWENTY-TWO

RENAISSANCE

"JENKINS, COME UP FRONT, RIGHT HERE. NOW!" IT WAS INEVI-
table that I had to take required English classes in high school, and there
was only one high school English teacher at our small school. I always sat
in the back of the room in all my other classes. Plus, my constant fidgeting
and inability to do the required assignments didn't work well if you sat
on the front row.

"Now!" Mrs. Addcock pointed her finger at the first desk in the front
row closest to her as she gave me what sounded like a final command. As I
warily shuttled forward, I heard giggles and chatter from my fellow classmates. Most of the noise was coming from my thug buddies. At the same
time, the higher-echelon students just looked astonished and waited for
whatever would be next. I took my newly assigned seat.

Mrs. Addcock was a tiny woman who looked fierce. I was confident
that there was not one kid in school who wasn't in some way afraid of her.
She smiled but never laughed. She always wore dark clothing with skirts
that stopped at her ankles. While lecturing, she would constantly walk
between the rows of desks while slapping a ruler in her open hand. She
added to this persona by wearing her cat-eyed glasses on the end of her
nose. She would cut those piercing brown eyes over the top of them when

anyone made an unsolicited sound. Sometimes the glasses would slide off her nose and dangle around her neck from the attached large beaded necklace. She had a mystique about her, for she was the only teacher no one knew much about. Where was she born, and where had she lived?

I tried my best to remain still. I was now in front of the whole class, though they were behind me and I didn't have to face them. This was the most uncomfortable I had ever felt in a classroom. Mrs. Addcock conducted the one-hour class while never looking toward me again. As I shuffled my papers in preparation to leave after the bell rang, she looked over her glasses, conveying that I should stay put.

She pulled up a chair and sat down facing me. "What's on your mind, young man?"

"Nothing," I responded in confusion. Why would she ask me that?

"So, what you are telling me is that you are an empty head? Is that it?"

"Yes, Mrs. Addcock, that's about it. My head is an abyss."

"I have been observing you since you arrived from grade school. You are a consummate smartass."

I had never heard a teacher say a cuss word other than the football coach who taught general physical science. He would say "hell" and "damn it to hell" when he was confused about what he was supposed to teach. "Excuse me, Mrs. Addcock," I responded with boldness.

She walked to her desk and pulled out some wrinkled-up notebook pages. She read a poem from one of the pages.

A line of lights today
Moving down the road
Straight Line, no sway
Another dead
Out of the way
The rest of us

A burden to stay

"Stop it. Don't read any more," I said.

"I have an extensive collection of your works. Your seventh-grade English teacher excavated these out of the trash. She was aware you were not diagramming sentences like you were supposed to be doing. I have plenty more of your writing. Ms. Drain either didn't have the time or didn't wish to waste her time on you. I can't say that I blame her. A horde of you little hoodlums all ended up in her class at the same time."

I felt the heat rush across my face, and most assuredly my face was flushed. My emotions were somewhere between embarrassment and anger. *How dare she lay this on me. What purpose did it serve? And how dare teachers talk to each other. Who knew?*

I had a flashback to my sixth-grade teacher, Mrs. Fellow. Her temper was robust, and the screaming would be followed by crying when she lost it. If you'd been the cause of her irritation, she made you give her a big hug afterward. She was a large woman with gargantuan boobs, and she'd squeeze you tight with your face lodged between them. Only the tallest in class could escape their smothering effect. At first it was an embarrassment to be called to the front of the class for one of her hugs, but after a while it became a game for some of us to see how many hugs you could acquire in a week. If Mrs. Addcock had a gimmick like that I might be more compliant, I thought. All of a sudden she slapped the ruler on my desk and snapped me out of my thoughts.

"Can I go now?" I asked.

"No, sir, you cannot," she replied with a tyrannical commanding voice.

"Why not?" That was the wrong question to ask, because it gave her an opening to lay down the doctrine according to Addcock.

"You will not waste my time or yours. You will learn. No, let me rephrase that. You will love to learn in my class. You will pay attention. If you can't sit still, stand up but always pay attention. Never be late for my class."

I counted the number of times the ruler struck her hand. *Ms. Drain had no right to dig my stuff out of the trash*, I thought. I was tuning Mrs. Addcock out.

"And don't you tune me out!" Mrs. Addcock demanded.

What the hell? She's reading my mind.

"These belong to you. I would say the punctuation is atrocious, and your spelling is dreadfully wicked," Mrs. Addcock commented as she handed me an overflowing shopping bag of my trashed writings. It was challenging to be any more deflated or depressed than I had already been most of my life, but she was doing a damn good job trying to get me there.

"Now, I have to say aside from all the beforementioned issues, I found your writings to be creative, unique, and highly imaginative. I assume this is word doodling from you, but I see the potential."

I had never had a compliment from a teacher before in my life. In fact, I couldn't recall ever getting praise from anyone other than my grandpa. His was simple, like "That's a good-looking bow you made from that persimmon tree. Can't believe an eight-year-old can do that." What Mrs. Addcock had to say was like a breath of fresh air.

Once I accepted the bag, her eyes indicated that my departure would now be permitted. I rode the bus home after school and walked to my favorite pecan tree, and began reading what I had trashed two years before. I was excited and positively reeling from being told I had potential. I was embarrassed about my work too. I felt like I had grown a lot since I'd thrown that stuff away, and even though I had written other things since then, I hadn't kept them. My songs, poems, and short stories seemed so depressing. I had even created three plays. For two hours that afternoon I tried to write something more upbeat, but to no avail. So I wrote a poem about a drunken Indian in honor of Leon. Then I threw all the old works in the old rusty oil barrel and burned them.

Then it began. I couldn't stop writing. I was searching for the sublime but couldn't get there. *Sardonic* best described my work during this initial period. As hard as I tried, I couldn't break out of the darkness that had always ruled my life. If writing was my escape, my therapy, then something had to give. This struggle allowed me to realize that I could not separate my home environment from school. Try as I might, the well-defined chameleon persona that had served me so well was faltering.

I was now making the best grades of my school life, though only in Mrs. Addcock's class. I was not sure where the inspiration came from. Still, as I was writing a poem, diving toward the darkness again, I recalled something my mother had once said to Jill and me when we were younger. We were getting off the school bus one day after some field trip. It was one of the few times our mom was at school to pick us up. Maybe she had noticed it before, maybe not. But that day she tore into us about hanging our heads down as we walked. Sounding both angry and caring, she impressed upon us that we should hold our heads high and not be ashamed of who we were.

Mrs. Addcock continued to motivate me, like a coach. She knew my syntax sucked, but she stayed focused on my creativity and passion for her writing assignments. I guess she figured the syntax proficiency would evolve. During one coaching session she challenged me to do better in all my classes. I decided that I'd try.

I met with each teacher to explain that I was going to do better. Most of them accepted what I was saying, but with reservations. None of them showed any indication that they expected me to follow through. The football coach and quasi-science teacher took a different approach. His counterproposal was that he'd give me a B if I played football for him. So just like that, I had a B and was on my way to a first honor roll.

The Devil was still at his extended-stay motel, also known as a mental hospital, so it was quiet at home. Doing homework was a new concept, as I had always ignored homework assignments before. It was still hard for me to sit still and focus, which impeded my homework. I tried everything: studying under my favorite tree, taking breaks to do a walk around the creek, and petting my dogs. After several weeks of making sluggish progress with homework and even staying focused in all classes, reality kicked the door down.

I smelled the oil before I saw the trail of blue smoke coming up the hill. Then I heard the muffler-less Devil's carriage, the old green Chevy pickup, clawing its way toward home. From the winding engine sound, it was stuck in second gear. The pickup came to rest once it hit the corner post of our yard fence. The Devil had returned from his hell to reintroduce us to ours.

He stared at me while dusting the glowing cigarette ashes off his dingy white T-shirt. His face was grayish, his eyes empty, and his movements were akin to those of a zombie. He said nothing to me as he shuffled and staggered into the house.

My progress toward improved homework and school attention took a giant step backward. Surprisingly, football became significant, not because I was in love with the sport but because it was an avenue to release hatred and violence. It wasn't football practice or games that made a difference. It was the cage.

I guess the cage was our Neanderthal coach's idea of fun. It was a mixed bag for the players. Some players—the biggest, roughest, and meanest ones—never had to enter the cage. The cage was a place where a player could challenge any first-string starter for his spot at the next game. It was a simple process where you told the coach what position you wanted to play, and then you were placed in the cage with that player.

The cage was the equipment storage area, built like a giant chicken coop with a locked screen-type door. Players would enter in full game-ready gear, including helmets and shoulder pads. Once inside with your opponent, there were no rules. The two would attack each other until one surrendered or the coach had had enough of the blood sport.

I was a newcomer to the sport, so initially I didn't challenge anyone. I watched as others extended and received challenges. Then I got my break and was a starter as a defensive tackle. This did not sit well with the players who had been playing the game in peewee leagues since grade school. That was when I started receiving challenges to dethrone my starting position. This was also how I discovered the therapeutic value of the cage.

The toughest and best players who would never be challenged encouraged everyone else to challenge me. I quickly learned that once the cage battle began, the sooner I could tear off my opponent's helmet and the easier it was to beat the shit out of them. Even when my challenger surrendered, I found it hard to stop pounding on the other guy. Sometimes the coach would see this and hastily send the next challenger in even before the last one had left the cage. To the coaches, it was all about having fun. That fun soon spread to other teachers, and even the janitors would come to watch.

I developed a reputation for being the kid who was marginal at best in football but who was never beaten in the cage. The only time I came close to being beaten was from a tall, skinny kid. I learned always to pay attention to the length of someone's arms, which was more important than weight or muscles. A player with long arms was able to break my nose.

If players sucked at football but won a cage battle, the coach would start them for only one play and then pull them for the remainder of the game. Oddly, this didn't seem to matter or reduce the number of challenges.

Between football, the cage, and improved grades, I was starting to experience something I had never felt before: confidence. However, this confidence did not carry over when dealing with the Devil. It was as if nothing had changed. Once again, the substance abuse and mental health treatment world had failed. While the Devil had terrified me as a child, as a teenager he was now an impediment to anything positive in my life. He was akin to a virus that keeps mutating.

Maybe it was football or improved grades, but encounters with the opposite sex were becoming part of my life. Nothing had changed about parents not wanting their daughters to spend time with me, so I had to get creative. At that age my sex drive was like an RPM red-lined 911 Porsche on the Autobahn, so whether it was fumbling through a bedroom window or getting entangled with a girl on a tree limb, they were risks I was going to take.

I needed a car if I was going to progress to the next level of sexcapades. A vehicle provided freedom. Ciphering whiskey from the Devil's bottles and a host of other nefarious deeds created a buffet of options to acquire the money to buy a car. I wasn't old enough to get a driver's license, but that didn't matter in the culture that surrounded me.

My first car: I thought I had died and gone to heaven. It was a 1960 Chevy Corvair and cost me a grand total of $225. Its top speed was 40 miles per hour, and that was going downhill. Standard transmission and a rear-engine could pop a wheelie upon a quick takeoff. Who cared if Ralph Nader said it was unsafe at any speed? The girls liked it. It had a new paint job but also had rusted-out floorboards and door hinges. I suspected it was one of Gumbo's hurricane-flooded cars he'd brought from Louisiana, and he'd tried to camouflage the water damage.

All was going well. One of the finer girls in town convinced her father to allow me to take her on a formal date.

I met the parents, opened the car door for her, and off we went driving to the county seat to see a drive-in movie. It was in full Camelot mode, until it wasn't. We were two blocks from her house when I turned a corner rather sharply, trying to impress her. The rusted hinges on the passenger door gave way when she leaned into it on the turn. The door flung open, and she fell out, bouncing off the road. Luckily she wasn't hurt: a few scrapes and scratches, nothing I thought was serious. I wired the door shut with some baling wire and was ready to continue with our date, but was shocked when she demanded that I immediately take her home. I barely stopped when I dropped her off at home, and I certainly did not want to see her father. She never spoke to me again.

Like most things happening during this time, and with Mrs. Addcock's encouragement to write, I began immortalizing my adventures in poetry. The car door incident poem was spectacular. Mrs. Addcock looked over her nose-end glasses several times while reading it. When finished, she couldn't hold it in any longer and burst out in laughter. Even if no one else was there to see it, I was the first student to make her laugh.

CHAPTER TWENTY-THREE

RECKONING

"YOU NEED TO DO THIS FOR ME. IT'S NOT TOO MUCH TO ASK. He is, after all, your father," Mom pleaded. She appeared conflicted and was clearly experiencing an emotional kaleidoscope. Her makeup was caked in an uneven fashion.

Jill responded first, "Why would I want to go see him? He was never a father to me."

"I'm with Jill on this one," I chimed in. "He never acknowledged our birthdays, and even when sober, which was a rarity, he didn't talk to us."

The Devil was hospitalized at the Veteran's Hospital in the state's capital city. I hadn't known he was a veteran. This forced Mom to let one of the skeletons out of the closet. He'd run off and left his family; no one knew where he was. Then he showed up later, having been in the military. Since we could never make sense of the things Mom and the Devil screamed at each other, we'd never been able to put the complete puzzle of their life together before we were born. The military was a new piece.

The county hospital had transferred him several days earlier. Mom said they did this because they didn't want to have him on their death records. The diagnosis was liver and kidney failure due to alcoholism. Jill and I knew better, or at least thought we did. We were convinced that we'd caused the illness.

We'd finally put our plan into action. The Devil had been on an extended terror binge, and Jill had to convince me to be patient when she saw me fish the old .22-caliber rifle out of the pond. Jill had been doing some research, and she told me that our state had no minimum age of absolution. This meant a juvenile could be charged as an adult at any age if the crime was severe enough. I did some research myself and countered that it could be self-defense or justified. But I gave in and decided using the gun was not a smart idea.

Executing the plan proved to be easy. Jill gave me the Valium she had been hoarding. I retrieved the open fifth of whiskey from his truck, poured a little more out, and dumped the pills in. I was careful not to wrinkle the bottle's sack. He never closed the sack by wadding the top. It always amazed me that a staggering foolish drunk always took the time to ensure his whiskey sack was folded and pristine. The next day, the Devil awoke and drove off. Two days later he stumbled into the liquor store and passed out, knocking over a vodka shelf. The liquor store owner was so used to him being staggering drunk he thought nothing of it, so he waited over an hour before calling an ambulance. He may have done us a favor.

I found out what had happened when I was onstage, practicing my extemporaneous speech. Mrs. Addcock had us rehearsing possible follow-up questions that would be asked after we presented our ten-minute memorized speech about the US Constitution. She had convinced me to enroll in her optional speech class, but had failed to mention this requirement. I was struggling to meet the speech's time requirement when the principal informed me that my dad was in the hospital, and that my mother was in his office to pick me up. I told him I didn't want to go. People around me seemed surprised by my response, but not Mrs. Addcock.

Mom was not accustomed to driving in the city. She knew that the state capital was in the middle of the city and used that as her only point of directional reference. My job was to read her the road map. I gave up and pointed to the tallest buildings downtown. "It's down that away somewhere," I suggested, and made a paper ball out of the map. So Mom zigzagged her way in that direction. It was like going through a maze, with the VA as the tallest building by which we navigated.

I could smell the stench when we walked through the hospital entrance. This was a place of death. A host of wheelchair-bound veterans occupied the lobby. Some wore caps that reflected the war arena they fought in. The Vietnam veterans were distinguishable by being younger. Most had ponytails and a peace sign patch somewhere on their clothing. My first elevator ride awaited me. Jill and I didn't want to make eye contact with the diseased and dying patients who accompanied us on the ride. Mom didn't seem to mind.

We stepped off the elevator on the sixth floor. *Maybe he's in room 66*, I thought. For the Devil, that would have been appropriate. Jill appeared more disinterested than me. We did not want to be here. We walked down a hallway lined with beds occupied by patients awaiting a room. The hospital was clearly overcrowded.

The Devil was at the end of the row of hallway beds. His breath seemed labored, and I could see his eyes twitching underneath his closed eyelids. His rusty feet with long yellow toenails were sticking out from under the sheets. His skin was scaly and gray. I looked at Jill, who had a slightly calm expression that cycled into signs of anger and then relief. Mom held the Devil's hand and allowed a few tears to trickle down her face. Once again, she was trying to play the role of a typical American middle-class wife. He looked like an alien with tubes in his nose, IVs in his arms, and compression stockings on his legs. Even in his semicomatose state, his evil shined through.

While I was trying to comprehend what I was beholding, we were interrupted by an elderly doctor clanking the metal medical clipboard attached to the foot of the Devil's bed.

"Are you the family?" asked the doctor.

Mom sheepishly replied, "Yes, we are."

"Well, let's see here—fatty liver—mid-level stages of cirrhosis. Kidneys are working at about 30 percent," the doctor said. "That doesn't match up well with what we see with his vitals. He was unconscious when we arrived and had only sporadically shown signs of coming out of it. A toxicology report will be necessary." The doctor explained all this while rubbing his gray-frosted unshaven face. His traditional long white medical coat had tiny faded bloodstains splattered across the front.

"Is he going to be okay?" asked Mom nervously.

I was thinking she should ask, *How long before he dies?*

"Well, we'll start draining the fluid from his lungs and stomach and give him treatments to kick those kidneys back into better working order. Now, his cirrhosis is a severe issue. I take it he has a history of alcohol abuse?"

Before Mom could respond, I blurted out, "Drinks like a fucking fish!" Jill turned away.

"Stop it, Jenkins. This is your father!" Mom admonished. The doctor didn't look up from the clipboard or make any discernible acknowledgment of my proclamation. I suspected this scenario had played out before him many times. "Yes, he drinks a little," Mom finally answered in a submissive tone.

"Well, I think if we can determine what's causing this coma, this lazy brain, as I call it, we could be out of the woods, so to speak. Assuming we identify that issue and it's treatable. His other issues can be addressed and somewhat controlled," the doctor added, continuing to read the medical charts.

"What does that mean? Are you saying he is going to live?" Jill asked.

"I can't speak in certainties, but I can say I am optimistic. Now, your dad will need to quit drinking. The liver damage is not reversible, so he will continue to have issues there."

"So he will be okay?" Mom asked rhetorically.

Damn it to hell. The son-of-a-bitch is going to live, was all I could think.

Jill whispered in my ear, "What do we do now?"

I took a deep breath and whispered back, "Who in the hell knows now?"

I knew Jill and I were both wondering why the Valium hadn't killed him. *Do they have an expiration date? What is their shelf life?* Panicked questions ran through my mind.

On the drive home, Mom kept talking about changing her work schedule so she could sit with the Devil at the VA. I explained to her how we didn't have enough money to pay the grocery bill, much less buy gas for multiple 200-mile round trips. Mom replied by reminding me that our gasoline was on credit, and we could sign more IOU tickets each time we filled up the tank. It was a long and arduous trip.

Once home, depressed and exhausted, I lay on my bed and imagined the flies on the ceiling engaged in organized warfare. I grabbed a pencil and paper and tried to write a poem about how I was feeling, but nothing could calm or distract me from what I'd heard from the doctor. I kept going back to the last conversation I'd had with Leon.

All of a sudden it occurred to me that Leon had given me a way out.

A pillow would be my weapon of choice. It would have been euthanasia for Leon; for the Devil it could serve as a weapon of destruction.

A righteous kill, one that would require extensive planning. I'd need to go to the VA Hospital at night, when less staff would be there. Would he be moved to a private room? How long did it take to suffocate someone with a pillow? Would he be strong enough to resist me if he was out of the coma? At that point I didn't dwell too much on what would happen to me if I were caught.

I was obsessed and could think of nothing else. I thought about what was right and wrong. The deed I had prayed for God to do was now before me as a choice I could carry out. Maybe God was finally answering my prayers after all those years of hiding under the bed and offering myself in exchange for the Devil's demise. Pastor Wayne had said that God worked through people, so maybe I was such a vessel, in an Old Testament kind of way.

How had I written off my previous indiscretions? I'd never thought of myself as a killer, eventually accepting Jill's rationalization that we had not killed Jaxs and Sonny. Our involvement was circumstantial at best. Randy had shot Charles, not me. Mr. Lewis was in self-defense. I was not a vigilante; I was a survivor.

"I don't understand why he's not dead," Jill announced in frustration.

"I don't know, but I'll handle this," I assured her.

"He'll know. If he wakes up and comes home, he'll figure out what we did," she insisted.

"Yeah, we'd be fucked. I said I would handle it. I'll take it from here." I knew that Jill wouldn't be able to be a secondary participant in another attempt to rid the world of the Devil. Besides, this would be physical, a hands-on assassination. It would be me, little brother, who would end this. She had a more promising future than I did anyway, and I could live with my plan of action.

Javier was confused about why I wanted to go see the Devil, but he agreed to give me a ride halfway. We went two days later. The ride on his Honda 90 in four lanes of fast traffic was much different than my first ride with him. The eighteen-wheelers and fast traffic scared me shitless. He dropped me off at the halfway point, which was at the largest salvage yard I had ever seen.

It was easier to thumb a ride when people knew you. On the interstate hundreds of cars passed by, but no one stopped to pick me up. Finally some hippies picked me up in an old station wagon with wood grain sides. Van and April were a lovely couple and appeared not to have a care in the world. He drove with both hands tightly wrapped around the steering wheel, muttering that he was high and didn't want to make a mistake and get pulled over by the police. April chimed in that pot sometimes made him paranoid. Then they both broke into song, Black Sabbath's "Paranoid." It didn't have the same effect without a heavy metal-pounding guitar riff.

They dropped me off several blocks from my destination, because they were concerned that there would be cops around hospitals. April gave me a parting gift of a string of handmade love beads, presented with a moist kiss on my cheek. The streets were dark, with an occasional homeless person stepping out of the shadows like zombies. I wasn't scared; I was mission-focused. I did take my time to survey the environment with every step I took.

The VA Hospital rose from the neighborhood like a begotten dingy red brick bastion. I envisioned it as a mountain I had to ascend to keep me in the mental state of mind I needed to maintain. Once it was conquered, I would reap my rewards. I approached, walking through the nonindigenous planted trees that had all died from lack of attention. The front sidewalk was crumbling, and the attempted repairs made walking more difficult.

I entered from the south side entrance. Fewer veterans were hanging out there exchanging drinks and smoking with the locals and homeless. Only a couple of them gave me a glancing look.

I entered and walked through an atrium. All the plastic flowers and plants that hadn't been dusted in years seemed to reach out and share their discontent. An elderly, overweight security guard in a too-small black uniform briefly peeked over his wrinkled magazine. If one of his shirt buttons popped off while holding that huge belly in, it would have become a lethal projectile. No one else stopped me or questioned me.

There were fewer beds with patients in the hallway this time. I approached the bed that the Devil occupied. The sheet was pulled over his head—I took a big breath of relief. The Devil was dead. I gingerly began sliding the sheet down while hoping he hadn't died with his eyes open. It wasn't until the sheet was down to his chest that I realized it was not him.

"Young man, may I help you?" a gorgeous blond young nurse inquired as she walked up behind me. I had not heard her approach, too shocked from finding the Devil missing. Maybe the Devil was already dead and had been moved to the basement morgue, or they had found him in an actual room, and he was alive.

"Oh, well, yeah, I'm looking for my dad," I finally stuttered out as a response. It felt so strange having to call him that. It felt like treason. "He might be in your morgue," I said, to narrow her search.

"What's his name?" she asked me.

Momentarily distracted by her good looks, I finally got out, "Jackson, Mr. Jackson."

Much too quickly, she said, "Your dad is in room 1492, just down the hall. Take a right, then left, then take the second right, and it will be on your left. If you get to the stairwell, you've gone too far. Are you okay? Do you want me to take you?"

I would have loved for her to walk me through this maze, but I needed to focus on the mission.

Some patients moaned; others talked to themselves; many stared at me. Their eyes seemed anticipative, hoping someone would visit them. I took a few wrong turns but eventually found my way to room 1492. I gently pushed the door open. There were two beds, both occupied. Lights from medical equipment illuminated the room. The patient in the bed closest to the door had two tubes in his nose and more than one IV going. I carefully and quietly worked around his bed to the next.

There he lay, labored breathing, snoring, eyes closed. I surveyed the room. There were extra pillows in a visitor's chair. I walked back to the door and looked right and left down the hallway. There was no one in sight and only the sound of patients' bodily functions. All the while thoughts were running through my head. *Remember you have to plan this one. Be careful, no witnesses. Do it right. Make sure he isn't breathing after you're finished.*

I stepped back from the entry and silently made my way to the Devil again. I stared at him. He appeared comatose, like when we'd visited. His chest slightly rose and fell, shallow breathing but labored. I didn't want to touch him, but I needed to make sure he was out cold. I poked his foot, then his leg, and finally the chest. No movement. The only tubes or hoses were a split T-type oxygen hose inserted into his nose.

He actually looked harmless like that. I shook off any feeling of sentiment. I reached for one of the pillows, gripping it tightly in my hands while I stood over him. Someone was walking down the hallway. I paused, then turned to see if they had passed.

Killing would be doing him a favor, I reasoned. Not only would I be saving Jill and myself from his torture, but I'd also be saving him from the suffering associated with his decrepit condition. Mom would be spared from having to nurse him at home. Maybe he'd been spared from the Valium death for a reason. He didn't deserve a quiet, peaceful death in his sleep.

"I need some water."

I jumped, and then I was frozen. "Water, get me some water!"

It was the patient in the other bed, who had momentarily awakened but looked to be asleep again. But then I heard, "Boy, get me some water, too. Can't get no fucking service around this damn place." I turned, and the Devil was looking right at me.

"Jenkins, what the fuck you doing here? Get me some water." The Devil spoke in a drained, raspy voice.

A thousand scenarios flashed through my mind. I obeyed and shakily poured a cup of water from the bedside metal pitcher. I tripped over his bedpan that was overflowing on the floor. His pee looked like varnish and was so thick it didn't even splash out. "Thanks," he said.

"You're alive?" *Stupid, stupid, fucking stupid*, I admonished myself. *What a stupid fucking thing to say.*

"Well, you dumb little shit, what's it look like?" he said with a smile.

"I just thought, you know, that you were in some sort of coma or something," I finally got out.

"Can't wait to get out of this hellhole."

Hellhole is correct, I thought.

"Seems I'm going to need some care. Won't get that here. Damn liver fucked up, and kidneys only working part-time. Then there's pleurisy. I need a drink," he rattled on. He reached for a towel and coughed up what looked like a yellow pound or more of phlegm. I had to turn my head.

I poured him another water. "Fuck boy, not that type of drink. I need a real drink. Yeah, need to get home. Your mother will take good care of me. There ought to be someplace around here to get a bottle."

At that point, I understood my mother would spend the rest of her life nursing him. She'd make sure all his medical needs were met, prolonging his life further into old age. She'd be waiting on him hand and foot. It had to stop. She deserved freedom in the last half of her life.

I gripped the pillow like a vise and hid it behind my back. I suddenly didn't feel the need to rush, for I wished to enjoy my contempt for this evil. "Why are you so mean? Why do you drink all the time and treat us like shit? Hell, why did you even have a family, you son-of-a-bitch?" I blurted all of this out.

I wanted answers. I'd never had a conversation of any significance with this man. Biologically, that was what he was. Did I actually think he was the Devil? As a child I had, but I'd vacillated back and forth for the past couple of years on what he really was. Now he'd survived a killer concoction of Valium that should have killed an elephant. I couldn't purge the memory of my grandpa calling him the Devil while I prayed for Grandpa to squeeze the trigger.

"Having fun," the Devil answered. "Guess I just like having fun."

"That's your fucking answer? Having fun?" I said through my clenched teeth. I pulled the pillow from behind my back like a quick cross-draw of a gun. I slammed it over his face with a force that popped my knuckles and placed all my weight forward. He resisted, amazingly strong. He made several swimming motions with his legs, flapped his arms around my head, and wiggled his whole body. For a split second he pulled at my hair. I pressed harder.

Time stood still. I was floating in space, holding a pillow over the moon. After what seemed like an eternity, his movements ceased. I released all pressure from my weapon of choice. Sweat dripped from my forehead and tears rolled down both cheeks. I looked at the other patient, who was sound asleep.

"I killed Gumbo for you, you little motherfucker," I heard the Devil gasp out.

"Thanks, and fuck you," I whispered while holding and compressing the pillow on his face with all my capacity. *Don't stop, don't let up, press harder, harder, harder*, I thought. I was in panic mode.

If he is the Devil, he won't die. But if he does die, will the evil pass into me? Does evil require another host to survive? I pressed even harder. It had been minutes since his last movements and my arms were aching, but I couldn't stop. I had to be sure. My wrists were weakening. Exhausted, I fell forward across his chest. I felt no breathing. I removed the pillow and saw purple lips and steely eyes staring at me. Had he died with his eyes open, or was he still alive? I pressed the pillow down again until I fell to the floor in exhaustion.

A cacophony of street sounds greeted me as I flung the window open and proceeded to fertilize the plants below with partial digestion of all I had to eat that day. My face raced with fever. I took in the night air and finished dry heaving. I sat in the visitor chair, clenching the pillow I had just used. His snot, sweat, and a few drops of blood left an eerie image on the pillowcase. A small amount of blood trickled from the creases in my fingers, reminiscent of the coat hanger squeezing phenomenon years before.

I placed the pillow under my arm and slipped out of the room, down the exit stairs. Once outside, I threw the pillow in the first trash can I saw.

CHAPTER TWENTY-FOUR

TIME FOR CHANGE

JILL AND I KEPT GLANCING AT EACH OTHER. WE HAD ARGUED with Mom that we did not want to attend the funeral. She acted like we had lost our minds for making such a request. Once again, she was back in her perfect middle-class family fantasy, taking in all the pomp and circumstance of collateral funeral benefits. She enjoyed the attention. The few flowers that were sent, the prepared food brought to the house, visits by friends, and, of course, Pastor Wayne were graciously and ceremoniously welcomed. Now here we sat after the circus.

"For heaven's sake, he is your father. Can't you two cry or something? Show some emotion," Mom kept imploring us. I thought, *She wants emotion?* Did she not understand that it was a lack of emotion that had allowed us to survive this hell?

"He was just a sperm donor, Mom. He never did what dads are supposed to do," Jill countered every time Mom reminded us that this evil was our dad.

"I didn't have a say-so for being born in this fucked-up family," I said. "Given the option, I would've stayed someone's imaginary fantasy." I rambled on, taking full advantage of getting my cruel hits in.

Maybe attending the funeral was our penitence for refusing to assist in choosing the casket and showing no interest in the choice of wreaths and other funeral decorations. Disgruntled and annoyed, we watched as the few in attendance paraded past the open casket.

Then she did it. I couldn't believe it. Mom was attempting to crawl into the coffin with him. I had a flashback when Red did that at my grandpa's funeral, and Mom was so insulted. Now I knew how she felt. Even though there was only Mom, Jill, Pastor Wayne, and the funeral home staff present, I was embarrassed by her spontaneous display of emotion. Two funeral staff gently talked Mom down and refrained her from being successful. I was humiliated. Jill and I turned away. Then, to top it all off, Pastor Wayne asked if any sinner among the handful of us present wanted to be saved.

The doctor had told Mom that the Devil had died of a terminal case of cirrhosis of the liver, though he was surprised that he died so quickly. With that diagnosis the coroner chose not to accept the body, and it was sent to a funeral home under contract with the hospital.

Then Randy showed up at our house four days after the funeral. "Old Duck says I need to talk to you about finding money," he said.

"What money?" I responded.

"Come on now. With Folgers and your old man dead, he wants to find it."

"I suggest he go find Gumbo," I recommended. "Bet he has some answers about that money." I was testing Randy. Did he know Gumbo was dead? Could I trust Randy? If he knew anything about what his grandpa was up to, would he tell me?

"Look, Jenkins. I'm only in town for a few days, and my grandpa asked me to check with you. That's all. Don't get your panties in a wad."

"How much money we talking about here?" I asked.

"Hell, I don't know! I just know it's a lot."

"So you do know then," I poked at him.

"All I know is that Grandpa said he'd need to leave town if it's not found," Randy said.

"Look, Randy, we have been through a bunch of shit together. Come on, look at what we did to Charles. I'd tell you if I knew anything about the damn money."

"Damn it, Jenkins, I know, but this is my grandpa we talking about. I got to do something to help him find it."

"I don't get you, man. I mean, if you are playing with all this trash, you goin' to get dirty. Old Duck made a calculated risk to get into this hillbilly mafia shit; he knew the consequences." I surprised myself. I had some newfound confrontational confidence. I had been feeling freer, empowered, and had more self-confidence. Now it was spilling over into my friendship with Randy. Maybe we had created some sort of détente as a result of our Charles episode.

But Randy was persistent. "Grandpa said your old man might know something about the cash, Jenkins."

"How would he know anything?" I asked. "He ain't never had any money; hell, he owes everybody in town."

"Maybe he bought drugs or drank with the crew," Randy said. "I know he was hanging out with Folgers and Gumbo a few times 'cause I saw that myself. Grandpa says your old man used to loan Charles money."

I wondered if maybe Randy was playing me. He knew how close I was to my grandpa and perhaps used that word to soften me up. We went back and forth for another 30 minutes, then agreed to disagree. I think Randy believed I didn't know anything about the money, but he needed me to volunteer to help find it. And I thought Randy knew more than he was letting on. But I didn't think he was aware Gumbo was dead.

I found my way back to Salem's store. I was drawn to it like a moth to light. "Tyranny, my boy. That kind of sums it up," were Salem's first words upon seeing me. I noticed that the store was dirtier than usual, and there was a drastic reduction in inventory.

"Say what?" I responded.

"That's what you have when one controls desire, emotion, and knowledge."

"What? Please, no riddles today," I pleaded.

"Power is the ability to influence people. If someone can push your buttons, cause you a hunger, create anger, or make you question your knowledge, you have given your power away."

I pulled up an old rope seated chair, interested in what else Salem might have to say.

"I miss that crazy Leon," he said. "Now he was never one to give his power away. Like you, he had an abundance of common sense; for him, it was a gift; for you, it is presently a punishment."

"A punishment?" I asked as a string to keep the conversation on the topic. Salem had the habit of quickly moving on and not explaining himself.

"Well, then, it's the punishment if you only surround yourself with those that don't have it. I think that comes from Voltaire. It's frustrating, isn't it, Jenkins, trying to deal with people with a real lack of common sense."

"I guess I get it, Salem."

"Time and patience will prevail, but not if you wait too long. A risk is not a risk if it is not a risk."

"Come on now, Salem. Give me a break, English, please."

"A risk is not a risk if you can calculate it. Is that better?"

"Yes, sir, thanks."

"So what are you going to do, Jenkins? I saw in the little local paper that you made the honor roll. Congratulations."

"I'm not sure. I know I need to get out of here."

"I have the impression that you have something to prove. Your expression would add credence to that," Salem continued, oozing with insight and philosophy. He walked from behind his counter and pulled up a chair to face me. The dust he awakened with his relocation presented a brown haze curtain between us, rendering him a mystical presence.

He was correct. I had developed a drive to prove to everyone that I could rise above where I came from and what I was. I'd started feeling this way after inspiration from Mrs. Addcock, and the desire had grown ever since. The Devil's demise fast-tracked my evolution.

"It is not like you and Randy are parasitical twins. You owe him nothing."

He knows, I thought. He must have understood what Randy and I had done. Or at least knew Old Duck was using Randy to locate the missing cash.

Then Salem stood up, dusting the toes of his shoes off with a dirty yellow handkerchief. Only then did I notice his exacerbated frailty.

"Sometimes, a good deed is a crime," he said. "They will never be able to identify those poor children. Their bones will stay in the evidence locker for eternity. The good news is there will not be any new ones on that sweet potato farm, now will they? I wish you the best of luck, my friend, and self-mastery." He gave me a soft military-type salute while slightly bowing. I gave him two thumbs-up.

Randy returned to Texas, and Old Duck closed his catch-all business operations. The word was that he also moved to Texas. I didn't care. Jill had one year of school remaining, and I was not far behind. I poured myself into academics. I couldn't get enough of Mrs. Addcock's teachings. I wanted to be an English teacher like her. However, that would be a problem. The rite of passage ran through the oil fields, and only there would I be able to finance my path to college.

CHAPTER TWENTY-FIVE

HORIZONS

AFTER THE EMBARRASSING EMOTIONAL DISPLAY AT THE funeral, Jill and I were surprised by how quickly Mom bounced back. The expectation was that she would stay depressed and wallow in pity. Instead, she started what we called her renaissance years. Maybe this was where we inherited our ability to overcome adversity. She evolved quickly into our newfound world. I kept waiting for the other shoe to drop, because that was how my world had always been. She started taking classes in oil painting, cake decorating, and computers. Who knew she could paint? She was making up for lost time, trying to squeeze as much positive aura as possible in the time she had left on this earth. Mom had never told us that Grandpa had a small whole life insurance policy on the Devil with her as the beneficiary.

Jill and I begrudgingly agreed to take a Greyhound bus trip with Mom to visit her father, our wife-beating grandfather, in California. It was a disaster. First, I was naïve and didn't realize that the damn bus stopped at every Podunk little town along Route 66. Second, I categorically did not care anything about seeing a grandfather I'd never known. I could only recall maybe seeing him twice for a few minutes before that trip, and one of those times was when he drove by our house and threw a bag of candy in the yard. He didn't even stop to say hello. Jill sat with Mom on the bus, and I was left to the mercy of whoever needed a single seat and deemed me an acceptable travel mate.

Fortunately I had some smarts, because I knew I was being watched. We were at the downtown Los Angeles bus terminal changing buses when a man approached and softly asked me if I could help carry his luggage, but the catch was I needed to go outside the terminal to help him retrieve it. He was younger than Charles, but I could see that same desolate but nefarious look in his eyes. He walked away, but I kept an eye on him. He circled the rotunda and probably asked the same favor of the two other young boys he approached.

I was coming out of the stall after holding my bladder as long as possible. I hated using the bathroom in bus terminals and preferred to use the one-holer on the bus. As I opened the stall door, there he was again. As he raised the palm of his hand, I head-butted him right in the face. It was over in a second. He grabbed his bloodied nose and I calmly walked out victorious, although my gait was somewhat quicker. I had a small bump on my forehead from the blow. I didn't tell anyone about this incident. Maybe I had attacked before asking any questions, but it had made me think of that time in Javier's cellar.

We arrived at the house where Mom's half sister lived in Bakersville. She was the father's caretaker. He wasn't allowed to smoke in the house, so they had configured an impressive living room look-alike in the garage where he could chain-smoke self-rolled Prince Albert cigarettes and drink cheap beer from sun-up until bedtime. He didn't say much, so I never knew if he was drunk or not. However, a case of beer a day was par for the course.

His pet desert tortoise named Tarzan was my only entertainment while we were there. He would gingerly crawl out of his wood Pepsi-Cola

crate home and eat clover. Every evening we would all sit in the backyard and watch the turtle. Tarzan was short on entertainment value, but
I enjoyed the quietness.

We stayed for only four days. Mom packed up the front two pocketed
square-tailed plaid shirts and other used clothing from her dad that she
thought I would wear. After some fake goodbyes, we were back on the
damn bus again. We had nothing in common with the California half
sister, who had never worked outside the home and seemed perfectly con-
tent with that.

Upon our return back home, we found a certified letter waiting for
us stating that Mr. Corbin Blackford, Esq., wished to be contacted in reference to the Devil's estate. I went along with Mom to the county seat to
his office. I was there for moral support, as Jill was off doing some senior
class extracurricular activities. I was calm until we entered town, when I
realized that my heart was racing and keeping beat to our car's rhythm as
it bounced over the red brick roads.

The man looked like Jackie Gleason. He had a pencil-thin mustache
and a colossal belly that I was sure obstructed his ability to aim his pee.
That might have explained the dusty splatters on his shoes. He moved
his forearms from resting on his stomach to adjusting his wide paisley
necktie, then repeated this movement frequently like a nervous twitch.
He spoke while chewing on a large black cigar.

Corbin Blackford was an attorney and also vice president of a bank,
which gave him dual power. Mom wore her best dress and a bucket of
makeup, though nothing could disguise the country in us.

"I will get straight to the point, Mrs. Jackson," he said, ignoring me.

"Your husband, being the sole proprietor of one-half of the original
estate inherited from his father, sold said property to me, one Corbin
Blackford, for the amount of $80,000, to be paid in annual installments

of $10,000 before the end of each calendar until paid in full. I also might add, interest-free." Blackford read and ad-libbed from some official-looking gold-sealed document.

"That's only $500 per acre for a quarter section of land. This can't be right, $80,000 for 160 acres when land sells at $1,500 per acre. Does that include the fenced ten acres with our house? Tell me no, please," Mom cried out.

"Now, Mrs. Jackson, your husband came to me with an offer to sell, and I tendered an offer he accepted. He seemed satisfied, and so was I."

"And the house?" I interrupted.

"Well, that was included in the contract," he said. "While you were out of state, I graciously paid the back taxes on the property to get a clear title. Before you thank me for that, I will forgive what you owe me for said taxes. There will be no expenses to pay as you vacate the property." He presented this information with counterfeit concern. He chopped the end of a new cigar off with his miniature French guillotine, smiled, and awaited our reaction.

"No, this is not right. This is not correct. I'll sue you and your bank. We have no place to go!"

"Now, now, Mrs. Jackson. Please calm down. This is just business. You may have your attorney look everything over. I actually encourage you to do just that, and I am sure no irregularities will be cited."

I stared at him and thought, *Man, I would love to take his nose and cut it off with that damn miniature cigar-cutting guillotine.* Mom was shaking, and I couldn't find it in myself to reach out and provide any comfort. Like her, this was a surprise to me too. But I was calloused to the point that I didn't care. This man was causing me to relapse on my anger management issues. I needed to stay strong on my path of positive changes.

Maybe Blackford developed some sympathy for Mom, or maybe it was just part of a plan to keep her from retaining an attorney. "Mrs. Jackson, I am in no hurry to convert the land. Plus, we will be developing the horse ranch on the property's north side first; therefore, you will not need to move immediately."

"I need a year," Mom stated.

"Mrs. Jackson, I don't believe that is reasonable."

Mom sat silent. Blackford waited patiently and took the opportunity to spit a wad of a chewed cigar in the trash can.

"Look, I did not wish to bring this up. Now, I know you think the price was too low."

Mom interrupted and said, "Too low, you damn right it's too low. Something ain't right here."

"Let me finish, please, and thank you," he answered. "What I was going to inject is that your husband owed the bank quite the sum of money. All that debt is forgiven, so the price is fair."

"What debt? What did he borrow money for? We certainly never saw any of it. Show me the paperwork on these loans," Mom implored him.

I was triangulating, connecting the dots. That was what Salem would do.

"Well, you see, some were with the bank, and some were personal loans from me."

"Who are you, the banker or the loan shark?" Mom shrieked.

"That was unnecessary," he replied.

"How much did he borrow? What did he put up for collateral?"

"He satisfied some of the debt after his father passed. If you are insistent on documentation, that may take a while. Now, I can give you six months in the house."

Hmm, this explains where all of Grandpa's antiques went, the crosscut saw, the mule skinner equipment, I speculated.

"We need a year," Mom reiterated.

"That is not doable," was Blackford's definitive answer.

"Give me our copies of the sale transactions and all that other legal stuff. We're going down the street to see a lawyer."

"That's your prerogative, but you will be wasting your money."

I'd been sitting quietly, studying Mom and this shady man. I thought about Leon and his description of how things worked and the hierarchy of despicable players he'd alluded to. I took a shot in the dark.

"So, Corbin, you or your bank here ever loan any money to, say, Old Duck, Charles, Folgers, or Gumbo?"

"Young man, who we make loans to is none of your concern," he angrily responded.

If looks could kill, I would be a dead motherfucker. He took the cigar out of his mouth, swung it in the trash, and told us he would be back in a few minutes. Mom asked me why I asked about those men. I told her that if this Corbin character had loaned money to the Devil, then he might have thrown some lends to other undesirables as well. All of whom most assuredly had no credit ratings.

I was anxious, twisting in my chair after getting up numerous times to look out the window. Blackford was taking his time. Maybe he was trying to wait us out, wanting us to give up and leave. He returned with a smile that would have put Carol Channing to shame. He was carrying a stack of papers.

"Mrs. Jackson, here's your copies as requested," he said. "That one-year residency you asked for is acceptable."

I was right, I thought. *This fucker was the one, or at least close to the one, a banker at the county seat and a lawyer also, so if he ain't the one, he should be.* I decided to test it.

"Corbin, sir, I think there has been some misunderstanding. We are asking for two years in our home." He looked at me with a crooked smile that faded into a frown. He organized a few papers on his desk and extended the pregnant pause we were locked in.

"I will have the agreement drafted for two years," he answered with biting indignation. "Satisfied?"

CHAPTER TWENTY-SIX

THE ADULT EDUCATION

JAVIER HAD MOVED TO NASHVILLE, AND I HAD FOLLOWED HIS progress. He'd decided to make it big in the music capital. We stayed in touch and I would occasionally receive a postcard with a few words about his auditions and his ever-changing housing situations.

It had been five years since that old kingpin and banker Blackford gave us two years to live in our own home. After high school graduation, Jill married her high school boyfriend and moved over 100 miles away. Mom stayed in the old hellhole of a home until the very last day of the agreement and then moved to the county seat to be closer to her job. I was going to a small college part-time about 150 miles east from my hometown. I split the rent for a shabby, roof-leaking, two-bedroom house with three other students. My share of the rent was $40. I continued to work part-time in the oil field.

I'd always thought Javier was an excellent guitar player. Maybe he'd inherited the talent from his father. According to Javier's dad, the famous country guitar player Chet Atkins, known as Mr. Guitar, had once told him that Javier had something special. Whatever the case, as long as I'd known him Javier practiced hours each day and lived and breathed guitar. He never went with guitar fads and kept playing the first guitar he ever owned, a cherry-red, hollowed-body Gibson electric.

But no matter how good you are at something, there will always be someone else who is better. The temptation for all of Javier's afflictions must have been tremendous in a city riddled with innocuous players like him. You can take the boy out of the country, but not the country out of the boy. Maybe he realized that thousands of players were as good or better than he was. The news spread fast when Javier died in Nashville of an overdose. His many relatives in the area made sure everyone knew.

Rumors abounded concerning the circumstances of his death: that he was homeless, had contracted terminal gonorrhea, was murdered, or had committed suicide. Whatever the case, he was the first of the old under-the-bridge gang to go. The local newspaper didn't list his cause of death.

The funeral, like most, was a conduit for a reunion. Pastor Wayne had moved on to greener pastures, and the new preacher awkwardly muddled through the ceremony. Freddy and Neddy were there, looking worse for the wear. Surprisingly, Randy attended, although he arrived at the very end. He must have had a growth spurt, for he had gained considerable height and muscle. I noticed Mike's name on a card attached to flowers by the casket. None of us knew where he was, but we joked he was probably still following his mom around the strip clubs collecting exotic bras. We all paid homage to Javier's red Gibson mounted on an easel at the church's entrance. "Stairway to Heaven" was played over the intercom.

Even though Javier had embraced the thug life, he was also a genuinely kind person and was liked by all. That would explain the other classmates' attendance. We assembled in the church's front yard under an old cottonwood tree. The twins' chain-smoking kept many at a distance. I could have stood there and visited all day, but then I saw Bella, Leon's mother, meander out of the church. I hadn't known she was in attendance. I hadn't outgrown that peculiar feeling that I had for her, either. Whatever it was, it moved me.

The fit of her dress and her aura of confidence, along with an infectious smile framing her pearl-white teeth and large eyes, beckoned me to come hither, and that I did. I meandered in her direction, trying to be discreet. I didn't want it to seem intentional.

"I was hoping I would see you today," Bella said.

"How are you?" was all I could muster as I battled with butterflies in my stomach.

"It's been challenging, but each day is a little bit better. First Leon, then my husband passed. It's been a heavy burden." She lit a Salem. I'd never thought smoking a cigarette was sexy, but my mind was enlightened at that moment.

"Sorry, I didn't know he had passed."

"It was expected, but that doesn't make it any easier," she responded quietly.

I watched the old gang out of the corner of my eye. They didn't seem to be looking our way or showing any signs of expecting my return. Besides Javier's failed foray to Nashville, I was the only one of the group today who had actually moved and not returned.

I shifted my weight from one foot to the other, trying to divert my nervous energy from the stomach to the legs. I was running out of small talk but didn't want Bella to leave. She slowly walked over to the church's side entrance and gingerly snuffed out her Salem.

"I don't feel up to attending the graveside service," she remarked on her return.

"I probably need to attend. I haven't had a chance to speak with his parents," I said.

"Yes, you should. Leon said you two were close. If you feel up to it, come by my apartment afterward for coffee."

I was not a coffee drinker and figured it was one of those learned tastes where you just had to keep doing it until your body gave up and accepted it. It was time for me to love coffee.

"Sure, I can do that," I answered.

"I've moved," she said. "I'm in a duplex on Second Street, across from the pharmacy, the one with a dream catcher hanging from the porch. See you later."

Less than one-third of those who attended the funeral went to the graveside. The mariachi band playing their version of "Amazing Grace" was fantastic. It was the only thing that broke my thoughts of visiting Bella. I hugged Javier's parents and shook hands with many there. Javier's dad gave everyone one of Javier's guitar picks. I decided I'd drill a hole in mine to make a necklace. I declined some of the old gang's offers to have beers and play pool. The twins asked if I wanted to assist them in harvesting Javier's pot crop. I asked them how they knew it even still existed, but they didn't answer.

"The door is unlocked. Come on in," Bella called out as I nervously and lightly knocked on the door. My heart entered, and my body followed. Bella was in the kitchen and had changed into a terrycloth jumpsuit. The bright red toe polish on her bare feet caught my eye. I couldn't explain it, but those polished toes were an instant game winner.

"Make yourself at home," she said. "I'll be right there."

I looked around the living room and chose a recliner to sit in. The room was sparsely populated with a few family photos, a porcelain Siamese cat clock-lamp combo, and a handwoven American Indian design blanket on the wall.

"It's a little late for coffee," Bella said, coming back into the room with two glasses of wine. "Is this okay?"

"Sure," was all I could say. I was not a wine drinker, but at that moment I was willing to learn. I didn't know what a Cabernet was, but I was aware of Boone's Farm and Mad Dog 20/20. She handed me the glass and our hands briefly touched.

She chose the sofa as she sat and crossed her legs, which caused her jumpsuit to climb higher on her thighs. I was at a loss for words. She lit up a smoke, leaned forward with both elbows on a knee, and said, "So, Jenkins, what have you been up to? I haven't seen you around in quite a few moons." She smiled. I relaxed.

"I knew I just needed to leave town and haven't had any desire to return," I said. "If I stayed, I'd just be another aging thug with no future. You know what I mean?"

"Of course. I'm glad you left. No, as a matter of fact, I'm proud of you. I told Leon he needed to escape. I wish he had. It's never too late to leave. I'll be going soon too."

"You're leaving? Where are you going?" I asked with a feeling of immediate loss.

Bella smiled. "I'd rather not say. I've been here my whole life, so it's time for my journey. I've sacrificed for everyone and ended up sacrificing myself. Now it's time for me." She refilled my glass of wine. I had unconsciously emptied the first one. Her pending move saddened me, but I understood.

Between lots of small talk, we drank several more glasses of wine. I wanted to know more about her soul, what she was made of. The wine was giving me courage and confidence, allowing me to ask probing questions. "What did you mean that it was now time for you?" I asked.

Instead of answering me, she reached out for my hand. "Here, Jenkins, come with me, and I'll show you." I followed her to the bedroom, which was sparsely furnished. There was a stack of books on a small nightstand and a brightly colored throw rug at the foot of the bed. A dream catcher hung over the door.

She stood facing the bed with me at her back. She said nothing, but I understood her unspoken invitation. I calmed my trembling hand and slowly unzipped the jumpsuit. It fell at her feet. Time stood still, and then she turned around. She was perfect, everything proportionate. She kissed me delicately, then passionately. Her body felt more firm than mine, surprisingly solid. I felt like I was just seconds from passing out, and I didn't believe it had anything to do with the wine.

Bella stood facing me for a few more moments, not in hesitation but in calculation. One hand placed pressure on my left shoulder, and the palm of the other hand mildly pressed my chest, compelling me to turn. She continued with the nonverbal hand maneuvers until I was in bed on my back. I quickly pulled my shirt off and attempted to wiggle out of my pants. With her long and sharp fingernails, she traced an invisible road map across my chest with routes snaking down my thighs. My breath and heart were now as close to normal as they were going to be. I reached out for her.

I tried to break into those soft dark eyes as her torso rose above me. With the tautness of all things beautiful, I reached up to explore the fruit that was so tensely suspended before me. Then I felt the indescribable detonation of contact. It was real.

She shook her head no, so I stopped my motion. She was in charge and was not ready to surrender it. "Slow, slow," she whispered.

I was convinced that the patience she was demanding would cause brain damage. Relief, I needed relief, finality to this exquisite torture. "You'll get your turn," she whispered into my ear. Her rhythm increased; we were communicating. The time was now.

Then she collapsed in a labored breath. I allowed myself to exhale. She lay face down beside me. After a few moments, she went to the kitchen and brought back two glasses of water. I wasn't thirsty. She noticed, took a small drink, and said, "Guess I underestimated a young man's recovery time." She reached for me again.

Among other things, I lost track of time. We exchanged explosions in every possible method. If I ever felt in control, it was because Bella allowed it. Everything seemed in sequence, and she was the architect. She was the conductor, and I was the orchestra. We knew it was over when it was over. I wished to visit her forever, but I knew better.

With all the passion drained from me, I covered myself with a sheet. Bella didn't bother. I yearned for that type of confidence. Propped up on one elbow, she smoked another cigarette and sipped a glass of wine. It was now night, and the moonglow discovered a route through the window shade and rested on her nakedness.

"We need to talk," she said finally.

"I know, I know," I said. "This was a one-time thing. Right? I mean, I get it." I wanted to say it before she did.

"No, not that. Just listen and don't say anything," she whispered while circling her fingernails on my chest. I was listening, but my body was begging for more pleasure.

"Look, I knew about Leon's business with that asshole Blackford. A mother always knows things even though it's often better not to let on. Then I got a little unannounced visit from him. Money, money, and more money. We all need some of it, but it can become a ferocious enemy. You following me here, Jenkins?"

"Yes, oh, yes, I am," I answered. I was now listening so intently that my brain, for the moment, was distracted from any thought of passion.

"Said he was paying respects, but in reality, he was checking out what I might know about that damn missing money that has now become folklore around here. I said fuck him and the horse he rode in on. I don't care about his money, and if I had it, I'd burn it all. Ill-gotten gains are for the Devil. What's important is you, Mr. Jackson. That old fart Blackford will die before us, but he'll keep looking for his damn money until then. Ask a wealthy man how much money is enough, and he'll say, 'Just a little bit more.'"

I didn't know quite how to respond. Then she changed the subject.

"You been to your old homestead lately?" Bella asked.

"No, and I don't plan to."

"I guess Blackford ran low on cash flow, because he never converted all that land to that fancy horse ranch he bragged about to everyone in the county. He only got roughly half of the creek brush burned off. Damn fool had to deal with the washout and new gullies. My guess is that cost him some money he hadn't planned on spending. Anyway, your old house and sheds are still standing, though looking rather shitty, in my opinion."

"They were always shitty," I responded.

"Let's just say you weren't at the very bottom of the food chain," Bella stated thoughtfully. "The point I'm trying to make is that maybe you should pay a visit to the old place and look around."

"I have no desire to go back there," I said. "Too many memories. I don't look backward, only forward. That's how I survived all that craziness that no child should ever have to deal with."

She sat up and looked at me intently. "Let me be straight-up with you. First of all, I don't want any of it. You earned it."

"I earned what? What do you think I earned?" Now I was feeling slightly defensive.

"Leon, once he knew he was going to die, kind of started talking about things."

"What things?" I interrupted. Bella sensed my apprehension and kissed my lips ever so softly, and gently pulled on my chest hairs. It was the best message that I ever received to advise me to shut up and listen.

"Two things. First, Leon was convinced that you knew what happened to Charles. He never came out and blatantly said you killed him, but I sensed that he thought it. Second, Leon went to Charles's house the day he heard he was missing and took the stash of money. I know you know Leon did jobs for that chain of command that trickled down from Blackford. Leon always skimmed a little off the top, so let's just say he was aware of the stash account."

At best, it was challenging to keep my mouth shut while listening to Bella lay this out. I bit my tongue and hung in there. Then she squeezed those fingernails into my chest and continued.

"Jenkins, Leon and your old man hid that money someplace on your old homestead."

"What the fuck!"

"They did," she insisted. "Leon told me."

"My old man, the fucking Devil, are you sure?"

Bella arched her eyebrows to telegraph the answer.

"Okay then, how much money?" I was getting straight to business now after the initial shock. Then I thought, *Why didn't Leon keep the money for himself?*

Before I could ask what I was thinking, Bella said, "I never understood why Leon did things the way he did. He constantly seemed to have some plan, some system of getting something in place for later use. I guess this is one of them. Maybe it's not ours to know. But I suggest you have a look around. If you don't want to, then let it rot back into the earth like all the rancid souls who coveted it."

I had nothing to say in return. I didn't know what I wanted to do, other than stay there with her.

We rolled toward each other again. This episode was abundantly unlike the others; there were no taking turns, no syllabus being followed, just unadulterated passion. We twisted, wrestled, and fought for who was taking charge. Who was in charge changed every five minutes or less. I was going to achieve satisfaction again or die trying, and dying right now didn't seem all that bad of an idea.

After, Bella collapsed with her face nestled at my feet and I just collapsed in place, flat on my back. Neither of us said a word for some time.

Then she gave me a soft kiss on the lips, and a softer one on the cheek. We hugged, not as lovers but as friends saying goodbye. I had no expectations that it would ever happen again. If we are all walking history books, then Bella had just written one of my best chapters.

On the drive back to college, I didn't overthink how the last 24 hours had started by attending Javier's funeral. I tried to count the girls I had slept with and how different Bella had been. Now I had little interest in any of them.

Once I arrived at my apartment I took a hot shower and settled into bed, but Bella was still on my mind. My cat Cosmo jumped on my chest. He was a rare male longhair calico that a girlfriend had left and never came back to retrieve.

I hadn't analyzed the possibilities of what Bella had told me about the money. Did I care about it? I was doing okay, and my biggest problem was keeping my hot-rod 1969 Camaro Z28 running. I tossed and turned until I couldn't take it anymore, and at three in the morning I called Jill.

"Jenkins, for heaven's sake," Jill said when her husband handed the phone to her. He was always so calm and nonjudgmental. He took the time to ask how I was doing and if I was okay. I admired his tranquility.

I didn't tell Jill about my night of passion with Bella. But I did summarize what she'd said about the possibility of money being hidden on the old property.

"Why would Leon trust the Devil?" Jill asked. "If he'd had money, he would have spent it. It makes no sense to me. I think it's just another twist on the old myth around that money. It's become some sort of legend. I don't think there is any money, and if there was, Folgers and Gumbo can't talk now, can they?"

"I guess you're right. It's logical." I took a deep breath. Jill had always been the voice of reason. It probably wasn't worth the risk to return to the scene of our childhood crimes. Then it dawned on me that if someone took this lost money so seriously they started digging around on the property, what was to stop them from unearthing Gumbo and Charles?

The next day it was back to my college classes, which was a good distraction from thinking about the past. I was an English major solely because of Mrs. Addcock. I was struggling and did not have a passing grade in Old English Verse. It was basically a foreign language, and the teacher was horrific. I thought about dropping out many times, but I had no passion for any other major.

My diminutive state-funded college was one of the first to be completely handicap accessible, so it attracted all the Vietnam veterans with major handicap issues. They were party animals, and I fell right in with them. The bar next to the local VFW was party central, and I tagged along for the ride. My grades worsened.

One night, I met Hank the Tank while driving back to the apartment from the bar. I had seen him traversing that final hill to campus in his wheelchair on many a night. Hank's biceps were more extensive than my waist. He was too drunk to make it up the hill that night in his wheelchair and was progressing at a rate of one roll up, three rolls back. I stopped and offered him a ride. After he cussed me out for some unknown reason, he accepted my offer. We couldn't get his wheelchair in the Camaro, so he said fuck it, kicked his chair to the side of the road, and crawled in. "Fuck the Germans, let's roll," he screamed out the car window. I thought, *Germans?* What the hell did that have to do with anything? But Hank was like that. If you asked him any questions he'd go into a raging dissertation to explain himself, so I learned never to ask.

Hank told me being an English major was for nerds and losers. He said the more he got to know me, the more convinced he was that I needed to change majors to one of the social sciences. He kept inviting me to attend the Sociology Club meetings, and I finally gave in just to shut him up. It was an awakening. Everybody talking about social issues was all new to me. He gave me books on Weber, Durkheim, and Parsons. I devoured them. Within a month I had changed my major to sociology but kept a minor in English.

The women were a collateral benefit of hanging with the club and going to sociology classes. They were outspoken, independent, and, best of all, proponents of uninhibited free love. I was the poster child for an American libertine for the next two years. I detached myself from all material things and focused on flesh. I rarely allowed a thought about the Devil during those years.

Bella came to mind many times. I had several forays with older women, and it seemed that was a preference I gravitated toward.

Hank must have been concerned with my communication issues and quick temper, so he called in a favor with his VA therapist. The therapist initially allowed three free sessions but decided to permit more. Hank said it was because it was obvious that I was so fucked up.

I refused to be open with the therapist involving my relationships. Still, she made a convincing guess with the slight information I gave that I had difficulty with intimate relationships. She said I had no frame of reference for healthy personal relationships because I had never seen one, which was a good point. My definition of intimacy was sex. She said I shouldn't judge myself too harshly, and then said I judged myself without mercy.

There were big eye-openers that were right on the money. The frequency of telling lies, for example. Or the inability to have fun. Humor was my mechanism to cover all other things, including insecurities. I took this all very seriously. The college library became my second home, where I researched every affliction that was reflected in my sessions with the therapist.

I was determined not to let the Devil define me. I'd learned what not to do from him, and now I needed to apply that. Extinguishing the Devil was my idea of relief—until it wasn't. I'd escaped my old hometown, but it was still going to be a long journey.

CHAPTER TWENTY-SEVEN

STEP BACK

THERE WAS NOT MUCH YOU COULD DO WITH A DEGREE IN sociology in the 1970s. It was a rude awakening that the college placement office had failed to mention. When there was an opening for a social worker or something similar that required a degree in social science, I was competing with hundreds if not thousands of other hungry applicants. Many were from that same group of veterans who had persuaded me that this was the way to go. Most of these job openings were in government. I was competing with veteran preference points, with which I had no issues. However, it kept me from making the final cut for job openings. So it was back to the oil field for financial survival, but it would cost me to remain tethered to my past.

I did my best to accept oil field assignments as far from my old hometown as possible. The oil field was always boom or bust, and the boom would move from one town to the next. It was inevitable that my old hometown was in the sites of the seismic crew of blasters, wildcatters, survey crews, and all the other activities that follow the money from oil. Once the drilling started and enough oil was discovered, the big oil companies would move in, followed by all the post-collateral businesses. Tank truck companies, pipe inspectors, welders, heavy equipment operators, and a host of others would migrate to the boom location. There was never enough housing, so the more prominent companies would establish mobile home villages, with housing as a recruiting perk. There was fierce competition for experienced employees; many were recruited from other states.

Try as I might, I could not break away from the allure of some of the best wages in the state. This, along with the fact that there were no jobs available where I could use my degree, created a destiny that I saw coming. The next big oil boom just happened to be the biggest boom in state history. And it was in my old hometown. It tripled in population. New beer joints sprang up, several restaurants opened, and the local bank built additional teller spaces and added its first drive-through window.

I moved into one of those company trailers with two other workers, one from North Dakota and another from Wyoming. The work schedule was seven days on the rig and five days off. At first I used my five days off to send out resumes and cold-call businesses across the state that required social science degrees. I was still desperate to get out of this culture that I once had escaped—a culture of drinking, fighting, womanizing, drugs, and violence. Plus, the work was hazardous. The drillers, tool pushers, and rig supervisors enhanced the danger by passing out liquor every holiday or sometimes just randomly. It was a young man's game, and I could tell the older workers by how many finger digits they were missing.

I wasn't as strong as I thought I was, and I soon found myself backsliding into the ways of youth. I was still trying to fit in and please everyone. I started going to the bars with my new friends. Sex was recreational. Everyone smoked pot daily, even while on the job. It only made me sleepy and dumb, so I faked smoking it in the motor shed of the rigs. The draw of peer pressure remained powerful.

"I know you." I'd had way too much to drink one night and was sitting at the bar of a rotting beer joint with my two roommates. This bar was not within anyone's city limits, and that should have been a warning to stay away. At first I didn't turn around to see who was speaking to me, nor did I care. This bar catered to the oil field, and everybody who frequented it knew each other.

"Hey, Jenkins, that dude there wants you to say something," my roommate ND muttered while sipping his beer. We always nicknamed our out-of-state working buddies by their state's initials or something to it. ND was my North Dakota roommate and W from Wyoming was somewhere in the bar, probably hugging the ugliest girl there. We'd eaten greasy pizza at some new makeshift café inside a truck stop earlier that evening. I was stuffed, full of beer, and not feeling too social.

"I said, I know you," I heard again.

"I guess maybe you do," I responded and turned to see who was trying to get my attention.

"You don't recognize me, do you?" he asked.

"I don't know. I don't think so." I smiled and tried to be pleasant. He was leaning forward with his hands in his pockets. He had a pink flush spattering his face.

"What about these?" He smiled and pointed to two gold front teeth.

I looked at him closer. Shaved head, short, stocky, and with a sleeveless T-shirt, he looked like a weightlifter. I was drunk and the gold teeth were amusing, but I wasn't sure why I should remember them.

"Little Joe, back then, they called me Little Joe," he said, tensing up as he identified himself.

Before I could respond, ND spun his barstool around and extended his hand. "Glad to meet you; I'm Ben Cartwright, and Hoss is somewhere in here." Little Joe was not amused.

"You and me need to go outside," Little Joe said. "We have some unfinished business. You owe me. I was drunk that night. I'm not now." He stood behind me without moving and presented me with this challenge.

"Jenkins, you want me to whoop his ass?" ND asked with a loud laugh. ND would fight anybody at the drop of a hat and never considered an evening finished without some skirmish. I didn't recall him ever winning, but he didn't seem to care.

I knew better. I was drunk and full of greasy pizza. It wasn't instantly apparent that Little Joe had been training and preparing for his revenge. Maybe the alcohol, pride, or just the younger and violent Jenkins emerged just then. "Sure, I'm up for that," I said. "Let's go."

ND yelled, "Fight, fight," and proceeded to rally the bar crowd and direct them to the parking lot. I walked out behind Little Joe. He quickly jumped into some type of kung fu stance and proceeded to dance around me. I followed his moments with my eyes, which made me dizzy.

He hit me and moved back. Multiple hits, and he moved away again. You don't feel the pain when you're in a fight, so his punches seemed weak. I needed to grab him. I was an in-close fighter. My first mistake had been agreeing to fight; my second was allowing him the advantage of an open parking lot. Whatever fight style he'd been training for was conducive to open spaces.

Finally, after taking some brutal punches, I was able to get in close and eventually throw him to the ground. He grabbed a large rock from the graveled parking lot and hit my forehead, stunning me. He rolled out from underneath me and reversed our positions. He was now on top, beating my face unmercifully. Now I could feel the pain. I was in trouble. I grabbed a handful of gravel and stuffed it in his face and eyes, hoping to blind him. This was not just a fight for revenge. We weren't kids anymore. It wasn't like when I'd stuffed gravel down Terry's mouth on the playground. No teachers were going to run in and stop this.

While the punches kept coming, I lay on my back and focused on protecting my face. Then he took a minute to rest, allowing me an opening. I kicked him to the side, rolled on top, and refunded the beating he'd been giving me. He fiercely fought back, but he could do only minor damage while he was on his back with me straddled across his chest. No one was going to pull me off. Nobody was shouting for me to stop or show mercy. No, this crowd wanted blood.

My fists were dripping in blood from his face, and his teeth gouged on my knuckles. My bloodied nose dripped across his neck. There was no fear or panic in his eyes, just hatred flaring. I was staring down into his face, a mirror of what I was and didn't want to be.

I stood up.

"You win, Little Joe. I quit. You got your revenge, whether you deserved it or not." I didn't know what to expect. Would he jump up and start again? Would he accept a surrender? I heard someone in the crowd yelling, "Pussy." These jerks wanted more entertainment. Standing there exhausted, waiting to see what Little Joe's response was going to be, I glanced at my oil field buddies. They looked disappointed.

Little Joe didn't say anything. He popped up full of energy, then walked over to a large rock and took a seat. His energized appearance quickly drained away. I was exhausted. Waves of pain rippled through my body. I don't know why, but I sat down next to him. We were too tired to be surprised anymore.

"Good fight," he whispered.

"You too," I said. "Round two was a motherfucker."

"You know, I thought I would feel different. That first time, you really beat me down; it took my pride, man. I had no choice. I thought revenge would feel better. I trained for this day," Little Joe said with no discernible emotion in his voice.

"So you came back for pride." I recalled old Salem Lowe laying his definition of power on me.

"Yeah, that's about right."

"I don't think anyone can take your pride, Joe. You have to give it away to lose it."

Little Joe looked at me as if he was trying to make sense of what I had just said. ND handed us a beer and said that they were rolling on to another bar and he'd see me later.

"So, who did I give it to?" Little Joe asked after thanking ND for the beer. He spit out some blood and then motioned for my answer.

"You probably gave it to those gangsters that brought you to our first fight. Maybe you gave it to anybody who's judged you. Your pride is a piece of what creates your power." As I said these things to him, I realized I had never experienced pride. I couldn't give mine away because I'd never had it. All I could do was talk about someone else's. It was a moment of clarity, a realization that my transformation was incomplete. Pride was the missing link. Why had it taken a brutal fight to awaken me to this? I recalled my mother admonishing Jill and me for not keeping our heads up.

We continued to talk for an hour or more. Joe wasn't the Neanderthal I'd thought he was. His insightfulness was startling. He was so much a product of his environment he couldn't see anything else. In that accord, we had many things in common. I still didn't like him, but I didn't feel hate or anger toward him anymore, even when I found out the next morning that I had a few broken ribs.

Two days later, I quit the oil field and signed up for unemployment for the first time. It was a scary move. But it was time for a change, and I couldn't wait any longer, expecting change to rescue me. I needed to take a larger stake in my destiny. I found a job before I got a letter denying my unemployment.

I went back to my college to get additional certified copies of my school transcripts, applying for any professional job where I could use my sociology degree. I read a sign in the admissions office advertising that human resources representatives were recruiting minority applicants for state agencies on campus. I wasn't a minority, but I thought I'd drop by and maybe run into some of my old Vietnam vets who were stretching their GI Bill as far as it would go.

"So, you were making that kind of money in the oil field, and you quit to get one of these low-paying government jobs?" asked Mr. Young, the representative for the Department of Corrections. I'd arrived at the job fair as everyone was packing up their flashy displays.

"Yes, sir. I know I'm not a minority, but I am unemployed and ready to start a career. I want to get out of oil work before I get old." He asked me to take a seat and said he was in no hurry to drive a hundred miles back to his office. We talked for over an hour. He took down my address and phone number, but I was under no illusion that he would ever call. After our visit, I felt like I had known him my whole life.

"Hey, fucker!"

I turned to see who had yelled at me. "Hank the Tank, what the hell you doing here?"

"I am proudly serving as a rehabilitation counselor. I'm the VA rep here on that stuff," Hank announced with pride. "What you up to, Jenkins, my boy?"

"Man, need a job. How you get so fat, Mr. Hank?" He was fatter than ever with his arms resting on his stomach as if it were a desk.

"I said I was a counselor; I didn't say I lost the taste for some good cold beer," he said, laughing as he held his sides. "Look here. I know some of these recruiters. I'll put in a good word." He rolled off to see his next client.

Three months passed. I had taken several short-term jobs working at a paint store and sacking groceries, where I also learned the butcher trade. I'd always had a fondness for knives, which helped me overcome the grossness associated with chopping, slicing, and cutting dead animal carcasses all day. Learning how to skin squirrels earlier in life helped a little bit.

I tried to control the desperation when the person on the other end of the phone line identified himself as an HR rep from the Corrections Department. He said that Mr. Young had given him my name and a good recommendation. The interview was set, and now it was time for a haircut and to get my one dress suit cleaned. That khaki bell-bottomed three-piece suit had never looked better.

Mr. Young called the morning of the interview and said, "They'll ask you if you believe in the death penalty. If you say no, they won't hire you. Oh, and tell Hank hello. He gave me a call about you. He's a good man."

About a month after the interview, while I waited for my background investigation to be completed, Mr. Young called again. "Jenkins, man, look here. They finished your background check, and you are not recommended for hire. I know we talked at college and you told me about your youth, but, man, this investigation."

"Mr. Young, what happened? I'm clean, no arrest or anything really bad," I managed to stutter back.

"No, no, nothing like that. We do thorough preemployment background investigations, and you got the bad luck of the draw—your investigator really got into it. You had only one high school teacher who said anything positive about you. Look, I'm going to lay this on you straight-up. Your father, back in your hometown, many believe you're like him. Sorry you had to hear that. It looks like your father left a lot to be desired."

I was devastated, to say the least. I thanked him the best I could, softly placed the phone down, then picked it up and slammed it down. A feeling of helplessness smothered me. The Devil was haunting me. *Would this follow me my whole life?*

CHAPTER TWENTY-EIGHT

THE END GAME

MY CAREER HAD STARTED AND ENDED IN WHAT FELT LIKE A blink of an eye. But Mr. Young changed the hiring recommendation from "do not hire" to "questionable hire," and I was able to take an entry-level job as a parole officer. I'd never planned on staying more than a few years with the Corrections Department, but 36 years later there I was, combing my hair in the mirror. I'd always had a high forehead, but I could tell my hairline was receding. I had already conceded that the battle was lost to gray hair. *Got to fight this aging process*, I thought.

I was now the state correctional director, preparing for a day that would not end until almost midnight. That evening I'd be required to oversee another execution, number 28. Many years ago I took Mr. Young's advice and answered the capital punishment question with a resounding yes. In other words, I lied.

That lie got me to the viewing chamber, where I watched condemned men take their last breaths, 21 grams of air that some say is your soul escaping. They had two minutes for their last words, while I'd have those words etched in my memory for eternity.

Over the years, I converted my liabilities into assets. My insecurities and PTSD became motivators to prove myself. I always needed to prove to people who had not even known me that I was better than my child-hood environment.

"Director, a lady on the phone wishes to speak to you," my administrative assistant said to me one morning. "She says she's the granddaughter of Mrs. Addcock. Said you would know who that was." I had just passed through security and was attempting to get organized and drink that day's first cup of coffee.

"Mrs. Addcock, you sure she said Addcock?" I asked.

"Yes, Director. Do you want to take the call? You don't have much time; you must be at the Capitol by 8:30. Remember, today is your first joint House and Senate budget hearing."

I took a deep breath and picked up the phone. "Hello," I said.

"Hello, this is Deloris Addcock. My grandmother was your English teacher in high school. She's in a nursing home now and would like to see you."

No matter how long it had been since high school, the thought of being summoned by one of my past school teachers instilled the same distress. It was particularly pronounced with someone as intellectually intimidating as Mrs. Addcock had been. After taking a few seconds to fight back the anxiety, I thought, *How can this be? She'd have to be over 100 years old.* But of course she wasn't that old. When you're in school every teacher appears old. In high school, I would have thought she was ancient.

"How old is she?" I blurted out, and immediately embarrassed myself for having done so.

"She'll be 87 this year, and she is not doing too well," Deloris said.

"Did she say why she wants to see me?"

"It's that book you wrote. She wants you to bring her a copy," Deloris responded. Just like Mrs. Addcock, granddaughter Deloris was straight to the point.

The book. I had written a book of vignettes, stand-alone short stories about some humorous and unusual cases I'd supervised as a parole officer. My oldest daughter had encouraged me to write it while reminiscing about the case stories I told when she was young. A publisher liked it, and my little book was in stores. The statewide newspaper decided to print a book review only because I'd become the corrections director.

I didn't like nursing homes and didn't want to see Mrs. Addcock in one. "I can mail her the book, or you can come to pick one up," I said to Deloris. "I'll sign a copy for her."

"She read the book review in the paper, and it intrigued her. Said she never had a student write a book."

The first student *to publish a book*, I thought. *How can I not go see her now?* My ego had been triggered.

My bravery and commitment were solid until I parked in front of the nursing home. "This is crazy," I said to myself. "I should just leave the book at the front desk and get out of here."

The smell reminded me of the VA Hospital: a mix of hospital and prison housing with a pinch of homeless shelter sprayed in. Your past follows you closely, so I always looked straight ahead and never slowed down, a never-ending race that I also believed to be winnable. As I walked inside that place to see Mrs. Addcock, my past walked beside me. In the sterile nursing home environment where employees made minimum wage, no one looked happy to be there. The receptionist never looked up while pointing toward the corridor and saying, "Last room on the left, sweetie."

There she was, Mrs. Addcock, propped up in bed and looking down through those same end-of-the-nose glasses. She turned to see me enter her room and motioned to the visitor's chair beside the bed. I sat down and asked her, "How are you doing?"

"I would say I am doing fine, but under the circumstances and you being an eyewitness, I will assume the question as rhetorical," she replied without looking at me. Her voice was gravelly and weak. I handed her the book. I had taken the time to wrap it and added a purple bow.

"It's not my birthday."

"Mrs. Addcock, it's the book, my book, the one you requested. I autographed it for you," I proudly declared.

"Not sure why you did all of that. I just wanted to read the book. It's not like it's a collectible or a bestseller. I can't take it where I'm going. There, leave it there on the end table. I'll get to it someday." When she pointed, I noticed her skinny hands, with road-mapped veins and barely enough flesh to cover the bones.

Silence. She watched television, and I was sitting there by her bed with nothing to say. It wasn't how I thought it would go down. I expected something different. Maybe she had a touch of dementia, or was just tired. I tried to make small talk. I even tried to joke about her having the same mini beehive hairdo that she'd had when I was a senior in high school.

"Jenkins, I'm tired now. I don't know if Deloris told you that I have cancer. The treatments exhaust me. If not for Deloris, I would have chosen the alternative of dying in peace. No damn such treatments to extend my life for another six months. The things we will do for grandchildren. Leave the book."

I said my goodbye, wanting to hug her but knowing it would be awkward and something she would more than likely reject. I didn't expect that she'd read the book. I sat in my car and watched the nursing home staff roll out a dozen wheelchair-bound patients, parking them in the morning sun to assist with the release of the body's vitamin D.

This is it? You worked hard, struggled to improve with each passing day, and ended up at the mercy of low-wage care custodians. Wardens were a better name. I thought of the twins. Neddy had died first, and Freddy five weeks later. That chain-smoking caught up with them at 50. I helped pay for their funerals. They'd never pulled out of that nosedive of a rough life, and in the end they had nothing. At least they hadn't ended up in a place like this.

Mike, on the other hand, ended up under a real warden. I was shocked when I heard he'd won some remote county sheriff's election. He lasted about two years before he was indicted on rape charges. He got a long sentence. He was the only one besides me of the old hooky bridge bunch who was still alive. Car wrecks, drugs, and violence took all of them.

I lost track of Randy for years. I called the office on my way back and asked my assistant to run a criminal records check on him. Two days later, she said that she'd located some misdemeanor arrests in Texas and Washington State. She took the liberty of checking death records in both states and found his obituary. He'd been killed in a lumbering accident outside of Seattle in 1997. I regretted not trying to keep in contact with him, but I had my reasons.

Three weeks later, Deloris was on the phone again. "Grandma says you can come to get your book now," she said. I didn't want to go back for a repeat performance. At first I told her no, I wouldn't go back. Deloris explained that Mrs. Addcock only had a few weeks to live, and she only asked to see me. How could I refuse?

Mrs. Addcock had oxygen tubes in her nose and an IV in each arm this time. "Your book is over there on the table. You can take it back now," she whispered hoarsely. I looked; she had wrapped the book in a plastic Walmart bag.

"Oh, no, I meant for you to keep it," I said, knowing that sounded stupid. She looked at me over those nose-hugging glasses as if to say, *Really?*

"Jenkins, now what do you expect me to do with that book? Did you forget our last visit?"

I didn't answer her, but I did pick up the bag. She asked me about a few of the others from her classes and what they had made of themselves. Unfortunately I didn't have much good news to tell her.

"Well, guess they were following tradition," was all she said. I could see she was struggling to speak, so I decided it was time to depart. I stood up and said goodbye.

"Aren't you going to look at it?" she demanded. I unwrapped the bag.

"Yes, that's my book," I confirmed.

"I said look at it, open the book," she said, attempting to raise her voice. I almost teared up. Then I opened the book.

"Mrs. Addcock, red ink? Did you edit my book?" There were corrections and red ink comments on at least every third page. For a moment I was indignant. "Mrs. Addcock, this book went through three edits with the publisher. Professional editors." Before I could finish, she raised the palm of her hand up. She'd used that same sign in high school. It worked to hush the whole class, and it worked again now. That woman had power.

"Well, it's apparent those so-called editors never took one of my classes, now did they? You can do better than this. I see you continue to cover up your darkness with a dose of humor. Jenkins, write what you know. Write what you know. You can do better than this." Those words seemed to take all her energy. Her eyes indicated she had more to say, but it was time for me to leave. Deloris called three days later to tell me her grandmother had died.

After seeing Mrs. Addcock that day, I decided to take a long detour on my way back to the office. Maybe I was just melancholy. Whatever it was, for the first time in over 40 years, I decided to visit the old homestead.

After old Mr. Blackford died, his successors didn't show the same interest in building a renowned horse ranch. The place was in disarray. They never finished the project, which left our old place untouched by anything other than time.

The old smokehouse was all that was left standing. It was leaning to one side, with a gaping splintered hole on the south side. The roof was partially caved down. Two hefty bull snakes were curled up by the door. They took a second to flick their tongues at me to remind me I didn't belong there. I walked carefully through the tall grass, loosened my tie, and grabbed a stick to warn the snakes I meant business.

I leaned into the splintered hole, stuck my head in, and looked around. A rat's nest, old bird feathers, broken fruit jars, an old metal handheld meat grinder, and an assortment of animal droppings covered the floor. Without someone farming and brush-hogging the land, nature had had its way. The once distant creek now annexed most of the area; vines wrapped around the smokehouse. They were probably the only thing keeping it from completely falling down.

The rain had finally destroyed most of that prized redwood floor. I used my stick to poke at the rotted spots. The redwood broke apart like Styrofoam. There was some loose gravel and white dust underneath. I assessed the roof to determine if it would cave in on me. I stepped inside. I brushed the dust and rocks away. Underneath appeared to be a concrete slab lid of sorts. I stepped out and walked around the area and found an old, rusty sucker rod pipe semiburied in the dirt. I picked it up and used it as a hammer to pound away at the slab.

The slab broke into many fragments. I dug them away with my hands. Underneath was a leather suitcase. I pulled on the handle until it broke off. I continued to tug at the suitcase until it split in half. There, displaying the effects of over 40 years of decay, lay stacks of rotting currency. The money, mostly one hundred dollar bills, was almost indistinguishable. The mold, rotting, and mud had made most of what I found unusable.

The Devil put this here, I thought. *Leon was right all those years ago.* Had he really killed Gumbo? The Devil had said he did, but I hadn't believed him. Maybe I was wrong, and it wasn't Gumbo who killed Folgers. Perhaps the Devil killed him too. Did it matter who did what? I sat in the tall grass and thought this all out, not caring if my suit got dirty.

Some of the money could have been salvaged, I guessed. I didn't care to dig in the stacks to find spendable bills. I didn't need money, and if I had, all I could think was that this money had perpetuated evil. If I took any, the Devil would haunt me more than ever. Mom had died after 24 years of being free of him. She had her peace and quiet. Now it was time for mine. I filled the inside of the smokehouse with dry grass and threw a match. I watched it burn until the pasture also caught on fire. I wished Jill could have witnessed this sacrificial burning. She had never returned to our childhood area after getting married, having children and a long career as a high school English teacher. I guessed she got that all-American family that Mom always tried to create.

As I drove away, Mrs. Addcock's words were on replay: "Write what you know." She had mentioned my darkness. I decided at that minute that my freedom, my exorcism of the Devil, was not complete. "Write what you know," Mrs. Addcock had said. She had mentored my darkness.

ABOUT THE AUTHOR

JUSTIN JONES is the author of two novels—*Tales of the Caseload* and *The Perils of Ms. Apple*—and various published articles and editorials. In addition to his writing accomplishments, Justin is a veteran of an extensive career in criminal justice, including as Oklahoma State Director of Corrections. He continues to provide expert opinion consulting in the corrections profession. Justin has and continues to serve on numerous nonprofit boards that focus on assisting the disenfranchised, and he established a foundation to support an alternative school that focuses on youth with various social challenges. He has been an adjunct professor and served as a suicide hotline volunteer. Justin has degrees in sociology and communications from East Central University in Oklahoma.

Made in the USA
Columbia, SC
03 November 2023

25406184R00164